Touch of Glory

BOOKS BY
ELIZABETH ANALISE

A Story of New Mexico Collection
Touch of Glory

TOUCH of GLORY

≣ A STORY OF NEW MEXICO ≣

ELIZABETH ANALISE

ROSE WOOD

PUBLISHING

Rosewood Publishing
300 Menaul Blvd NW, Suite A
PMB #205
Albuquerque, NM 87107
www.rosewoodpublishing.org

ISBN 979-8-9919758-0-3 (hardcover)
ISBN 979-8-9919758-1-0 (paperback)
ISBN 979-8-9919758-2-7 (ebook)

Library of Congress Control Number: 2025910146

Content Notice: There is a scene in this book that describes an attempted rape. In addition, there are descriptions of war and battle including injury, trauma, and death. Some readers may find these scenes to be disturbing.

Note: Throughout the book, Spanish words and spelling may be used to convey the setting and language used by the characters. The use of the term "Indian" in reference to Native American, American Indian, or Indigenous American people is only intended to be representative of the history and time when this story is set.

For my Father

≡ Introduction ≡

"A house divided against itself cannot stand. I believe this government cannot endure, permanently half slave and half free. I do not expect the Union to be dissolved. I do not expect the house to fall. But I do expect it will cease to be divided. It will become all one thing or all the other."
~Abraham Lincoln, Illinois Republican State Convention, June 16, 1858

The United States was in turmoil. By 1860, the last year of peace, one in seven Americans belonged to another. Four million men, women, and children were slaves. Abraham Lincoln won the Republican nomination for president, and he was elected in November with sweeping support from the North.

Lincoln's election was the signal for seven Southern slave states to declare their secession from the United States and form the Confederacy. In February of 1861, former Senator Jefferson Davis was elected president of the Provisional Congress of the Confederate States of America.

On March 4, 1861, on a cold and windy day in Washington, D.C., Abraham Lincoln was sworn in as president of the United States before a large, tense crowd gathered at the Capitol building. Riflemen were watching from every window, and cannons stood, manned and ready, on the Capitol grounds.

War was imminent, and Lincoln ascertained there was no other way. The Civil War began at 4:30 a.m. on April 12, 1861, when Confederate forces opened fire on Union soldiers at Fort Sumter in South Carolina's Charleston Harbor.

The Civil War seemed a long way from the New Mexico Territory, which was bordered by the Territories of Utah and Colorado, the States of California and Texas, and Mexico. The vast territory had originally been occupied by Native Americans, was colonized by the Spanish, and was once part of Mexico. In 1846, United States General Kearny had marched into the territory with his army and declared it to be United States property.

The territory was lightly populated and boasted a beautiful landscape of rugged mountain ranges, barren deserts, and wide-open blue skies. The population was a mix of Native Americans, Mexicans, Spaniards, and New Mexicans with deep ties to both Spain and Mexico. The industry was based on agriculture and cattle, and the stagecoach line allowed merchants to trade goods between Mexico, California, and Missouri. In the capital of Santa Fe, the citizens found themselves swept up in the ominous winds of the Civil War.

Many United States officers were serving in New Mexico when the Civil War began. Edward Richard Sprigg Canby was a career officer and led the Department of New Mexico. Christopher Houston Carson, known as Kit Carson, was a fur trapper, Indian agent, wilderness guide, and U.S. Army officer. He helped organize the 1st New Mexico Volunteer Infantry Regiment.

Henry Hopkins Sibley had a distinguished and long military career with the U.S. forces prior to the Civil War. He fought in the Seminole Wars in Florida, the Mexican-American War in frontier Texas, and the Utah War. He resigned his commission almost immediately after the Civil War began and accepted an appointment as colonel in the Confederate army. In the summer of 1861, Sibley traveled to Richmond, Virginia, to meet with Confederate President Davis. Sibley had devised a master plan to have the Confederates gain control of the Southwest and Intermountain West.

He proposed to lead a mounted force to New Mexico, garner food for his men along the way, and defeat the Union forces to secure the territory for the Confederacy. He then planned to march north to Colorado and then west to Salt Lake City and on to California. If he were successful, the entire Southwest, with its gold and silver mines and coastal seaports, would be under Confederate control.

The scheme was lofty, but Davis approved the plan and commissioned Sibley as a brigadier general, granting him the authority to raise an army in Texas. In December of 1861, Sibley claimed possession of New Mexico in the name of the Confederacy.

≡ 1 ≡

L ydia Sena stood on her balcony and watched the sun rise majestically over the Sangre de Cristo Mountains. Her vantage point encompassed the glorious sunrise from north to south. She felt moved by the beauty and serenity of the golden rays carpeting the snowy landscape.

She usually greeted the sun with hope and inspiration. Today, she felt dread. A war that might entangle her family and a betrothal she didn't want were about to change the life she had known forever.

She moved from the balcony and closed the doors as she entered her bedroom. Her attention was drawn to the daguerreotype photograph of her mother set in a hinged leather case. Lydia looked directly into her mother's deep-set eyes, as if her intent focus could bring life to the picture and allow her to speak with her mother. She thought, *If only this lovely woman were here today to help me find the right path forward.* Lydia had never known her mother, but she had formed an extensive personification that resided in her head and was wrapped inside her heart. She had no doubt her mother was with her in spirit, and that relieved some of her anxiety.

Lydia had a long, grueling day ahead of her, and she had to steady herself as she was the mistress of the household. She removed the soft blanket wrapped around her shoulders and laid it with care on the chair close by. She took a deep breath and cleared her head, mentally preparing for the day's tasks and calming her emotions—she had never experienced such turmoil during her young life.

Lydia began her toiletry while she waited for her maid to help her into her stays and her day dress. She could already hear the activities downstairs and let her emotions out with a heavy sigh.

*   *   *

Much had already been completed for the gathering planned for that afternoon, which was being held for the townspeople to hear the latest news of the war. Lydia, overseeing the final touches, was directing two young boys who were moving chairs into the large ballroom located on the second floor of the west wing.

"Rico, please be sure you place these close together. We are expecting a good-sized group this afternoon." The boy nodded and pushed the wooden chair with an embroidered seat closer to the adjoining one.

Lydia, with her petticoat bustling under her dark gray wool dress, purposely moved down the staircase and into the large kitchen. She was greeted by a variety of delicious aromas. The family's cook, Maria, an abundant woman with a permanent frown, was bent over a large pot on the cast iron stove, checking to be sure the cut of meat was well on its way to being done for the family's dinner that evening. Lydia peeked over Maria's practiced hand, wrinkled with age, and watched as she used a wooden spoon to toss the cut potatoes, carrots, and turnips alongside the meat.

Knowing dinner would be ready in time, Lydia turned her attention to the long table in the middle of the kitchen. An assortment of fruit empanadas, steam still escaping from their crusts, sat on top of the well-worn wooden table, which was uneven in some places and bore a battery of nicks and grooves from years of use. Lydia's maid was stacking small China plates on the tall sideboard.

"Alita," she said, "these desserts look beautiful." Alita smiled in response.

Lydia spoke in rapid Spanish to the cook about making the coffee and checking the lemonade for sugar. She then signaled to Alita to go upstairs and prepare for helping Lydia to change for the afternoon gathering. Remembering one last detail, Lydia grabbed her heavy shawl from the wide entryway and stepped through the heavy front door into the cold, early winter air. Workers were busy clearing snow from the paths within the spacious courtyard.

Hugging her shawl around her, Lydia looked around to make sure all was in place. She briefly admired the great cottonwood tree with gnarled, snow-covered branches reaching towards the sky and the long portal held by sturdy posts that framed the entire first floor of the Territorial Style house. The white lace curtains at every window looked crisp and inviting. She gave one last look at the arbor standing in one corner of the enclosed patio and recalled the lovely wild roses that covered the structure in the spring and summer months. Her thoughts turned to the deep history of her family home.

The Sena home had been built by her great-grandfather and was passed down to Lydia's father, Manuel. Many additions had been added to the original structure over the years, including the courtyard with a permanent fountain that served as the center of the home. In the warm months, the courtyard was filled with vibrantly colored geraniums, daisies, and roses. Flowers had long been a passion of Lydia's, and she spent many hours tending to them. The spacious kitchen, dining room, parlor, and her father's study were on the bottom floor, with several bedrooms, the ballroom, and a variety of storage rooms upstairs.

The house itself was made from thick adobe bricks. The ancient method of making adobe bricks had begun with the Indians who had occupied the New Mexico Territory land for thousands of years. Water and sometimes straw were added to the local dirt, and the bricks were molded by hand and allowed to dry in the sun. The adobe bricks were long-lasting and provided a natural insulation by absorbing and radiating heat in the winter and retaining the cool air in the summer.

The exposed beams that ran through the interior had been cut many years before from the aspen trees growing nearby and supported the layers of dirt that made up the roof. The house had a total of thirty rooms, some of which had been added by her father for storage, along with a chicken coop, coach house, a horno for baking bread, a vegetable garden, and small orchard.

Manuel had paid little attention to the furnishings in his home, and as Lydia grew older, she took a great interest in the interior design of her father's house. Most of the furniture had come from Spain or Mexico and dated back many years; the pieces radiated both elegance and timeless beauty, and yet there was a ruggedness about them. She'd had some of the more massive pieces put in storage or had given them away. What was left reflected Lydia's uncluttered and simple taste. The finer pieces, such as the mahogany armoire in the parlor and the massive dining room set, were set off by the whitewashed walls and wooden floors adorned by Indian rugs, artistically woven with earth tones of browns, reds, and greens that enhanced the simplicity and warmth of their home.

The large windows on the back of the house framed a perfect view of the gentle hills surrounding the city of Santa Fe. Hills that wore each of the seasons like a mantel. They now slept quietly, covered by a thick blanket of white snow.

Satisfied with the courtyard preparations, Lydia made her way up the stairs to her bedroom. The sound of her soft leather shoes was hardly noticeable against the hardwood floors that lay the length of the upstairs hallway. The brass lamps gave the passageway a warm glow. The house was quiet now except for a low creaking from the weight of the snow on the roof. Lydia pushed hard on the solid wooden door leading to her room. As the door gave way, cool air and a light scent of flowers greeted her.

Alita had already lit the lamps on the nightstand and the dresser and was drawing the heavy curtains. "We will need to stoke the fire," Lydia instructed. The days were getting cold, and any warmth left by the brief bursts of the early winter sun did not linger.

Alita knelt at the opening of the rounded kiva fireplace and put in pieces of piñon wood from a woven basket placed near the rounded banco, a ledge that circled the fireplace. She blew on the embers, enticing the wood to burn brightly. In a short time, the flames rose and crackled to chase away the drafts and chills.

Lydia moved to stand in front of the fire and allowed the warmth to penetrate her face and hands. The musky aroma of the burning wood swirled around her. Alita brought over a simple wooden chair with a paisley brocade cushion, and Lydia sat down gratefully. The light from the fireplace illuminated the white plaster wall of her room, creating a glowing, almost magical effect.

The tension in Lydia's body slowly released as she leaned back. Turning her head to one side, she glanced around the room that had been hers since she was a small child. The bed, dresser, and armoire were all made from cherry wood and decorated with delicate floral carvings. The wood had been taken care of and protected for many years, and the different red hues shone against the polished darkness. A quilt with a festive pattern lay on top of her thick goose-down mattress. A large mirror with a gilded frame and a large silver crucifix tied with a piece of leather adorned the white-washed walls. A full-length mirror held in a stand was pressed into a corner.

The finest and most precious piece of furniture was the elegant dressing table with a low bench covered in deep burgundy velvet worn from wear. The dressing table had belonged to Lydia's mother. The top of the table held toiletries, a small crystal vase filled with dried flowers, and the photograph of her mother.

Lydia gazed at her mother's picture, and it was almost like seeing her own reflection. Lydia had thick, dark auburn hair that cascaded down her back in a cloud of curls. The darkness of her hair was a sharp contrast to the light color of her skin, and her black eyelashes set off the deep blue color of her eyes. She was slightly built with a long, graceful neck. The picture of her mother reflected a light in her eyes, the same light that shone in Lydia's eyes—as though there was a great expectation from life.

It was hard for Lydia to imagine what her mother had really been like. Elise LaFollet de Sena had died shortly after giving birth to Lydia. Her father and older brother, Eduardo, had kept Elise's spirit alive by telling and retelling their favorite stories about her. When she would slip off her shoes and stockings and wade in the stream while they picnicked in the nearby forests, or how she would fill her home with food and music to entertain the townspeople during the holidays. Lydia's father would break into a smile when he told how Elise would always make sure to include everyone in the festivities, and she would eventually end up in the kitchen, preparing baskets filled with posole, tortillas, and tamales for those neighbors who might not have a decent Christmas meal.

Her mother's family originated from France and settled in the upper fertile hunting grounds of Rio Chama Valley in a small town called Los Brazos, which hosted a lush landscape and stunning waterfalls as a backdrop.

Elise and Manuel met during a harvest celebration in Santa Fe. She had known she would marry him the minute she saw him. Despite continuous objections by both their parents, by the end of the winter season, Elise had become Manuel's wife in a traditional Spanish ceremony. They'd had many years together, but her father had never truly recovered from the death of his wife. He raised his two children to further cement their deeply rooted heritage. The history of her father's family and Santa Fe, the city of Holy Faith, were intertwined and wrapped in tradition that had begun long ago.

≡ 2 ≡

Manuel was a son of one of the oldest and most distinguished Spanish families in the area. The Sena family, headed by Don Fernando de Sena, had come to Santa Fe in 1760 when it was a Spanish colony. Don Fernando had been commissioned by the King of Spain to help settle and bring prosperity to this untamed region of New Mexico.

Over the next several generations, the Sena family grew and flourished. They acquired huge tracts of land and managed prosperous businesses, including cattle and sheep ranching, wool production, and a mercantile store. The family was proud of their heritage and took care of one another. Even though Lydia was raised without her mother, she was surrounded by aunts, uncles, and cousins who loved her, as well as a devoted father and brother. She had grown into a well-rounded and self-assured young woman, but she felt uncertain and confused by the recently disclosed plans that had been laid out for her future.

Lydia, still lost in her thoughts and glancing again at her mother's image whispered, "Please Mama, send me strength for the future."

One of the burning logs in the kiva fireplace popped and startled Lydia back to the present. The sight of Alita contently brushing Lydia's dark blue velvet dress was comforting. Her back was turned, and Lydia looked fondly at the long black braid that hung down to Alita's bright red skirt.

Alita had been Lydia's primary caretaker since the day she was born. She was mestizo, part Spanish and part Indian, and had been trained at an early age to be a house servant—even though she was not able to speak. Her family had been killed during an Indian raid when she was a young child, and she had been brought to the Sena home. No one ever knew if her lack of speech was a result of the physical attack or from the psychological trauma. Alita was devoted to the young infant and spent all her time looking after Lydia. They learned to communicate with one another through sign language, touch, and eye contact.

Alita laid down the brush, then turned and smiled at Lydia. "Muchas gracias," Lydia said. "I must hurry and change. You know how Papa is about being late." Alita nodded in acknowledgement.

Lydia washed her face, hands, and neck with cool water from a ceramic bowl. With Alita's help, she slipped off her day dress and was left in her lace-trimmed chemise, stockings, and corset. Alita helped her climb into her hoop skirt and white petticoat. The velvet dress went over her head, and Alita began working on the many buttons up the back. The deep sapphire color of the dress set off the rich blue color in Lydia's eyes. The collar and cuffs were trimmed in a cream-colored, floral pleated Spanish lace which illuminated her skin. The dress fit Lydia snugly around her waist and flared out widely at the bottom. Alita held her satin slippers as she slipped into them.

Lydia sat down at her dressing table and Alita began brushing her thick, curly hair. "I am so happy Eduardo has come home," Lydia said with a smile. "It seems he has been away at school for such a long time. It was good Papa sent for him as soon as we knew of the war."

Alita nodded gently at the words. She watched Lydia's reflection in the mirror and smiled to herself as she regarded her young mistress. The girl's face was beautifully shaped, with high cheek bones and a strong chin with a cleft just like her father. The years had gone by so fast, and it seemed Lydia had grown up overnight.

Alita continued to brush Lydia's hair as the light from the fire reflected in its shiny weight. She pulled all the strands together and twisted them into a circlet at the back of Lydia's neck, holding it in place with pins and a black net studded with pearls. Lydia had just begun to wear all of her hair up, demonstrating that she was a young woman and no longer a girl. Even though Alita used many pins, several unruly curls escaped their restriction and framed her young mistress's face.

Lydia chose a simple amethyst and seed pearl necklace with matching earrings and placed a small bit of perfume at her throat and wrists. With a last look at her reflection, she made her way along the long hallway and down the staircase. Lydia could see the bright light emanating from the kiva fireplace and hear the low voices of her father and brother coming from the formal sitting room.

For a moment, Lydia felt very much alone, and her steps quickened. She wanted to feel encircled and protected by the two men who meant the most to her. Just before she entered the room, she stood up straight and squared her shoulders. Above all, she was strong inside, and these trying circumstances would not defeat her spirit.

"My darling Lydia," her father said as he stood up from his chair to kiss her warmly on her cheek. "You look so beautiful, so much like your mother looked when I met her."

The years had been kind to her father. His hair was still thick with light touches of gray, and he was still just slightly taller than his son. His eyes were a dark deep brown with flecks of green that lit up at the sight of his only daughter.

"Thank you, Papa," she said.

"I have to agree with Father, you seem to become lovelier each day," Eduardo said as he kissed her cheek.

"It is so nice to have you home again."

"It is wonderful to be here," he replied. "I just wish I had been called back under better circumstances."

Lydia stood for a moment and basked in the presence of her older brother. He had grown taller and broader in the shoulders, and his frame had filled out while he was away at school. He was a young man. His hair, now cut short, was light brown, and he gazed back at her with clear blue eyes. She detected the tug of a smile playing on his lips. Today, he wore his uniform representing the Union, a dark blue flannel coat with a series of gold buttons down the front and lighter blue wool trousers. She sensed a vibrancy and excitement within him that had not been there before. She was filled with pride and fear, acknowledging the deep connection they shared as brother and sister.

"I must say, you both look so official in your uniforms, and it might take me some time to get used to all of this," Lydia said tenderly. "All the preparations are ready, Papa, and our guests will be arriving any moment."

They turned upon hearing a loud knock. A house servant standing nearby opened the large front door.

≡ 3 ≡

The first to arrive were Colonel Edward Canby, accompanied by Colonel Kit Carson. The two men walked into the entryway, brushing fresh snow from their dark blue wool cloaks. The house servant stepped behind them to help remove their outer cloaks.

"Captain," Canby said as he reached to shake Manuel's hand. "Thank you for having us this afternoon and for giving us the opportunity to speak to the townsfolk."

Lydia stepped forward so her father could introduce her.

"You must be Lydia," Canby said warmly. "Your father has talked about you, and you certainly are much more beautiful in person."

She smiled and took his hand after he had settled down his unruly hair. She looked into his deep set, serious eyes. His face was etched with lines caused by sleepless nights, ceaseless work, and unease over the current situation. "Sir, we are honored to have you in our home, and please, make yourself comfortable."

Lydia then turned to Colonel Kit Carson and extended her hand. "Colonel, so nice to see you again," she said. "We must visit as I want to inquire about your lovely wife, Josefa, and the children."

A seasoned tracker and Indian agent, Carson was short and lean, with a stern mouth and gaze. He smiled slightly as he greeted Lydia.

"Nice to see you, Miss Lydia," he said as he removed his hat and took her hand, looking into her eyes with his own that held a twinge of wildness and adventure.

Right behind them stood Governor Connelly and his wife, Dolores. Connelly, who had served as a representative in the New Mexico Territorial Legislature, had recently been appointed governor by President Lincoln. Originally from Kentucky, he had been in New Mexico for the past twenty years. The governor was older, with white hair and soft brown eyes. Lydia noticed a weariness about him as the house servant helped him remove his dark wool overcoat. He removed his hat and greeted Manuel, who he knew very well, with a great bear hug.

"We are going to need everyone's support in this matter," he said as he pulled away and Manuel nodded.

"Eduardo, will you please see that our guests are escorted upstairs? Father and I can greet the rest," Lydia said politely. The group started down the hall and up the flight of stairs to the ballroom.

Within minutes, there was another knock and Lydia opened the door to see Carlos Aragon. He leaned over to kiss her check, and she hesitantly accepted.

"Carlos," she said, feeling surprised. "I didn't realize you would be here today."

"Your father sent word and so I decided it must be important," he said. With that, he turned to Manuel. "Good afternoon, Señor Sena," he said with an air of formality. Her father nodded in return.

"Carlos, please come in." Lydia did not look at Carlos but focused her attention on greeting her remaining guests who were now entering the front door.

Before long, the ballroom upstairs was filled with a mix of military personnel and prominent members of the community. Many were circulating, while others were enjoying a cup of coffee or tea and a piece of pie. Manuel caught Lydia's eye across the room and gave her a quick smile so that she knew he was pleased with her preparations.

"Ladies and gentlemen," Manuel said as the conversations quieted down. "I would like to thank you, first, for joining us today. Please take a seat."

As the group settled, he continued. "Our community, our territory, has now become a part of the Civil War, whether we like it or
not, agree or not," he said solemnly. "It is now up to us to stop the
Confederate forces. I would like to introduce Colonel Edward Canby
to explain more about the situation. We are fortunate to be led by such
an experienced soldier."

Canby walked to the front of the room, his footsteps in his tall
black boots creating the only sound. "As Manuel said, we are now
considered a crucial area in the war effort. We have received word that
General Sibley, who oversees the Confederate forces, is currently in
San Antonio rounding up troops and supplies. Texas, as you know,
has declared itself a part of the Confederate campaign, and they would
love nothing more than to take possession of this territory and, more
importantly, to move forward on to California where there are seaports and gold mines. I can't emphasize the importance of stopping
their efforts here," Canby said over mumblings from the gathered citizens.

"Due to the seriousness of the situation, we have received permission from Washington to hold our regular forces, who were slated to
travel to the east, here, where they will be desperately needed. We have
made additional requests for troops from Colorado and California,"
Canby said.

Colonel Carson stood. "Colonel, if I may. I have been honored to
make a life here, and I don't doubt for a second that the men of this
territory will come forward and help defend against the rebels. Already, we have enough men who have volunteered to create two regiments and most of them are farmers, herders, and tradesman. Each of
you sitting in this room knows one or all of them."

There was a loud burst of applause from the group and Governor
Connelly stepped to the front of the room. "We must protect what is
ours," he said passionately. "Our families, our homes, our way of life."

The group erupted with questions and comments for both men,
and they answered, careful not to disclose details that could threaten
their own plans.

Breaking away, Colonel Carson joined Manuel at the back of the room. "Good turn out," Carson said.

Manuel leaned his head close to Carson. "Yes, hopefully, they will understand the significance and do their best to get on the right side." Carson looked perplexed and Manuel offered an explanation. "It's been difficult to determine which side some people are on. Many felt we would never be a part of this war, and since we still reside in a territory and not a state, they believe they have the luxury of not committing."

"That's not hard to believe," Carson said. "I know up north there were many who felt like the U.S. government had done nothing for them and wondered why they should join or support the Union."

"I understand, but now, we have no options," Manuel said as he folded his arms. "Either they are with the Union, or we consider them to be Confederate sympathizers. I suspect there are some who are taking this risk."

It was nearly evening when the guests started to leave, and Lydia was busy saying goodbyes and giving reassurances to the men and women. As she turned to see an older couple to the staircase, she noticed that Carlos Aragon was standing across the room with an irritated look on his face.

He was tall, with jet black hair, chiseled features, and wore a custom-made suit. Many women considered him extremely handsome, and with his father's wealth at his disposal, a very good catch. Lydia had known Carlos most of her life. Their mothers had been the best of friends, and as a result, after her own mother died, Mrs. Aragon had made it a point to watch over Lydia as much as she could.

Carlos made his way across the room to her. "I feel you have been avoiding me all afternoon, Lydia," he said sternly.

"Oh no, Carlos," she said lightly. "I was only making sure that all our guests were comfortable."

His frustration showed with an agitated sigh, but before he could reply, Vicar Lamy joined them. "I want to thank you, Mademoiselle Lydia, for your hospitality and for giving us the opportunity to understand our situation," he said with a heavy French accent. He wore his simple brown Franciscan robes and gestured with his hands as he spoke, with genuine concern about the situation reflecting in his eyes. She nodded in acknowledgement, and he turned to Carlos.

"Señor, I hope I will have the honor of marrying the two of you," Lamy said. "I was informed of the engagement by your father, Lydia, but I understand the war would cause a postponement."

"Thank you, Vicar," Carlos injected. "We are working on other arrangements right now that might hasten the wedding."

Lydia gently reached for the Vicar's hand. "Nothing has been decided yet. It would be an honor to have you perform the ceremony," she said and escorted him and Carlos to the front of the house to collect their wraps.

As Carlos was leaving, he leaned over and kissed her on the cheek. "I am staying in town for a few days with my father to take care of some business. I will call on you tomorrow and we can discuss the wedding arrangements." She waved goodbye as he started toward his carriage and closed the front door with a sigh.

After all the guests had departed and the plates and cups had all been cleared, the family sat down for dinner in the formal dining room. Alita had overseen the setting of the table with the white porcelain dishes and crystal wine glasses.

"How did the troops look today, Papa?" Lydia asked as she served a warm vegetable soup from a tureen.

Manuel had hoped they would at least get through the main course before their discussion again turned to war. He had always talked openly and honestly with both his children. It had never occurred to him to limit Lydia's education because she was a woman. On the contrary, he had always challenged her intellect and understanding by discussing serious issues with her. Both Lydia and Eduardo had learned the inner workings of the family business at an early age. Each of them had worked behind the counter of the mercantile store, helping customers and entering figures into the ledgers. They both knew how to care for livestock and understood their value. They were also familiar and knowledgeable about territorial issues.

"I have news but I'm afraid it is not promising," Manuel said. "I was a part of the military exercises today. The territory's militia turned out for Governor Connelly and Colonel Canby." Manuel paused while he unfolded his napkin and placed it on his lap. "Most of the men that make up the territory's Union army are poorly armed and untrained."

Lydia frowned, creating a familiar wrinkle between her eyebrows. "But you said there were close to one thousand men. That sounds hopeful. Surely these men can be trained and armed."

"If only it were that simple, Lydia," Eduardo said. "The wealthier families are fronting the funds for supplies, but we have only a few trained soldiers who can train others. We are simply running out of time. We will have to demonstrate a strong show of force against the Texas troops, especially since they have already seized parts of the territory."

Alita brought in the main course, a slow-cooked brisket with hearty vegetables and homemade bread. She also filled the slender crystal wine glasses with a deep burgundy wine made at a monastery to the north of Santa Fe.

Lydia was about to ask her father another question when Eduardo raised his wine glass toward her. "Let us talk of happier occasions. A toast, Lydia, to your marriage. May you and Carlos always be happy."

Lydia did not respond immediately, but she slowly and carefully lifted her wine glass up to acknowledge the toast. "Thank you, Eduardo," she said as she sipped a small amount of the dark wine. She kept her eyes cast downward for a few moments. She didn't want either of them to see the emotional turmoil she was feeling inside. When she finally looked up, she was composed, even though her face was slightly flushed.

Dinner moved along between conversation, and the three eventually returned to the small parlor to share more stories and savor the warmth of each other's presence. Lydia and Eduardo were playing a game of checkers, as they had when they were children.

"I beat you again," Lydia said as she stifled a yawn. "But you will have to get revenge another day. I am off to bed. Good night, Papa," she said as she stood and leaned forward to kiss his cheek.

"Good night, my dear," he said as he held her hand tightly.

"I am feeling the long trip home," said Eduardo. "I will walk upstairs with you, Lydia. Good night, Papa."

Alone with his thoughts, Manuel sipped his brandy and focused on the roaring fire but not seeing it at all. In his mind's eye, his memory wove scenes of his wife, Elise, young and alive. Her face was radiant and glowing proudly as she held Eduardo when he was just a baby. The many wonderful memories of the laughter and the joy and the life he'd shared with her drifted by. Eventually, there was the final vision of Elise shrouded by blankets, lying in her death bed, pale and ashen, holding Lydia, who was a tiny bundle at her side, asking him to always take care of the children. Manuel remembered how weak she was when she barely whispered, "I want my son to be educated in the East, and I want Lydia to marry Carlos. His mother is the best friend and woman I have ever known, and she will look out for my little girl. Please Manuel, promise me these things." Holding her hand and stroking her face, he could do nothing but agree with his wife. She was so close to death, and he could only think of her wishes.

As Lydia began to grow, her father never truly worried about the promise he had made. Being both mother and father to two small children made his days very full. He had toyed with the idea of marrying again, but never found another woman who compared to Elise. He thought the children would be young forever, but one day he realized they were growing up.

True to his word, Manuel sent Eduardo to a private school in Alexandria, Virginia, when he turned fourteen. Lydia was fast becoming a young woman, and Manuel had begun to wonder why Elise had wanted this marriage for her daughter. Both the families had kept in touch over the years, and Mrs. Aragon had always taken a special interest in Lydia, being fully aware of her mother's dying wish. He'd finally realized that, in Elise's mind, this might have been the only way she could have some impact on Lydia's adult life. Her true friend would eventually become Lydia's mother-in-law and become a permanent female fixture in her life as she traveled through adulthood.

Manuel ran his left hand through his dark hair, now touched with streaks of gray. He had never taken off the simple gold wedding band Elise had given him so many years ago.

"My love," he whispered to himself, "I will keep my promise to you. I only hope it is the right thing." Lydia seemed so young and vulnerable to him and now, with the war, he cared about nothing but the safety of his children.

Upstairs, Lydia lay awake in her bed. Thoughts of marrying Carlos, thoughts of the war and what it would mean, were running through her mind. When sleep finally came, it was troubled, and she tossed and turned late into the night.

≡ 4 ≡

Over a hundred miles away at Fort Garland in the Colorado Territory, Lieutenant Colonel Eli Stevens was in a deep sleep when the private came to wake him. "Colonel Riley wants to see you right away."

Eli moaned, and the private, afraid to touch him, raised his voice. "Please sir, wake up." Eli did not respond and the private again began his plea. "Sir."

"All right, Johnson. I heard you. Tell the Colonel I'll be right there," said Eli. He pulled the thin wool blanket back and rolled his long legs over the edge of the cot as the private exited the small quarters. Eli had been sleeping soundly, but he was used to these late-night meetings with the Colonel, it was the time Riley was at his best and he often called Eli in for discussions.

Eli struck a match against the wall and bent to light the kerosene lamp, which cast a shadow on the few pieces of furniture including a cot, a small armoire, chest, and washstand.

The fire had long since faded to smoldering embers, and the air in the windowless room was crisp and cold as he pulled on his light blue wool uniform pants along with thick socks and his tall black boots. Eli removed a freshly laundered white cotton shirt from his wooden chest and stopped to appreciate the clean smell of the starched fabric as he pulled his arms through the sleeves and adjusted his leather suspenders on top of his broad shoulders.

He poured a small amount of water into the large metal washbowl and washed his face, which was showing the early beginnings of a heavy beard. Taking some of the cold water into his hands, he ran them through his dark wavy hair.

The navy-blue coat with red piping hung on a hook at the edge of his cot along with his hat. Eli grabbed both as he made his way towards the door. Pulling the heavy wool coat on, he paused to secure four gold buttons in the front. He placed his wool forage cap, with a brass infantry horn in the front center, firmly on his head, quietly opened the door, and stepped into the dark night.

The cold air assaulted his senses. The early winter moon, covered partially by clouds, offered little light. As he made his way toward the Colonel's quarters, Eli's breath created a misty steam. The walls of Fort Garland surrounded him. The adobe fort had been built in 1858 on land that was part of the Sangre de Cristo land grant. It was established to protect surrounding settlers from Indian resistance but now served as a base camp for over 200 Union soldiers. He tried to step quietly as he passed the small tents where his men lay sleeping. They had worked hard today, learning the tedious exercises and drills it would take to become a united army.

As he came closer to the Colonel's quarters, his strides were long and determined and the crackling sound of his footsteps could be heard in the crusted, frozen snow covering the ground. Eli nodded at the soldier standing guard at the Colonel's room and knocked on the door before turning the knob.

Eli entered the dimly lit room clouded by a blue haze of smoke from the Colonel's constant cigar. The Colonel looked up with gray eyes set in dark circles and heavy bags, and Eli raised his hand to his head and straightened his body in a salute.

"At ease, Stevens. Take a seat. Private, pour the Lieutenant Colonel some whiskey," said Colonel Riley, nodding at the young man pressed into the shadows of the room who returned to place a small glass on the desk.

"Thank you, sir," said Eli as he sat down in one of the hard, wooden chairs in front of the desk.

Sitting back, Colonel Riley took a long puff on his cigar. "I felt it was necessary to call you in, Stevens. We've had a messenger arrive today from the New Mexico Territory," the Colonel said. "It seems the war effort is moving more quickly there than we thought. As you know, Texas seceded from the Union, and Texas troops have captured both Fort Fillmore at El Paso and Fort Bliss in the southern part of the territory."

Eli nodded his head as the Colonel continued. "The Texas commander, Sibley, has declared himself military governor of the territory." He paused. "And he has claimed it as Confederate territory."

Eli took a long drink of the whiskey from his glass. He could feel the hot liquid burning as it traveled down his throat. "What about their troops? What can we expect?" he asked.

"The territory is sparsely populated. Most of the New Mexico militia is made up of volunteers. They were left without direction when the commander of the U.S. troops left his post and joined the Confederates last spring. I daresay they can't defend the territory on their own, although I have faith in Colonel Canby. I have received letters from Governor Connelly and our Governor Evans, and they agree two of our companies should immediately be sent to New Mexico to assist."

"Stevens, I want you to lead a small group of your men to Santa Fe to assess the situation and get back to me immediately so I can correspond with the Governors. My gut feeling is that the Texans will try to take Fort Union next, and they will have to go through Santa Fe. We'll have to be prepared for any circumstance. They may have another route planned and we may have to move all our troops in quickly."

"I understand, Colonel. I will keep you posted on any developments in the area. Who should I report to when we arrive in Santa Fe?"

"Colonel Canby. I hope he will remain in the city until he knows which direction the Confederate troops will be moving. You may be in the area for many months or just a few weeks."

The two men talked late into the night about their plans and the best strategy to use, depending on what the Confederates did. Revelry sounded at dawn, and Colonel Riley decided Eli and his men would leave that morning.

Stepping out into the cold morning air caused Eli to shiver. He paused for a moment in the soft morning light. He had been sitting in the same position too long and it felt good to stretch his muscles.

The camp was alive with activity. Many of the men were preparing for the day's chores and routine exercises. Most had come out of their tents and were stoking their fires to make coffee, a precious commodity. Other rations included hard bread, salt pork, sugar, and salt. Fort Garland was surrounded by farms and ranches, and this morning the soldiers would enjoy eggs and biscuits courtesy of the townspeople. The clanking of pots and pans, small bits of conversation, and the scent of burning firewood drifted toward Eli.

The horses could be heard from the corrals as they waited for their hay and oats. Most of the soldiers had brought their own horses, not risking the possibility that they might have to engage in battle without one. The men who had joined the Union army in the Colorado Territory were ranchers, hunters, miners, and even some Indians. They were rugged and self-assured; this land was harsh and savage at times, and they were seasoned by its temperament.

Eli approached his captain, a young man close to his own age with a ready smile. "Edwards, we will be leaving this morning for the New Mexico Territory," he said. "Let Davis, Armstrong, Hale, and Carter know. It will take us several days, so make sure each man has enough food and ammunition."

"Yes sir, Lieutenant Colonel Stevens," Edwards replied briskly as he held his hand in a salute.

Eli returned the salute and continued on his way. He was still trying to get used to his position. It had come as a surprise when Colonel Riley requested that Eli be appointed lieutenant colonel of the troops at Fort Garland. He had joined the U.S. Army at the tender age of seventeen and had been involved in suppressing Indian uprisings over the last few years.

Eli was headed toward his quarters when he passed a small group of the men who would be riding with him. They were brewing coffee in a tin pot over a fire. "Good morning," Eli said as he stopped. "Can you spare a cup of coffee?"

"Yes sir," said Hale, a middle-aged man with a cheery disposition. He poured the bitter coffee into a tin cup with hands calloused from farming. "Here you go, sir."

"Thank you, Private Hale, and you all eat a hearty breakfast. We'll be pulling out today for the New Mexico Territory."

One of the older soldiers, who wore a heavy beard splattered with gray and a deep scar across his eyebrow, let out a joyful whoop. "We're finally gonna get a chance to whup them Confederates!" he cried.

Eli grinned at the soldier. "Save that enthusiasm for the battle-field, Davis." He drank the coffee in one easy gulp then handed the cup back to the Private. "Be ready to leave at noon. I'll see you men shortly," he said.

As Eli walked away, one of the older men spit tobacco into the snow. "What a lot of nonsense, having that young'un as a lieutenant colonel in this man's army. The Colonel ought to be hanged for choos-ing him. Why, he probably couldn't find his way out of a gunny sack."

"I'd be careful about what you say, Armstrong," said Davis. "The way I hear it, he's one hell of a gunman and he can charm the mocca-sins right off the Injun's feet. It appears to me that's the kind of man we'll need to win this here war." Armstrong shrugged and spit again into the snow.

Eli opened the door to his quarters. A fire blazed in the small pot-bellied stove and radiated warmth through the room. He needed a bath, breakfast, and his gear packed for the journey.

First things first, he thought as he gathered his soap, shaving brush, razor, mirror, and towel and headed towards the stream that ran out-side the walls of the fort.

The bubbling sounds from the running water were soothing, and Eli enjoyed the escape from the noise and confines of the fort. Even though the temperature was cold, Eli removed his wool jacket, leaving him in his white cotton shirt. He set up the mirror in the branch of a tree near the stream, dropped his suspenders, rolled up his sleeves, and unbuttoned his shirt to reveal the dark hair on his chest.

Mixing a small amount of the frigid water with the soap, Eli used the shaving brush to create a thick lather, which he spread in a circular motion across the lower part of his face and on his neck. He picked up the razor, and with a practiced hand, slid the sharp blade up from his neck to his square chin. His mouth was set in a straight, determined line. Life had handed many blows to Eli, and it showed in his intelligent brown eyes that looked older and wiser than his twenty-five years.

Completing his shave, Eli knelt and rinsed his face with water from the stream. He then removed his shirt, pants, and socks and jumped into the clear water. The water was freezing, but he spent some time washing, not knowing when he would have another opportunity. Feeling fully refreshed and invigorated, Eli climbed out onto the bank and spent little time drying off and getting dressed.

He walked back to his room to find Private Johnson waiting with a plate of steaming food. "Sir, the Colonel thought you might want a hot breakfast this morning."

Eli's mouth began to water at the sight of golden biscuits, fried eggs, and ham. Eli truly appreciated the Colonel's gesture; he knew he would be eating hardtack and dried beef for the next several days. "Please send the Colonel my thanks, Private," Eli said as he sat down to enjoy the warm food.

Popping the last piece of ham into his mouth, Eli rose and packed his rations, ammunition, gear, and some clothes into his haversack and saddle bags. He had spent some time the day before cleaning and polishing his rifle and his .44 caliber revolver, and he carefully inspected the guns before slotting them into their holsters. He also spent a few moments inspecting the edge of his bayonet before placing it in its leather case.

Eli had requested his horse be brought up from the grazing fields. He carried his gear outside and laid his saddle on the wooden fence outside his room. Looking out toward the field, he saw the private leading his horse with a tether and headed in his direction. Eli whistled loudly and smiled as the stallion broke into a quick gallop, pulling the reins out of the private's hands.

Coal had been a part of Eli's life for many years. The black horse had been young and wild when he was captured and brought to the family ranch. His upper leg had been injured during his capture, and Eli's stepfather was ready to let the colt go free and fend for himself, but Eli begged him to let him work with the animal. After much discussion, Eli won out and became devoted to making sure the colt overcame the injury. As a result, Coal had become a loyal and obedient horse. Eli had chosen his name, not only for his color, but also because he had several white spots on his right rear quarters that reminded Eli of the white edges found in coal when burned.

The horse nuzzled Eli's chest with his head. "Okay boy," Eli said soothingly. "Stand still now while I saddle you up." He placed a finely crafted leather saddle on Coal's back. It had been a gift from his mother and stepfather when Eli left the ranch to join the army and begin his own life.

He carefully fastened the straps underneath the horse's stomach. Eli noticed from the sun's shadows that midday was approaching. He cinched his bulging saddle bags, making sure they were secure. He threw a heavy navy-blue wool cape over his uniform, pulled on his long, gold-colored gloves, and climbed into his saddle.

Five men on horseback were waiting for Eli. He nodded his head at them, and the men formed a column behind him as they made their way outside the fort. Colonel Riley stood outside his cabin headquarters and saluted Eli and the other men as they rode past. Under his breath he said, "May God travel with you, son, and protect you in all your battles."

*　*　*

The trail they took led them through a steep and narrow canyon. A light snow was falling, and the horses carefully selected their footing. Eli hoped the weather would improve as they came down from the higher elevations.

The distance between Fort Garland and Santa Fe was about 130 miles, and it would take them several days. Eli wanted to pace his men so they could make good time without being exhausted—he wasn't sure what would be waiting for them when they arrived.

As they rode, his ears became accustomed to the sounds from the horse's hoofs, the men's voices, and the noises of nature. Tall pine trees protected them from the bitter cold wind sailing down through the canyon. When the day's light was beginning to grow dim, Eli decided they would make camp for the night.

They stopped at a clearing with a stream running through it. Two of the men watered the horses then set up tents, while the others gathered firewood and made a temporary corral out of fallen trees. Within a short time, the horses were fed and content and the men were warming themselves by a roaring fire.

"Nothing can beat a warm fire on a cold winter's night," said Davis as they ate dried beef and hard biscuits. "Too bad we don't have a pot of beans or fresh stew. That would sure warm us up. How far along did we get today, Lieutenant?"

"We covered about seven miles," Eli said. "We'll need to move as quickly and quietly as possible. There is still a threat of Indians, and there could be Confederate soldiers scouting the area."

The men were listening intently, but Armstrong, who was using his knife to carve on a small piece of wood, acted as though he wasn't.

Carter, a young man who had recently left his parent's home to join the newly formed army, asked, "Why New Mexico, Lieutenant? Shouldn't we be protecting our own territory?"

"The Texas troops have already entered the New Mexico Territory on the southern side. We believe they will try to get through Albuquerque, then Santa Fe, and on to Fort Union," Eli said. "It's the only fort between the Confederates and Colorado. We need to stop them there, Private. Once we arrive in Santa Fe, we will survey the area and report back to Colonel Riley."

Armstrong spit a wad of tobacco near the fire and muttered something under his breath.

"Did you have something to say, Armstrong?" asked Eli.

Armstrong locked eyes with Eli. "No sir," he finally said.

Eli could feel his temper rise as he snapped back, "Good, you'll take the first watch tonight. Hale, you'll relieve him." He threw the rest of his biscuit in the fire. "Get a good night's rest men, we'll leave at dawn tomorrow."

Sleep did not come quickly to Eli as he tried to make himself comfortable on the bed roll, the only thing between him and the hard, snow-packed ground. He could physically feel the lack of sleep from the previous night, but he wasn't able to relax. He was concerned about Armstrong's attitude and the effect it might have on the other men. A lack of respect could destroy a troop of men just as easily as a lack of control. Eli could feel the anger rise in his chest as he remembered the look on Armstrong's face. He had wanted to take him to the ground and hit him with a cold, hard fist, but Eli had learned to control his temper during his struggles with his stepfather. After taking some deep breaths, he finally slept.

The next day, the small company rode nearly seventeen miles. The men only stopped once at the edge of a stream to water the horses and eat their midday meal. At the campfire that night there was little conversation. They were tired from the day's ride and the continual pounding, frigid wind. Davis softly played a harmonica as the men tried to stay warm in the cold grip of the winter night.

Eli finally stood, his legs and back stiff. "I'll take the first watch tonight. Carter, you'll relieve me."

"Yes sir," Carter replied as he rubbed his hands together over the fire.

Eli selected a site a few yards from the camp and horses where he had a good vantage point of both. He stood and watched as the small camp finally fell silent; he was alone except for the sounds of the night. He placed his rifle close by and, out of habit, placed his hand on his holster.

The sky was clear, and the stars shone brilliantly against their dark backdrop. Eli relaxed as he sat down and leaned against a pine tree. The stillness of the night and the lulling sound of the nearby stream forced his mind back to an easier time. He was filled with happy memories of hunting trips together with his younger brother and father. The time they shared was very brief, but Eli would never forget.

Eli's parents had come to the Colorado Territory from Pennsylvania when the boys were very young. Eli's father had a dream of starting a cattle ranch in the rugged territory. They sold most of their belongings, and with one wagon and a small herd of cattle, made the treacherous journey west.

The first few years were lean, and they barely survived. But as the two boys grew, so did the family's commitment to making Colorado their home. Eli had come to cherish those early memories and, as a young man, realized the importance of all the things his father had taught him. He loved his mother, Anna, who he had fond memories of working in the garden on a sunny day. After his father's death, he never thought she would remarry and was shocked when she broke the news to her two sons.

The sudden crack of a branch made Eli's heart jump and he was instantly alert. He held his rifle ready. If it wasn't an Indian or a Confederate, there was always the danger of mountain lions. He sat very still and eventually made out the shadows of a small group of deer drinking from the stream. Had the circumstances been different, Eli would have used his expert shooting skills to kill one of the deer for its meat. He waited and watched as the graceful animals slipped quietly back into the thick trees and the darkness.

When his shift was over, Eli silently walked to where Carter was sleeping to wake him. "Carter, wake up," he whispered. The young man's eyes opened quickly, as though he hadn't even been asleep.

Eli noticed the apprehension in Carter. "Is something wrong, Private?" he asked.

Carter sat up and gathered his rifle. "Not really, sir. I'm fine," he said.

"Follow me, I'll show you a good spot to stand guard," Eli said.

Both men, wrapped in their heavy coats and wool blankets thrown over their shoulders, walked up towards the ledge through the heavy snow on the ground.

Eli waited until Carter was settled. "I'm going to get some rest now. Wake me if you hear or see anything suspicious," Eli said as he turned his back.

"Lieutenant, can I ask you something before you go?" Carter asked. Eli nodded. "Have you ever killed a man?"

Eli drew a deep breath and sat down next to the young man. "Before I answer, why do you ask?"

"Well, to be honest with you, sir… I'm scared. Here we are marching off to a fight in some strange place against men we've never seen before. I've never even shot at anyone before, much less killed a man, and I don't know if I can pull the trigger when I must."

"Well by God, why did you join?" Eli asked with a smile, trying to break the tension. Before Carter could respond, Eli continued.

"It was right after I left my parent's ranch. I was seventeen years old, and I had been riding with a small group of cattle drivers. We stopped in Golden one night and went into the saloon for a drink. There were two drunken fools playing poker. We were standing at the bar minding our own business. Pretty soon, this dusty, old miner came in and accused one of the two men of stealing his mule and his equipment. The man denied it and began beating the old man. I told the man to stop. He stood up straight, smiled, and reached for his gun. I drew mine faster and killed him."

The sound of the wind rustled between the two men. "I was protecting someone," Eli said, "and that's how you'll feel, Carter. You're protecting the people and the land you love. We can't let them take what belongs to us without a fight. The strength will come to you when you need it, and you'll do the right thing when the time comes. You'll have no choice." Eli patted Carter on the shoulder and left him to his own thoughts.

The next morning, the small unit continued to make their way south. The weather improved slightly, and the men became accustomed to the demanding pace. On the fourth day, one of the horses began limping badly, which caused the group to slow down.

Eli knew they were approaching the village of Taos and remembered that a friend's father owned a ranch nearby. He had an idea of the approximate location and hoped that he could find the house for a hot meal and good night's sleep for his men.

It was late in the afternoon when he ordered the troop to stop and wait in a secluded area. "Captain Edwards," Eli ordered, "Hale and I will try to locate the Sutton Ranch. You're in charge while I'm gone. Be on the lookout, there are different Indian tribes in the area. There's no telling whether they are for or against the Union army."

"If you don't return before dark, Lieutenant, we'll make camp here," Edwards said. Eli nodded his head in agreement as he and Hale headed out.

After an hour's ride, the two men came to the top of a ridge over-looking the entire Taos valley. From that distance and vantage point, the ranches scattered about looked like doll houses and it was difficult to tell one from the other. As they scanned the area, their attention was drawn to something moving at the top of one of the homes. It was hard to make out at first, but then Eli realized it was an American flag waving in the breeze.

"Hale, I believe we have found the place we're looking for. Go back and get the rest of the men. Bring them to that ranch," Eli said as he pointed. "I'll be waiting for you."

It didn't take him long to get down to the valley, and he cautious-ly approached the entrance to the sprawling hacienda. An older man with broad shoulders and a slim build came out from the main house. He wore a leather vest with a white shirt, dark wool pants, and rugged brown boots, and a bright kerchief was tied around his neck. "What can I do for you, son?" he asked.

"Are you Mr. Sutton?" Eli asked. "Thomas Sutton?"

"Yes. I am," he replied gruffly.

"I know your son, sir. I am Lieutenant Colonel Eli Stevens, United States Army. I was hoping my men could spend the night here. We need fresh horses as well."

"I would be mighty honored to be of service to you," the old man said. "Please, come in." Eli swung his leg over and came down from his horse.

"Raul," Sutton called loudly then said to Eli, "My man, Raul, will see to your horse and watch for your men."

"Thank you," said Eli as he tied Coal's reins to the porch.

He followed Sutton into the spacious front room of the house and removed his gloves and cloak. The furniture was made from thick slabs of wood from the forest nearby. It looked uncomfortably sturdy, and yet when Eli sat down in one of the chairs, he leaned back and felt the softness of the thick cushions. A fire burned brightly in the corner of the room, and Eli noticed there were many books strewn about the tables with bookmarks securely in place.

Sutton filled two small glasses with whiskey from a glass decanter and handed one to Eli. As he turned, he revealed a face that had been exposed to the elements over the years. Deep lines etched his forehead and around his mouth, making him seem timeless. His hair was a silvery gray, but it was hard to tell whether he was forty-five or seventy-five. As he took a seat, he asked, "How did you know my son?"

"We worked together running cattle in the Colorado Territory. It was only for a few months. He used to talk about this ranch, and you. I feel like I've been here. How is your son, where is he now?"

Sutton, standing in front of the fireplace, answered in a low, gruff voice. "He was shot and killed by some cattle rustlers in Colorado. He was on his way home with the herd he had picked out."

"I'm sorry to hear that," Eli said. "He was a good man." Sutton looked at Eli and nodded, the look on his face showing the depth of his pain.

"My son and I talked about the war before it came to this part of the country," Sutton said. "He would have joined the Union army, that's part of the reason I put up the flag—in his honor." Eli nodded in understanding.

"There's another reason too. I have a strong suspicion the people who killed my son and stole the herd are just south of here. I know of some ranch owners who have a brand very similar to mine."

"Go on," said Eli as he leaned forward in his chair.

"I've suspected it for a long time, but I never had enough proof to accuse them of it outright. Hell, I still don't," Sutton said as he moved to stand in front of Eli. "You need to be careful. There's talk in the territory. There seem to be some who want nothing more than to see the Confederates win. My sources tell me it's the same group that took my son's life. I understand they intend to help with food, money, horses, anything the rebels may need. I decided to fly the flag to show them where I stood, along with many others in this territory,"

"Let the Union army take care of this," Eli said. "You could be putting yourself in a great deal of danger."

Sutton laughed sarcastically. "No offense, son, but that's a chance I'm willing to take. I've lost everyone I ever had any feelings for, my wife many years ago and my son. It doesn't really matter what happens to me now. But I swear to you, Stevens, I'll find the men who killed my son before I die."

Both men's attention turned to the sounds of Eli's men riding into the ranch.

"I'll find a way to let you know if I find out anything worthwhile," Sutton said. "In the meantime, watch your back. It may be hard to tell your enemies from your friends."

After settling in, the men enjoyed steaming bowls of mutton stew, plenty of fresh bread, coffee, and small preserved fruit pies.

After dinner, they spread their bed rolls out in the massive front room with its roaring fire. Well-fed and warm, the men slept quite soundly. The next morning, Sutton exchanged four horses with the small troop.

"Santa Fe is about a three day's ride from here," Sutton said.

"Thank you for the night's lodging and the horses," Eli said. "Try to get word to me if you have any information." Sutton shook Eli's hand and watched as they rode off into the mountains towards their destination.

They arrived in Santa Fe late at night, riding into town quietly so the sleepy village remained undisturbed. The adobe buildings glowed in the moonlight. Eli knew that Fort Marcy was serving as the military headquarters, so he led his men there. The fort building was long and narrow and held barracks, corrals, and offices for the Union army.

Eli slid out of his saddle, tied Coal up along the hitching post outside, and walked toward the front gate. Suddenly, a wiry, nervous private stepped right in front of Eli and pointed a rifle at his chest. "State your name and your business," he said forcefully.

Eli, tired from the long journey, slowly raised his hand and moved the tip of the rifle away from his chest. "I am Lieutenant Colonel Eli Stevens, United States Army, here to see Colonel Canby," he said.

The young man shouldered his rifle and saluted. "Bring your men inside. I'll have someone show them where they can bunk. I'll let the Colonel know you're here."

≡ 5 ≡

Lydia was awake early, but she remained in the warmth of her bed and listened to the sounds of melting snow dripping from the rooftop. Light from a brilliant morning sun crept through the slight openings of her thick curtains. Usually, she would have been up and ready for breakfast, but she felt worn out after having a few restless nights.

There was a soft knock at the door and Alita entered with a small tray holding a steaming cup of tea in a dainty porcelain cup.

"Buenos días," Lydia said as she pulled the thick quilt aside, smoothed out her ankle-length white nightgown, and sat up on the edge of her bed. She shook her hair to get out some of the tangles and tied it back with a wide ribbon from the top of her nightstand.

"I had the feeling I'd like to stay in bed all day today and do nothing," Lydia said as Alita placed the tray on a chest at the bottom of the bed. Both women looked at one another and smiled broadly.

Alita knew Lydia had rarely been ill and was never one to stay in bed. Alita opened the dark burgundy curtains, allowing the bright sun to pour into the room. She stoked the sleeping embers in the fireplace and they slowly came to life. In a short time, she had the fire up and going.

Lydia sipped her tea and enjoyed a few quiet moments. Alita had already pulled out a dress for the day's activities. After washing up, Lydia slipped the light chemise over her head and stepped into her corset. At times, she hated the restraining feel of the awkward garment and wondered why women wore them. Alita didn't need to bind the stays too tightly; Lydia was petite and narrow in her waist. Lydia moved closer to the fire as she had begun to shiver in the cold morning air, and she pulled her black woolen stockings over her slim calves and thighs.

Alita tugged gently on the white silky petticoat as it went over Lydia's head, and she stepped into the heavy wool dress. The deep purple color was accentuated by narrow black embroidery trim fashioned into a delicate flower pattern on the front lapels of the dress. The top was fitted to the waist. The cuffs of the sleeves and the front of the skirt held the same black embroidery. Many of Lydia's dresses were made by a local dress maker. Being the daughter of the owner of the town mercantile, she was able to select and order all her fabric and trims which left room for expression and creativity.

After lacing her ankle boots, Lydia sat down on the bench at her dressing table. She shook her hair loose from its ribbon and began brushing through it with a silver-plated hairbrush. With Alita's assistance, all her dark auburn hair was pulled back from her face, braided, and rolled into a chignon at the back of her neck. The final touch was a pair of earring bobs that were set with black onyx stones.

As Lydia gazed at her reflection, she noticed the deep purple color from her dress emphasized the lack of color in her face. As if on cue, Alita reached over and gently pinched both of her cheeks.

Leaving Alita to tidy up the room, Lydia made her way down the narrow stairway and stepped into the quiet hallway. Both her father and Eduardo had eaten breakfast earlier and were already out of the house. Sunday was normally a day of rest and relaxation for the Sena family. They would have a light breakfast, attend mid-morning mass together, return home for a huge meal shared by family and friends, and finally, spend an afternoon of visiting and socializing in the plaza, if the weather permitted.

Since the war had come, however, the simple customs that had been taken for granted were replaced by more pressing tasks for the men, leaving the women to contend with the emptiness. Lydia sat down at the dining room table, the only sound being the settling of her petticoat. The cook had left a warm plate of eggs, bacon, and tortillas on the sideboard.

The slow rhythm of the ticking clock made Lydia more aware of the stillness in the house. It left her feeling unsettled, and she decided she wasn't very hungry and would wait to have something after mass. *Just as well*, she thought to herself. *I will fast before communion this morning.*

She took her plate of food into the warm, cheery kitchen and spent a few moments giving directions for the evening meal to the cook. "Rico killed two chickens this morning," she said. Maria looked up momentarily and nodded as she kneaded her bread dough with patient, practiced hands. Lydia embraced the warmth and smells of the kitchen, and for a few moments, she was comforted by the soothing environment.

She eventually made her way to the parlor and checked the time on the ornate grandfather clock on the fireplace. It was later than she thought so she hurried up the narrow stairs to her bedroom, hoping to catch her father or brother at the mercantile before she went to church.

The small black hat with a veil sat on her bed along with the short spencer coat that matched her dress. She took a few moments to secure the hat with pins. Always watching over and caring for her charge, Alita held the coat so Lydia could pull it on over her dress. Nodding in final approval, Alita placed her own heavy wool shawl over her head and shoulders to face the winter morning.

Lydia picked up her black leather gloves and small satchel sitting on the wooden bench in the entryway and headed for the front door. She pulled hard to open the ancient, thick piece of wood and slammed it soundly behind them so that it would close properly. She was leaving Maria alone in the rambling house to prepare the evening meal, and Lydia wanted to make sure she would be safe. Their home had always been secure and well-fortified in the event of an Indian raid or any kind of trouble. Normally, she wouldn't have worried about such precautions, but along with the prospect of war came feelings of uncertainty and distrust.

Since Lydia was an unmarried young woman, custom dictated that she be accompanied by her maid when she went out in public. They made their way down the steps, across the patio, and through a large wooden gate secured with a heavy latch. Lydia and Alita walked gingerly down the narrow sidewalk, being careful not to step in the thick mud created by melting snow.

Their first stop was at the end of their street just before the plaza. Manuel's store, Santa Fe Mercantile, sat on the corner of Palace Avenue and Shelby Street. The two women went around to the back side of the tall building and entered through a small door in the alleyway, passing through a storeroom with stacks of crates and barrels. As they entered the front end of the establishment, they saw Ramon dusting among the many shelves filled with jars, material, farm tools, lumber, flour, sugar, and other food items.

"Buenos días, Señorita Sena and Alita," Ramon said as he came out from behind the large wooden counter. He had been working at the store since he was a young man many years ago. On Sundays, the store was closed, and the morning was reserved for cleaning and accounting.

"Buenos días," Lydia replied warmly. She looked around the store. "It doesn't look like my father or brother have been by the shop this morning."

"No, I have not seen them, Señorita."

Lydia was disappointed, for she'd been hoping they could join her for mass. She exchanged small bits of conversation about Ramon's family. "Ramon, please say hello to your wife and hurry with your work so you can get home to your family," Lydia said as she and Alita stepped back outside through the front door.

Knowing there was still time before mass, Lydia decided to visit her cousin, Claire. She motioned to Alita to follow as they walked towards the plaza. The morning sun glimmered through the barren branches of the huge cottonwood trees lining the enormous square and fell upon the tiniest remainders of forgotten snow still lingering. There were one-story buildings around the plaza that contained shops, offices, the post office, a saloon, the Fonda Hotel, and the Palace of the Governors. The small town had grown over the years, and the arrival of the stagecoach had brought new residents and goods to satisfy the need for many types of services and commodities.

Although the plaza was quiet and deserted now, Lydia remembered the many times she had laughed with family and friends, swayed to music, and enjoyed the many celebrations held there. It was a place to see friends and neighbors, exchange greetings, discuss the latest fashion, talk about crops, gush over new family members, and mourn the loss of loved ones. It was also a place for the young people to promenade and exchange pleasantries.

When Lydia thought of these wonderful occasions, Claire immediately came to mind. The two girls had grown up together; she was Lydia's closest female relative and two years older. Claire's father had named her Antonita Claire, in honor of her grandfather. Her mother despised her only daughter's first name and called her Claire from birth. Lydia and Claire had both attended the academy for girls, overseen by the sisters of Loretto, where they received religious, math, English, and social training from a very young age. Having only men to turn to at home, Lydia felt a strong bond to her cousin. She had always looked to Claire for consolation and advice, and their intimate relationship progressed naturally as they both grew into young women.

The girls were fully aware of the goings-on in the small town and occasionally took some liberties. They had conspired and succeeded in pushing beyond the unseen social boundaries that held them. One of their habits was to sneak into the brothel in Burro Alley and play poker with the local prostitutes who were clad only in their lacy undergarments and robes. Their games always took place late in the afternoon, when the girls wouldn't be missed at home. They were always brought into the back room and were never exposed to what went on behind the bedroom doors; but the girls understood what occurred, despite the strict rules by the owner, Dona Rene.

Claire had blossomed into a beautiful and high-spirited woman with dark features, including her long, straight hair and almond-shaped eyes that glittered with intelligence and gaiety. As the girls become older, Claire's parents began to worry that she would never marry. It was not that she was unattractive or lacked a dowry, it was that she rarely showed interest in any of the local young men, even though many had come to court her.

She and Lydia spent much of their time riding horses, working in the mercantile store, and hosting teas centered on literature, art, or games with the young men and women of the town. Out of this group, natural couples emerged, began courting, and eventually married. But Claire seemed to shrug off the responsibility of marriage. She would often tell Lydia she wanted to see the world and live independently. "Marriage will bring some joys," she would say, "but I believe it will also bring many crosses to bear."

Lydia occasionally exhibited the same attitude. But, deep down, she knew she wanted to find someone to love. Every so often, she practiced flirting with the young men. She was not unaware of the effect she had on men, and yet, she was truly innocent and naive about using her charm to manipulate and get her own way.

Claire's parents were quite surprised and delighted when a young lawyer from back East came to Santa Fe to live with his grandmother, and Claire showed more than a casual interest in him. After a few months, they were planning a wedding for their daughter, and in the month of May, with Lydia as her maid of honor, Claire became Mrs. Cecil Murray.

Marriage had been both a wonderful and frustrating experience for Claire. She loved Cecil dearly and realized he wanted to be involved in every part of her life, as was expected. She had cherished her freedom but slowly she gave way, knowing it would strengthen their marriage. They were both delighted when she gave birth to a lovely baby girl, who they named Violet.

Cecil, who was tall with bright red hair, hazel-colored eyes, and a soothing manner, had a charming adobe home built for them on a huge parcel of land, not far from the plaza, which had been given as a wedding gift by Claire's family. He had paid close attention to all the details, and it was the first home in Santa Fe to have a bay window. He had the window sent all the way from Boston by train and stagecoach. Several townspeople gathered to watch the window being installed, and Lydia fondly remembered how proud Claire was on that day of her new home and her new husband.

Lydia smiled to herself as they approached her cousin's home. She noticed the fine handmade lace curtains nestled comfortably inside the bay window. *How well Cecil has tamed my cousin*, she thought, wondering if that was a direct effect of love. Alita knocked softly on the front door, and after a moment, the guests were greeted enthusiastically by Claire's maid, Rita, who took their wraps.

Lydia, feeling comfortable in her cousin's home, walked back to Claire's bedroom. "Mi linda!" Claire exclaimed as Lydia entered the room. She was arranging her hair, but she stood up and hugged Lydia tightly. "What a wonderful surprise. I am so happy to see you," she said.

"You look lovely, prima," Lydia said. "Marriage and babies do suit you." Claire smiled broadly as she smoothed out the waist of her dark brown silk dress.

"Please, sit down while I finish my hair, we have time for a quick visit before mass." Claire asked Rita to bring a tray and Alita joined her to help.

Lydia sat back in a chair and let out a long breath. Claire could see her cousin's reflection in her mirror. "You have dark circles under your eyes. Tell me, what is troubling you?" she asked as she put the last few pins in place.

"I am just overtired, is all," Lydia said. "I am also worried about Papa and Eduardo. Who can tell what this war will bring," she said with concern.

Claire stood up from her dressing table and sat in the ornately carved, rosewood chair opposite Lydia. The entire bedroom set was made from the exquisite wood and had been a wedding gift from her grandfather.

Claire rested her hand on top of Lydia's. "I am also worried about Cecil and my brothers," she said. "My mother keeps telling me we must be optimistic and pray each day for strength, but I think it is very difficult being a woman who must sit and wait. At least the men know they will be training and fighting. Have you heard anything at all about where the Confederate troops are now?"

"Not really. Papa said last night they are moving in and are thought to be somewhere in the far southern part of territory. The winter weather is forcing them to travel slowly."

Both women turned at a knock on the door. It was Cecil carrying a small tray with two cups of brewed herbal tea.

"Muchas gracias, mi amor," Claire said with delight.

"I knew Cousin Lydia was here and I wanted to say hello," he said as he placed the tray on the table. He bent down and gave Lydia a kiss on her cheek. "Congratulations on your engagement," he said. "I am sorry I was not able to attend the dinner."

Lydia smiled and held his hand for a moment. "Thank you, Cecil."

As the three continued to talk, Claire stood up from her chair and removed a small piece of lint from Cecil's coat. Lydia could see the love between them come to life through their exchanged glances and touches.

"I'll leave you two to talk. Lydia, will you join us at mass today?" Cecil asked.

"Yes, that was my plan and thank you for asking," she said. With that, the bedroom door closed, and the two women were once again alone.

"Now tell me," Claire said as she sat back down and reached for her cup of tea, "why have you not talked of Carlos. I heard he attended your father's meeting yesterday."

Lydia looked straight at her cousin. "We spoke only briefly. I was very busy with our guests," she said defensively and then sighed deeply. "I am not sure about my feelings for Carlos. He seems a stranger to me." Lydia stood up and walked towards the window. "It was a match made to benefit each family in a different way. A match without love or feelings," she said as she stared vacantly out the window at the still winter landscape. "I don't know which frightens me more, the coming of this war or my marriage to Carlos."

Claire rose and stood behind Lydia. She placed her hands on her shoulders. "Perhaps it was meant to be this way, perhaps you will fall in love with him in time."

Lydia's eyes turned a steely blue as she continued looking out the window but seeing nothing at all. "Yes, I have to continue believing my father and my mother were correct in making this choice for me."

Claire turned towards a large hope chest sitting at the bottom of her bed. "I was saving this for your wedding shower, but I think it will brighten your mood today," she said. After lifting the lid and reaching inside, she turned around with her arms full of a creamy white cloud. She laid it out on her bed and motioned for Lydia to come closer. Very carefully, she unfolded the crocheted tablecloth until it covered the entire bed.

"Mama, Rita, and I have worked on it together for many nights since your engagement was announced. I wanted to give you something very special," Claire said proudly.

"Oh, it is beautiful," Lydia said as she gently examined its delicate detail. "Thank you. I will cherish it always," she said, hugging her cousin tightly.

The moment was interrupted by a gentle knock at the door. It was Rita holding Violet in her arms.

"Ah my lovely," Claire said softly as she took the baby into her arms. "Come and see how much she has grown and how beautiful she is." The two women gushed over the tiny girl until it was time to leave for church.

Cecil was finally able to herd the entire group of women outside, and after making sure the baby had all that she needed, they started off to mass at the parish church. Religion was a large part of the lifestyle in the community. Almost every celebration included a religious ceremony. Baptisms, communions, weddings, and funerals bound the people and the church together in both custom and tradition.

Lydia and Claire held their skirts high as they walked across the muddy sidewalks toward the plaza. They exchanged greetings with family and friends who were headed in the same direction. The sun was shining brightly, and it lifted Lydia's spirits. The mission bell sitting proudly atop of the church was ringing loudly, summoning all to hurry inside.

A large group of people were waiting in front of the massive adobe structure lovingly called La Paraquia. Many were walking through the thick wooden doors, while others spent a few moments catching up on any new information about the war. Lydia lifted the veil from her hat and carefully scanned the group, anxiously looking for her father or brother. Many of the men of the community were missing, and it was obvious there was some type of training taking place. Finding neither of them, Lydia sighed as she and Alita walked up the stone steps and paused to make the sign of the cross with holy water at the font.

The church had been established by the Franciscan friars, who came to this new land along with the Spaniards, and had not changed much in the last hundred years. The pews were simple wooden benches lined up in two rows on either side of the middle aisle. Lydia sat at the pew that was designated for the Sena family. The stone altar glowed from the radiant candlelight reflecting off the white cloth that covered it. A hand-carved, wooden retablo stood behind the alter, holding a host of painted saints with their eyes looking up towards heaven.

Soft chords of guitar music drifted through the sanctuary and the people began to sing a familiar Spanish hymn. Vicar Lamy entered through the back door of the church, dressed in the traditional white robes with red vespers, and was preceded by altar boys bearing tall, blazing candles.

Lydia bent her head in prayer as the mass began and tried to focus on the words of the priest, but her mind began to wander and drift to the pressing issue of her upcoming marriage. The time she had just spent with her cousin and her husband made her realize again that she lacked feelings for her betrothed.

*   *   *

Lydia had memories of Carlos and his parents from when they had spent time together as children. Carlos tended to sulk and stand back from the group of children when they played a game of tag or hide-and-seek. When he did join in, after much encouragement from his playmates, he was quick to anger and lashed out if he did not win. In a way, Lydia had felt sorry for him. His mother, on the other hand, was always very involved in the community, and even though the Aragon ranch was in Chama, nearly 100 miles away, Mrs. Aragon made certain the family was in town for the harvest, the holidays, and during Holy Week. She and Lydia were close during those early years, but as time went by, the Aragon family drifted away. Rumors swirled within the community that Mrs. Aragon had fallen ill.

Lydia remembered with some bitterness the day Mr. Aragon came into the mercantile store with Carlos to speak to Manuel. Lydia was helping Mrs. Vigil select fabric for a dress for one of her daughters. The tiny bell on the glass door jingled as the two well-dressed men walked in with a heavy step.

"Señorita Lydia, como estas usted?" asked the stout, gray-haired man who looked at her with intense dark eyes and a tight-lipped smile.

"I am well, Señor." She hesitated for a moment and then recognition set in. "Señor Aragon," she said as she made her way to greet him. He had aged excessively; his once tall stature was now bent, and he held tight to the cane in his right hand. His hair had grayed, and his face was lined with wrinkles and wear. "How are you and how is Señora Aragon?" she asked. Removing his hat, he said, "She is not well, Lydia. She has been ill for quite some time and is now almost completely bedridden."

"I am sorry to hear that," Lydia said with genuine concern. She then turned to greet Carlos who had been admiring the case of cigars.

"Lydia, you must remember my son, Carlos," Mr. Aragon said as the tall young man stepped forward. She noted his cold stare that evaporated quickly as he took her hand.

"It is a pleasure to see you again," he said.

"Hello, Carlos. It's been so long, and I am very sorry to hear your mother is not well."

He shook his head in acknowledgement, and looking straight into her eyes, he lifted her hand to his lips. She noticed how soft his hand felt in her own and his well-manicured nails. She removed her hand quickly and became flustered as she met his gaze. He was dressed impeccably in a crisp white shirt with a ruffle at the collar, a dark wool suit, and highly polished ankle boots. He had grown into a good-look-ing man with black hair, dark sharp features, and a slow smile.

"Would you let your father know we are here?" Mr. Aragon asked, interrupting the moment.

"Ramon," Lydia called without taking her eyes from them, "please tell Papa the Aragons are here."

There was an awkward silence, which Lydia filled by asking, "We bought cattle from you last year, is that what brings you here?"

The two men exchanged a glance, and Mr. Aragon raised his eyebrows slightly. The women in their lives were quiet and subdued, but Mr. Aragon saw Lydia's strong spirit as an asset for his son. "No, Señorita, we have come to speak to your father of other matters to-day," he replied mysteriously.

Just as Lydia was preparing to ask what those matters were, Man-uel came through from the back room and invited the two men into his office. He smiled at her but did not ask her to join them. Carlos gave her one long last look, which sent a shiver up her spine, before following his father. Lydia had errands she needed to take care of and left the store, never thinking the topic of the meeting might be her.

Later that night, after dinner, she and her father were sitting qui-etly in front of the fire in their front parlor. Lydia was curled up in an overstuffed chair, reading a favorite book.

"What did you think of Carlos?" her father asked gently.

She thought for a moment before she answered. "I'm not sure. I hadn't seen him for so many years, not since we were children. Why do you ask, Papa?"

Manuel was not sure he should talk to his daughter about this yet. "I was just curious, my dear. They are a very good family and have been in the territory for generations," he answered, and their conver-sation ended.

Three weeks later, Manuel called Lydia to his study and gently in-formed her she would be marrying Carlos in the spring.

At first, Lydia was sure her father had taken leave of his senses. "Oh Papa, you cannot be serious. I don't even know him," she said.

"Yes, my dear, I have thought about that. But his family is very secure and stable, and you will never want for anything. I have had many people tell me this is a good choice for you," he said.

Still in disbelief, she replied, "That's just it, this is your choice, not mine. I will not marry him, I refuse to marry him," she said with anger and frustration. "I will run away, Papa," she exclaimed as she broke down in tears.

Her father held her tight. "I would not hurt you for anything in this world, my darling. But I have agreed to this marriage. It was what your mother wanted and what I want for you. Please try to understand," he said soothingly. "With the uncertainty of the war, I must know you will be taken care of if something should happen to me."

Hearing those words touched Lydia deeply. She realized she must set aside her own needs for the time being. She would offer no resistance now; her father had so much to contend with.

Her mind continued spinning with thoughts of her mother's death, remembering the pain she'd felt when told her mother had died shortly after Lydia's birth. She had always wondered, in some part of her heart, if she was the cause of her mother's death. She could never speak openly about her feelings of guilt and remorse, and so they built up over time. She sometimes wondered what her father's life would have been like if she was never born and her mother had been able to share a full life with her husband and son.

Lydia remembered feeling numb at the La Sena de Compromiso, a formal dinner to announce the engagement, held at the Fonda Hotel. The entire evening had seemed like a dream. She could not believe the man sitting next to her would be her husband. Family and close friends offered her congratulations and good wishes. After dinner, the celebration continued with a fandango, a lively dance that included all the guests.

But Lydia's heart was not a part of the celebration. She was withdrawn and formal as Carlos saw her home in his carriage. He placed a heavy gold ring with his family's crest on her left hand. "I should have given you this sooner," he said. "It belongs to my mother."

Looking down at her own delicate hands, she responded, "Thank you, Carlos. It is lovely."

When she returned home and was alone in her room, she felt the heavy burden placed not only on her hand, but on the rest of her life. She removed the ring and dropped it on her dressing table. She was determined not to wear it until she became his wife. In many ways, she felt betrayed by her father, for as much freedom as she felt she'd had growing up, she realized she was still held tightly by the customs and traditions of the past. She maintained hope that she could convince her father to postpone and eventually rescind the marriage commitment.

* * *

The sound of the church bell ringing at the altar signaled the start of the liturgy. Lydia automatically sat down in her pew along with the other parishioners. Vicar Lamy reminded them all the Christmas celebration was just days away.

"In the midst of all this anxiety and fear, let us remember the significance of the Christmas season," he said. "Try to remember our traditions will be felt even more deeply since change may be at hand. We must pray our friends, families, and town are not destroyed by this war. Let us hope there will be some good that comes with it."

At the end of mass, Lydia stopped at the grotto that held the statue of La Conquistadora, an ancient statue of the virgin mother, and lit a candle asking for peace of mind and peace for her family. Looking at the many small flames dancing in the semi-darkness, she thought how each one represented a special need and said a prayer for all.

She kissed Claire and Cecil goodbye outside the church and made her way home with Alita. She would have liked to have them over for dinner, but not knowing what her father had planned, she saved her invitation for another day.

The two women entered the house quietly. Removing her gloves, cloak, and hat, Lydia was surprised to see her father's military coat hanging near the doorway. Anxious to see him and to hear of any news, she quickly walked to his study and knocked soundly on the door.

"Come in," Manuel said.

Lydia opened the door and walked to where her father sat in his chair behind his desk, not noticing there was someone else in the room. "Hello, Papa," she said as she threw her arms around his neck from behind. Father and daughter, their faces side-by-side, held each other tightly for just a moment.

Manuel patted her arm gently. "Hello, my dear. I didn't expect such a warm greeting from you," he said. Their relationship had been strained since her engagement to Carlos was announced. Their conversations had been centered on daily chores and activities but lacked the usual affection.

Eli Stevens did not move from his vantage point across the room in the wing chair. He felt suspended in the moment. Initially, he felt uncomfortable at having witnessed a private moment between a father and his daughter. But at the same time, he realized it was all very natural. Something deep within him stirred as he looked upon Lydia's face. He could feel her warm beauty and strength draw him to her. He noticed the gracefulness of her hands and the glow of her skin. He wondered what it would be like to touch her.

He was so deeply immersed in his thoughts he didn't realize he was staring.

Manuel cleared his throat. "Lieutenant Colonel Stevens, may I present my daughter, Lydia."

By then Lydia had stepped away from her father to the side of his desk.

Eli stood also and felt his heart pounding. He leaned toward Lydia and took her hand.

"It is a pleasure to meet you, sir," she said in a soft voice. She gazed up at his face and noticed how tall and straight he stood in his uniform. She could hardly take her eyes from his warm, inviting, deep brown eyes. When he finally smiled, she noticed the dimples in his cheek and could not help but smile herself.

Being this close to her sent a shiver through Eli. "The pleasure is all mine," he said. There was a long silence in the room while their hands remained joined.

"We still have many things to discuss," Manuel said briskly. "Perhaps, Lydia, you could have a tray sent in."

"Yes Papa," she replied as her hand fell to her side. "I'll have one prepared right away."

As she closed the study door behind her, she leaned against it and closed her eyes. She breathed deeply to calm herself and tried to quiet the flutter in her chest.

Alita walked by with clean linen in her hands and noticed Lydia finally had some color in her face—for the first time since she was told of her engagement.

Meanwhile, Eli was having some difficulty trying to focus on what Manuel was saying, but as the conversation turned back to the Confederates, he quickly remembered he had a job to do.

≡ 6 ≡

Colonel Canby stood in front of the roaring fire at Fort Marcy, New Mexico's Union headquarters in Santa Fe. In full uniform, he stared out the window at the overcast sky, collecting his thoughts. Now in his late forties, he had spent his whole adult life as a member of the United States military. Originally from Kentucky, he'd served as a major in the Southwest during the Indian wars and the Mexican-American War. His brow was furrowed as he turned his attention back to the room. Tension was thick as a small group of men studied a map spread out on a round table.

"Do you have an idea how many men they are bringing and what equipment?" Canby asked the young soldier whose uniform was caked with mud.

"I saw two thousand or so, but I know there were others camped on the back side of the mountain," he replied. "I just couldn't get there without being seen. I was there for nearly ten days, and the troops arrived in groups, not all at once."

"What about their guns?" Eli asked.

"I know they had some cannons, but it was hard to see how many," the young soldier replied. "They were covered with tarps, but if I had to guess, I'd say eight or ten."

"Why don't you get something to eat and get some rest," Canby told the young man. "You've done a good job, and if we need more information, we'll send for you."

"Yes sir," the soldier said as he saluted. The door shut quietly on the remaining men.

"We'll need to decide how to proceed, gentlemen," Canby said. "I do believe General Sibley is collecting both men and equipment and is headed this way. If he is already at Fort Bliss, that's only 325 miles away. We are probably not under immediate threat, but we do need to plan, and quickly. Stevens, would you go and find Captain Sena? I need to get his opinion."

Eli nodded. "I'll return as quickly as I can," he said.

*　　*　　*

The sweet aroma of biscochitos baking in the kitchen lingered and drifted throughout the Sena home. With the holidays quickly approaching and Lydia needing a distraction, she was busy rolling out the dough as Alita entered the kitchen with more piñon nuts for the empanadas, the meat pies they would be making next.

Alita noticed her young mistress was humming to herself. She picked up both of Lydia's hands with her own and looked right into Lydia's eyes. Something about her mistress had changed, but it was very subtle. Alita knew the tension in Lydia came from worry about her father and the war. She also understood the confusion Lydia felt about Carlos. She had seen it many times in her own life: a man and woman joined together for practical reasons and with little emotion or passion for each other. Feelings of friendship and tenderness sometimes existed as couples grew to know one another, but only a few were fortunate enough to find love.

Both women turned to a hard knock on the kitchen door.

Alita pulled open the door, revealing Eli looking refreshed and handsome in his uniform as he tipped his hat and made his way inside. Lydia wiped her hands on her apron and reached out to greet him.

"Good morning, Miss Lydia," he said. "I tried knocking on the front door, but there was no answer."

After removing his gloves, he took Lydia's extended greeting and held her hand for a long moment. It seemed to fit perfectly inside his own and was soft and silky from the flour. He had the sudden urge to place it to his lips.

Very aware of one another, Lydia was the first to gently release her grip. "How can I help you this morning, Lieutenant?" she asked brightly.

"I came for your father, if he is in."

Lydia sensed the sudden urgency in his voice. "I am sorry, Lieutenant, he is not here right now. He and Eduardo rode out early this morning to check on some cattle we have grazing on the outskirts of town. I expect them back soon."

Before Eli could respond, she continued. "Please sit and I will pour you some coffee. They will be back here before you could ever reach them." She placed her hand on his for the slightest moment.

He thought about riding out to find Manuel and Eduardo, but he decided to trust her instincts. "Thank you, I will wait," he said.

Alita reached for a cup from the cupboard and placed it in front of Eli who took a seat at the kitchen table. She used her apron to grab hold of the hot coffee pot that was warming on the cast iron stove.

"Would you like cream or sugar?" Lydia asked.

"No, thank you," Eli replied. He was trying to remember his manners. He hadn't spent much time in his young life learning how to be refined, but his mother had taught her sons to be courteous.

The kitchen was usually reserved for family and close friends. But it never occurred to Lydia to move Eli to the parlor. It felt very natural where they were. She had never felt so close to a man who was considered a stranger.

"Alita, would you get more flour from the storage shed?" Lydia asked. "This sack is almost gone." Alita nodded and left through the kitchen door.

Lydia moved back to the center of the table. "I hope you don't mind if I finish rolling out this dough while we wait," she said, needing to perform a task to distract her mind from her nervousness.

"No, not at all," he replied and took a sip of his coffee. He never took his eyes from her as she kneaded the dough. Several soft curls surrounded her face, and she brushed them off with the back of her hand. She had flour up to her elbows and her white apron was dusted with flour and the spices used for the cookies. She smiled at Eli through radiant eyes veiled by thick lashes. He found himself smiling back.

"What kind of cookies are these?" he asked. "It's a smell I'm not familiar with."

Lydia reached for a plate of cookies and walked to his seat at the table. "Forgive my manners," she said. "Please try one, they are called biscochitos. We use anise seed to flavor them."

"Very good," he said with a mouth full of the warm cookie. Lydia laughed.

Eli noticed she had some flour on her cheek. Looking deeply at her face, he was taken aback at all he saw. She had a blush of color on her cheeks, and her eyes glittered with amusement and excitement. Everything around him seemed to stop—there was no war, no fear of what was to come. He was simply suspended in that moment with her.

His hand rose to touch her face. Her eyes were penetrating. Their color changed from blue to violet in an instant, reflecting the depth of her emotion. His fingers moved along her cheek and brushed the flour away.

Suddenly, they heard her father's voice in the front hall. "Lydia," he called.

"In the kitchen, Papa," she called back.

Never removing her eyes from Eli's, she boldly placed her hand on top of his when he tried to remove it from her face. He smiled softly and moved both their hands down as her father entered the kitchen.

Manuel walked through the doorway and noticed Eli and Lydia leaning towards one another. He raised his eyebrows. Eli stood to break the tide of emotion.

"Lieutenant Stevens," Manuel said with some surprise. "What brings you here?"

"We've had word from the southern part of the territory. Colonel Canby would like to see you immediately."

Manuel nodded. "Eduardo," he called to his son who came in from the other room. "Lydia, we will be back soon." He motioned for the two younger men to exit through the kitchen door before him.

As Manuel followed, his eyes fell on Eli's broad shoulders. *Who is this young man?* he thought to himself. He trusted his instincts, and he'd noted a change in Lydia, one he had not seen before—openness and excitement that made her glow from the inside. Why would this man have such an impact on Lydia, a woman who was very much spoken for? For a moment, Manuel's mind went to the first time he saw his wife, Elise, and remembered he'd been captivated from the moment they met.

As they neared the Union headquarters, Manuel shook such thoughts from his mind. *I will set this aside and ruminate later. There is much to protect in the here and now.*

*　*　*

Lydia, finished with all her baking for the day, had changed her simple outfit for a dark blue silk dress with white-dotted Swiss sleeves. The dress made her feel festive. She had delivered baskets of food to neighbors and to Sister Teresa and Sister Cathleen who lived in a small house near the church and parochial school. Lydia had spent many years under their roof and appreciated their basic instruction. They had introduced her to classic literature, art, and history. She made it a point to make sure they had food and necessities; they lived mainly from the charity of the community.

Restless, she sat in the small parlor and tried to work on the Christmas gown she was embroidering for Claire's baby. Her hands worked swiftly as her fingers wove the white thread into the delicately shaped roses. Many thoughts drifted in and out of her mind—the war, her family, the Christmas holiday—but certain thoughts kept returning, and they gave her great pleasure. They were of Eli. She could see his broad forehead, strong nose, angular cheekbones softened by a deep set of dimples when he smiled—and she recalled the power she felt in his hands. He made her tingle on the inside, a tingle that traveled through her whole body. She thought of how handsome he looked in his uniform, with his dark wavy hair and wide-set eyes that shone with determination and kindness.

The fire burned brightly in the large kiva fireplace, and, for the moment, she felt content and wonderfully happy.

There was a knock at the front door and Lydia rose to answer. She was dismayed when she saw Carlos. Dressed in a dark brown suit and vest with a starched white shirt and a silk tie fashioned into a flat half-bow, his manner was reserved. He removed his top hat and stopped in front of Lydia as he walked inside.

"Hello, my dear," he said as he leaned over to kiss her cheek. "I was in the area and had an urge to check on you." His touch felt cold and rehearsed.

Lydia cleared her throat and turned away from him, walking back to the parlor. "Please come in. I was working on my sewing, but you are welcome to join me," she said. "Give me a moment. I will ask Alita to bring coffee."

He watched her in silence as she walked down the hallway. *My father chose well. She is beautiful and rich*, he thought to himself. Being quite experienced with women, he imagined what it would be like taking Lydia to his bed; she had such a warm and inviting look about her. *Soon enough*, he thought. He was here to talk about their wedding plans. He placed his hat on the low table at the entrance and showed himself into the parlor.

Lydia returned and took her seat by the fire. She sat up straight, feeling very self-conscious. She gestured to Carlos to sit, but he leaned against the fireplace.

Trying to make her voice sound cheerful, she asked, "What brings you here today?"

Ignoring her question, he watched closely as she smoothed the front of her dress and picked up her sewing.

"You do not have on your ring, Lydia. Why?" he asked.

"I was baking earlier today, and I did not want to spoil it," she replied honestly. "I must have forgotten to put it on when I changed clothes."

His temper rose slightly, and in a frustrated voice he said, "It's good you want to take care of it, my dear, since it once was my mother's, but you should always have it on your hand."

She could feel the blood rush to her face, and she bit the inside of her cheek to control her embarrassment. He spoke to her as if she were a child.

Alita entered the room and laid out coffee and cookies.

Carlos said, "My father is having dinner with friends this evening. I thought I would join you and your father."

"Claire and Cecil will be with us and one more will be no trouble," she replied with a slight sarcastic edge.

A dark look crossed his face before the corners of his mouth turned into a wicked smile. "Thank you for your graciousness, Lydia."

Lydia excused herself to finish last minute preparations and check on dinner. She opened the cast iron oven door, and the delicious smell of roast pork filled the air. Lydia left instructions with Maria to prepare the table for six and finish up the side dishes.

She walked up the back staircase to change for dinner. After she entered her room, she paused for a moment to rest her head on the closed door. She knew deep down she could not marry Carlos. He disturbed her on some level, and she had to find a way to explain this to her father.

Lydia walked towards her dressing table, and Alita came into the room quietly. Lydia smiled at her, and Alita began helping take her dress off to change for dinner. She selected a lilac-colored silk taffeta trimmed with black lace and layered with flounces at the bottom.

Alita had Lydia sit at her dressing table while she took down her waist-length hair and brushed through it to get out any tangles. With practiced hands, she braided the thick, curly mass and rolled it into a bun in the back. She finished by securing the braid with a pearl encrusted comb that had belonged to Lydia's mother. Lydia selected simple pearl earrings for the evening and made her way downstairs.

She could hear her father and Eduardo speaking to Carlos in the parlor as she lit the candelabra on the dining room table, which was set for dinner. She heard a knock on the front door and then her father warmly greeting Claire and Cecil.

"Please come in," Manuel said as he hugged Claire tightly. "Cecil how are you and how is baby Violet?" he asked as he shook his hand.

"Very well and thank you for asking after her," Cecil said.

Alita took Cecil's heavy wool coat and Claire's heavy shawl. As they entered the parlor, Manuel said, "You remember Carlos."

"Of course," Claire said as she offered him her hand and then moved to greet Eduardo with a hug.

Lydia entered the room and moved directly to Claire and grabbed her hand. "You feel so cold," Lydia said. "And you look beautiful in that color." Claire smiled and touched the ruffled lace at the wrist of her burgundy gown.

"Dinner is almost ready," Lydia said as she poured six small glasses of wine. "We are down to our last two bottles, so I thought we could celebrate the Christmas season with these tonight." Lydia touched her glass to Claire's with a clink, and then she directed her cousin towards the fireplace where a warm wrap was waiting on the settee.

The men formed a natural group across the room. Colonel Canby had asked Cecil to be his personal assistant, and they were discussing this recent appointment that they all very much approved. Cecil had never been inclined to outdoor activities, his interest had always been in books, reading, and studying maps. He had studied law at his father's knee and later as his clerk until he attended law school where he'd graduated with honors. Canby had recognized his high intellect and decided his talents and sharp mind would serve him well as the war developed. Both women noticed the persistent tension around the group, especially shining in Manuel's eyes. The women sat close together and sipped their wine.

Claire leaned close to Lydia and said, "Cecil and I were fighting as we rode over. He is now insisting I take the baby with my mother to stay at my grandfather's house. We will leave right after Christmas." Claire held her handkerchief to her face for a moment. "I don't think I can leave him. But I know I must go, the Confederate troops are getting closer, and I must keep my baby safe." Lydia rubbed Claire's arm gently and offered unspoken comfort.

Alita gave a small clap and motioned to the group to make their way to the dining room. Lydia took her father's arm and led the group to dinner. The candlelight, wine, and good food softened the atmosphere, and for a while, the serious issues and tensions were set aside. The conversation was lively and fun as they all talked about times before the war.

Carlos watched as Lydia leaned toward Claire to share a secret. The lilac-colored dress brought out the brilliant blue of her eyes. Once again, he felt aroused by her beauty and recognized her fortitude and resilience. Carlos enjoyed taking the luster from innocence and purity. He felt these things were signs of weakness, and, with little regret, he was adept at exposing the cruel and harsh side of the world.

He would never allow Lydia to stay as she was. He relished the opportunity to have her submit to him, regardless of the circumstances. The wedding would be soon, and he would take her home to his ranch. There, without her father or brother or cousin, she would be alone and vulnerable to his words and actions. The thought made him smile.

"Manuel, Claire will be traveling with her mother to her grandparent's home in Madrid right after Christmas," Cecil said. "The town is very well protected by the canyons surrounding it, and her grandfather has hired gunmen for protection. It might be a good idea if Lydia joined them." Both women looked at Cecil with surprise.

"Cecil, I have not agreed to leave, and I don't want to discuss our family business here," Claire said as she looked at Carlos.

"Lydia, that may be the best thing for you, my dear," Manuel answered with relief in his voice. "Eduardo, don't you agree? Cecil, when would they leave?"

Before Cecil could answer, Carlos jumped in with a need to have a say about his bride's future. "If Lydia must leave, I will take her back with me to my ranch," he said resolutely.

"No Carlos. You must be married before you can run off with my daughter," Manuel said sternly.

Claire turned to Lydia to engage her support on why she should stay in Santa Fe, and at the same time, Manuel looked to Lydia to speak about the proprieties of an engaged couple. Her eyes grew cloudy as she clasped her hands together tightly in her lap and felt a wave of anger passing through her.

"Cecil, as much as I appreciate your concern, whether or not Claire and the baby leave for safety does not depend on me," she said, her eyes and voice softening as she looked at Claire. She turned to her father. "But, more importantly, I will not be going anywhere, Papa. I will not leave you at a time like this. My sense of duty is just as strong as yours, and I will stay to help take care of the wounded or prepare meals or assist in any way I can. It is the last thing I will do as a single woman."

Manuel had calmed down and spoke with gentleness in his voice. "We can talk later, Lydia, we do not have to decide right now." The group collectively relaxed and returned their attention to dinner.

"Carlos, would you like more wine?" Manuel motioned to Alita to fill Carlos' glass, who felt he had lost a battle. He nodded to Manuel in thanks and watched Lydia intently. He wanted her with him and would just have to find a way.

Claire looked over at Carlos and noted an almost sinister look on his face as his eyes devoured Lydia. Feeling protective, she asked, "Carlos, I have been wondering why you have not officially joined the Union army?"

Carlos looked back into Claire's penetrating eyes. "My father and mother are not well, and since I am their only son, I must run the family ranch. I would be honored to join, but some of us must make sure there is something to return to at the end of this war, Señora," he said as he lifted his wine glass in a mock toast to her.

Claire raised an eyebrow and thought to herself, *It is not for lack of desire, but out of a family need. How convenient. If only we were all so fortunate.*

After dinner and dessert, the group moved back to the parlor for coffee and brandy. The evening was getting late, and Claire turned to Cecil with bright eyes. "We should go. Tomorrow will be very busy with all the preparations for the Christmas Eve celebration." Cecil took her hand tenderly and nodded.

Alita had already gathered their wraps, and Cecil placed the heavy shawl around Claire's shoulders. As they took their leave, Carlos also pulled on his gloves and reached for his hat. He asked Manuel to walk outside with him.

They paused in the courtyard as Manuel closed the front door and Carlos pulled on his overcoat. He again tried to convince Lydia's father. "It would be in her best interest to have her stay with me. Surely, you can't be serious about letting her stay here. My ranch is isolated and away from danger."

"I have thought about this. Rest assured, her safety is my main concern, as it has been all her life."

Carlos realized he was pushing too hard. "I know you will do what is best. If you change your mind, I will be leaving early tomorrow morning."

"She will stay here for Christmas and then I will decide the best course," Manuel said as he placed a hand on Carlos' shoulder before turning to return inside.

≡ 7 ≡

Carlos was in a foul mood as he walked back to the hotel where he and his father were staying. He jerked his horse's reins brutally and thought to himself, *How dare Manuel dictate to me?* It had been difficult to maintain his composure in front of his future father-in-law. Carlos knew his current disposition would only make his father's incessant questioning more agitating.

Instead of turning in the direction of the hotel at the corner of the plaza, he got down from his horse and walked down a dark alley he knew well. Sounds of laughter and music drifted towards him as he tied his horse to the post outside and made his way to the entrance.

The dimly lit brothel was thick with smoke and the strong smell of liquor. The bartender noticed Carlos and wiped down the faded wood plank as Carlos approached. "Whiskey," Carlos said in a low, controlled voice. The bartender poured a healthy amount into a tall glass, and Carlos swirled the golden liquid for a moment before taking the whole amount without flinching. He laid a gold coin on the bar.

Angry voices erupted from the corner of the room. "We don't deal in credit! Don't come back unless you have gold, old man," yelled the young dealer, touching the gun sitting comfortably in its holster as he roughly pushed the man across the room. Others in the brothel snickered as the old man picked himself up and left.

As the dealer sat back down, he looked towards Carlos and smiled an invitation. Carlos joined the small group and stood near the vacant chair. The dealer, who had slicked-back dark hair, knew him and his money well. "Have a seat, my friend," he said, the tone of his voice light and easy.

The man to Carlos' right was middle-aged with a long black braid down his back and wore a deerskin tunic decorated with beads. Carlos assumed he was an Indian trader. The man slurred his words as he spoke. "You want to join this game? We don't want any of that useless Confederate or Union money. Gold," he said. "Only gold."

Carlos looked at him with disgust.

"Do not make our guest feel unwelcome," the dealer scolded, knowing Carlos always had gold coins in his pocket. "Señor Aragon, would you like another drink?"

Carlos nodded, laid his hat down, and settled into the chair. The dealer motioned to the young woman at the bar. With a tall glass of whiskey in hand, she sauntered to the table and laid the glass down in front of Carlos. She shifted her hand to her satin-covered hip and raised her brow. The strong smell of her perfume mixed with cigar smoke drifted through the dark shadows in the room. Carlos' eyes never left hers as he easily drained the glass. A sly smile crossed her face.

Private Armstrong, sitting to Carlos' left, was beginning to grow weary of this sideshow. "We're here to play cards, aren't we?" he asked sarcastically.

The dealer shuffled the deck, expertly placed the cards in a stack, and pushed them across the table to Carlos. He cut the deck and pushed them back. Armstrong moved restlessly in his seat, and Carlos felt a twinge of anxiety as he realized this man and the dealer had cleaned out the old man's money.

Carlos twisted the gold ring with his family's Spanish crest around the pinky finger of his right hand and said, "Just a warning, gentlemen. I have a gun and I will kill anyone who tries to cheat."

"Calm down, Señor Aragon," the dealer said, taking a long puff from his cigar. "There is no cheating at this table, just a good time.

Place your bets." He nodded to the young woman who placed her hands on Carlos' shoulders and leaned her upper body into his back.

"Five card stud, deuces are wild," the dealer said as the well-used cards landed precisely next to the hands of the players.

Armstrong casually lifted his cards from the table—a queen, two eights, and the rest were useless. He had acquired the ability to stay completely unattached and unresponsive to the cards. It had allowed him to bluff his way to winning more times than he could count.

Carlos anteed up the bet. "I raise you twenty-five."

The pile of gold coins grew as each man parted with more. The dealer handed out the rest of the cards. Carlos' fingers fondled the five cards. "I call," he said. Armstrong laid out his cards, knowing they would not win him any money. Carlos arrogantly laid out his full house and pulled the money towards him with a smile.

The Indian trader, realizing he had lost once again, threw his cards on the table, mumbled profanities under his breath, and pounded his chair down as he got up to leave. Armstrong smirked and imagined how the trader would explain to his woman how he had lost so much money at the card table.

The dealer ordered another round of whiskey to ease some of the tension in the high-stakes situation. Armstrong sipped the whiskey, savoring the taste and the burn.

Carlos glanced at him as they waited for the dealer to start the next round and noticed his blue uniform. "Shouldn't you be preparing to defend our territory instead of playing cards?" Carlos asked.

Armstrong's face broke into a devious grin. "I suppose I should be, but as far as I'm concerned, it wouldn't do much good." He snorted, looked around the room, and lowered his voice. "We don't have a snowball's chance in hell of winning."

"And why is that?" Carlos asked, leaning in slightly.

"The men, the equipment, you name it," Armstrong replied as he leaned forward in his chair. "There ain't much to work with here. Between you and me, I'll probably head for home before there's any real fighting. You know, before we have our asses kicked." Carlos only smiled and sipped his drink.

Armstrong grabbed a hold of the barmaid's hips as she sauntered by the table and pulled her into his lap. Armstrong turned her head roughly and kissed her with force on the mouth. "That was for luck, darlin'. Now you stay right here while we play the next round."

Carlos noted the look of disgust that crossed the dealer's face. *This rough man may be the one I need*, he thought to himself.

The men played cards long into the night. The dealer was relieved to see them both leave the table when the early morning light began creeping in through the curtained windows. Both men had won and lost some, but it was obvious now that Carlos was the superior player.

"Let me buy you one more drink," Carlos said to Armstrong and suggested they move to a secluded table.

Once they were settled, Carlos looked at Armstrong as he rolled a cigarette and said, "I have a proposition for you." Armstrong folded his hands on the table and waited for Carlos to continue.

"You seem like a smart man who can handle himself, especially when it comes to this war." Armstrong looked at Carlos smugly through red-rimmed eyes and nodded for him to continue. "There are a group of us who do not want the Union army to succeed in their efforts here in the territory." Shattering glass and a loud crash made them both turn to a young man who'd had too much to drink and knocked over a table.

Carlos continued in a quieter voice. "We need someone on the inside. To have eyes and ears and then get the information back to us." Carlos stopped to let Armstrong think about what he was asking.

Armstrong sat up straight in his chair. "I don't know how you folks do it here, but back where I come from, they hang people for treason."

"Yes, the risks are great, but so are the rewards. If we succeed, you will be quite wealthy, and we will pay you in gold for your efforts." Carlos could tell by the satisfied look in Armstrong's eyes that he'd made up his mind.

"What will I have to do?" Armstrong asked.

Carlos smiled and leaned back in his chair. "Get information. What they plan to do and when. How many troops they have and where. It should not be too difficult."

Armstrong nodded. "Who will I contact?" he asked.

"There is an old Indian who takes care of the horses at the hotel. He will be waiting to hear from you."

Carlos rose and put money on the table for the drinks. He tossed a gold coin to Armstrong who watched it turn and roll in mid-air before he captured it tightly in his hand. "Consider this a down payment, Señor." Carlos tipped his hat before walking away.

He felt satisfied as he walked into the early morning light. It had been a long night for Carlos, he could feel it in his body as he mounted his stallion and headed for the hotel. But finding Armstrong had been just what he needed to change his mood. *Everything seems to be falling into place*, he thought to himself as he maneuvered his horse through the deserted streets.

For months, he and a group of men in the territory had been help-ing the Confederates. Stockpiles of supplies, guns and ammunition, and cattle had been stored and would be used at the right time. It had not been easy, and he had spent a great deal of money, plus a large portion of the supplies, including cattle, had been stolen and men had been killed. But the rewards he had been promised suited him: a share of the gold once the Confederate troops reached California and a great deal of say in how the new government would be run.

It would be a new day in the territory, and he would play a promi-nent role, maybe even be appointed governor of the territory, when all the dust died down. *Lydia will make a charming first lady*, Carlos thought.

Only a trusted circle of people knew of his involvement. Carlos steeled himself as he approached the hotel where he and his father were staying. He needed to rest and refresh himself before embarking on the long coach ride home.

He slid down from his horse and handed the reins to the stable boy. He walked into the rustic lobby and stared at the smartly dressed clerk behind the rich wood of the counter. "Do I have any messages?" he asked impatiently, expecting to hear from Lydia's father. He tight-ened the grip on his hat as the clerk's hand searched the message box and came out empty.

"No, nothing, Señor Aragon." Carlos turned and walked down the long hallway to his room.

*   *   *

Armstrong slowly sipped his last bit of bourbon. He wanted to keep the lightheaded feeling before he had to return to the barracks. He had slipped away from headquarters early the night before. He couldn't find Stevens, so he'd left word he would be scouting the outskirts of town. A reasonable excuse because of the rustle of excitement over the sighting of Confederate troops. Armstrong laughed to himself as he lit a rolled cigarette. "Stupid, patriotic fools. They aren't going to win this war, not if I have anything to do with it."

Even early in the morning, the brothel still had a lusty feel about it. He was the only patron left at the bar except for a young prostitute exchanging a laugh with the bartender. He walked up to girl. He put both arms around her longingly, wishing he could spend a little more time with her. She smiled up at him and he winked. "I'll be back soon, Señorita. Very soon."

*   *   *

Eli opened his eyes as the light of the new day came through the curtains. He felt exhilarated as a warm rush ran through his body. He thought of Lydia, her face, her hair, her smile, the way she smelled. Everything about her appealed to him, and he wanted more than anything to be near her. A smile crossed his lips, and for the first time in a long time, he felt the future held a promise. "All I need to do is get through this damn war," he said aloud to himself.

Eli jumped out of bed, a sense of urgency nagging at him, there was so much to be done today. He and Colonel Canby had been desperately trying to get the local troops in shape with constant drills and procedures. The news from yesterday had only made things worse.

Eli dressed quickly. Many of the men had a devil-may-care attitude, which made the drills and training difficult. *Today*, Eli thought to himself as he slammed the door to his room behind him, *they will get it right.*

Even though it was light outside, not much of it entered the long hallway. Eli heard a noise before he saw the dark figure moving cautiously ahead. All his instincts were heightened. He placed his hand on the handle of his gun and called out, "Who's there?" There was a tense moment of silence.

"It's me, Lieutenant," Armstrong called out.

"What the hell are you doing?" Eli asked angrily as he walked towards him.

"I was out last night," Armstrong replied casually.

"Out where?"

Armstrong's head was spinning, and he had to get control of himself. He'd decided to cooperate with the enemy, so he would have to accommodate Eli in order to get what he needed. More important matters were at stake. He tried to remain calm as he answered. "I was playing cards and the time just got away from me." He looked up at Eli and even managed to appear remorseful. "I'm sorry, sir. It won't happen again."

Eli was surprised at Armstrong's response but still felt he had to admonish him for staying out all night. "I expect you to help with the drills today. Report to Captain Piño in one hour." Armstrong nodded and turned to go.

Eli watched Armstrong's retreating back. He realized his men were bored and anxious and needed to blow off steam. But something about Armstrong made Eli uncomfortable, and he had a nagging sense of doubt and suspicion.

These thoughts slipped away as he walked into the courtyard.

The area was alive with activity. Wagons filled with supplies were being unloaded and stockpiled in storage areas. Local farmers were bartering with one of the soldiers to get the best price for the coveted dried meat and flour they were trying to sell. At the far end of the yard, two rows of men were practicing with their guns. Some of them looked very young and seemed out of place, but Eli sensed the resolve and purpose at the fort this morning and it fueled his own feelings to get the job done.

On his way towards the drilling area, Eli heard a voice call behind him. "Lieutenant Colonel, Colonel Canby wants to see you." Eli nodded and followed the young man across the courtyard to a solid wooden door. Walking inside the office, Eli noted Canby was efficient and professional in his approach and appearance. Eli saluted and stood formally in front of the desk.

"At ease, Stevens. I think it's time we send word to your Colonel Riley," Canby said. "The more information I receive, the more I realize the Confederates will be here soon." Eli nodded.

"I don't want you to go. I may need you here. Select one of your men, one you can trust and who can make it back to Colorado quickly, unnoticed, if possible."

Eli thought of Rivera. "I have just the man," Eli said.

"Good. Bring him here this afternoon and we can brief him. He can start out as soon as possible. It is essential we keep this quiet. I don't want the townspeople to panic, but it seems the rebels are determined to come to us," Canby said as he returned to his paperwork.

Later in the afternoon, as the winter shadows crept across the town, Eli and Rivera waited to enter Canby's office. Eli looked over at Rivera. He was a solidly built young man with dark eyes and hair. He knew the territory well from all the hunting and fishing he'd done as a child. Eli was confident Rivera could make his way to the Colorado Territory, deliver the message, and get back safely.

The Colonel's assistant called out and they both entered the room then stood at attention. Canby quickly told them to be at ease. Manuel was also there, and he and Eli nodded a greeting to one another.

"Sir," Eli addressed the Colonel, "this is Private Rivera. He will be making the trip back to Colorado. I have already given him some specifics."

The Colonel motioned the young man to sit down, and the Private adjusted himself in the hard wooden chair so he was sitting with a straight back. Eli sat in the chair next to Manuel.

Colonel Canby referred to a large map lying on his desk. "The Confederate forces have come together, and we believe there are two and a half thousand men about three hundred miles south. We are sending our own reinforcements but lack the manpower to cover the entire area and also protect Santa Fe. We need more men from Colorado. Tell Riley I have written to Washington as well."

Eli, his arms folded, watched Rivera's reaction. Rivera looked back at Canby with confidence as he tried to memorize the facts about the campaign.

Canby continued. "The first fort they will come to is Craig. Tell Colonel Riley we are attempting to fortify Craig with men and cannons. We will need as many men as he can spare. Can you read, son?" Rivera shook his head no. "Here is a short note to Colonel Riley. If you are captured, get rid of it, do you understand?" Rivera nodded. "Good, then be careful and God speed."

Eli had already selected a horse for Rivera earlier that day. They walked to the stall together. Eli could sense the anxiety in Rivera but encouraged him. "You can make it there and back in about six days. Just move quickly and quietly. I have every faith in you."

"I know, sir, I'll do my best," Rivera said as he climbed on top of the chestnut-colored horse.

Darkness had fallen across the courtyard with no moon to light the sky. Eli never saw Armstrong buried in the shadows behind the stalls. Seeing Rivera off, Eli turned and walked toward the main building.

*   *   *

Rivera had made good progress over the last several hours, but he knew he needed a break and so did his horse. Daylight would be breaking soon, and he stopped by a stream to quench his thirst. He never heard his murderer come up behind him, and the surprise attack left him defenseless. The knife pierced his lung and liver through his back, and he fell to the ground, his blood seeping into the snow. His death was long and painful.

The note, tucked away on the inside of his coat near his chest, was easily removed by Armstrong.

*   *   *

In San Antonio, General Henry Hopkins Sibley took a slow, steady sip from a bottle of bourbon and placed it on the table by his side. He gazed into the roaring fire at the corner of his office at the temporary headquarters. *War is never an easy thing*, he thought to himself.

In his forty-three years, he had seen many battles. It hadn't taken much for him to pick the side of the South. The Confederacy was well supplied now and had sent him forward to the New Mexico Territory with more than 3,000 men. They were mostly from Texas, well trained and prepared to fight.

Sibley picked up the official looking piece of paper and read his orders once again. "Gold and the whole west coast are at stake here, General," President Davis had written. "The area must be penetrated and held. After consultation, we want you to proceed north, following the Rio Grande River."

Sibley nodded his head slowly; it was time to gather all his colonels and captains so he could issue orders for his troops to proceed further into the New Mexico Territory.

≣ **8** ≣

L ydia called out to Eduardo who was in the courtyard. "Are you
finished yet? Can I help you bring it in?"

"Almost," he said as he straightened out the branches of
the pine tree he had just put in a stand. Lydia's enthusiasm was contagious, and Eduardo started humming a Christmas song as he dragged
the great tree inside the house to the parlor and into a corner near a
large window.

She clasped her hands together. "It's beautiful and you said it
would be too big," she exclaimed with delight.

"Once again, my dear sister, you were right," Eduardo said with
a smile on his face. He remembered that on each Christmas, Lydia
insisted they have the biggest tree possible.

"I have pulled all the decorations out so we can place them on the
tree. I expect Papa any minute, and we still must get ready for La Posada at Claire's," Lydia said as she handed Eduardo a basket filled with
small candles nestled in holders with a clip. Alita brought in a huge
bowl of popped corn and began stringing it on thread.

"Eduardo, you put the candles on and make sure they are even,"
Lydia said as she turned her attention to the dried rosehips carefully
wrapped in tissue.

He positioned the ladder and, starting at the top of the tree, he clipped a candle holder to the fragrant, lush branches and then continued with the next one in the basket. As Lydia looked over to examine his work, he teasingly said, "Can you show me how to put these on? I am not sure I am doing it right."

"Oh Eduardo, give me that!" she exclaimed as he held the basket out of her reach. She stood on her tiptoes, playfully struggling to get it out of his hand.

"What a delightful sight," Manuel said. He stood in the doorway while the brisk air from outside rushed in behind him. Both of his children looked up with smiles and mischief all over their faces.

"It's like a Christmas past when you were both so young and full of excitement. Here, give me the candle holder, Eduardo," Manuel said as he stepped towards them. "Let me show you both how this is done. Your mother was an excellent tree trimmer and taught me well."

For the next couple of hours, they shared a peaceful time decorating. Lydia tied dried bunches of rose hips together and placed them gently on the pine branches. She and Alita had spent hours beforehand weaving small flowers from colored paper, and the results now adorned the tree. Eduardo and Manuel wove the rows of popcorn and dried berry strands through the branches. Afterwards, they all admired their work.

"It's a lovely Christmas tree," Lydia said. "We did a fine job, but there is one last thing." She left the room and returned with a wooden box. Carefully, she removed the lid and removed, unwrapped, and placed each piece on the table.

Manuel picked up the delicately carved St. Joseph from the Nativity set. "This always meant Christmas to your mother. Her mother gave it to her when she was a little girl," he said softly and looked at his children. "She would have been so proud of both of you." His voice was thick with emotion. He cleared his throat. "I would like to sit for a moment, have some coffee, and enjoy this tree with my children."

"Alita, will you have a coffee tray prepared? Papa, I will have to leave that to you and Eduardo," Lydia said. "I must get to Claire's. I'm sure she has her hands full preparing for tonight's La Posada. I am just going to finish up the decorations in this room before I go."

As Manuel and Eduardo sat down on the couch, Lydia scooped up loose pine branches and walked towards the mantle to place them along with tall white taper candles.

"I am looking forward to Claire's gathering," said Manuel. "I have heard from so many of our friends and neighbors, and from many of the soldiers, that they plan to attend. It will be nice to have a normal evening."

"Yes Papa, I agree. This will probably be the last time we will all be together. I have been wanting to ask, did you invite Lieutenant Stevens to join us? I know you wanted to make him feel welcome, especially on Christmas Eve," Lydia said. Her back was still to her father so he could not see the apprehension on her face.

"Yes, I did see him today and I did mention the party."

She closed her eyes and sighed, thanking her father under her breath. Somehow, having Eli there would make all the difference.

Alita entered the room with steaming cups of coffee and some of the biscochitos they had baked. Lydia made sure her father and brother had all they needed before heading for the entryway and her coat. "Alita and I will be back soon. No peeking at the gifts while I'm gone," she said and walked back to hug them both.

As they sat before the fire and sipped their coffee, both men were lost in their own thoughts. Manuel sat up straight in his chair and turned to his son.

"I have been wanting to speak with you about Lydia's situation," Manuel said.

"I have as well. I am just not sure which alternative is better for her. I hate the thought of her being at Carlos' ranch without much supervision, but I am also worried about sending her with Claire. There would be no way to get her back if she were in any danger there. We will be called to fight," Eduardo said. "I just know she should not remain here for the next several weeks."

"I have decided she should go to the Aragon ranch," Manuel said. "I can send a note ahead to Señora Aragon. Although we have not seen her the last few years, I know she still has kind and warm regards for Lydia. I will never forget she was your mother's best friend."

"You would know best, Father," Eduardo said. "I suppose now it's just getting her there. I don't think you or I can afford to be gone that long. The Confederates are getting closer each day."

"Yes, I agree. She won't be happy about this decision, and I will have to see how conditions develop over the next few days," Manuel said as he rose from his chair. "I have some reports I need to go over and then we must get ready for this evening. It will be our last gathering for long while, and we can all pretend for a short while that there isn't a war at our doorstep."

Eduardo nodded calmly and drank the rest of his coffee.

*   *   *

As Lydia stepped outside, she could feel the excitement in the air. Was it the spirit of Christmas or the fact she would see Eli tonight? She didn't know but smiled at the deep warm feeling she felt inside that seemed to come from thoughts of him.

The plaza was alive with activity. A group of children was playing tag, trying to work off some of their energy. Mothers sat and visited, enjoying the winter sun. Everything seemed right to Lydia. Even the small sparrows were out and picking at the seeds under the crusty layer of snow. The feeling of impending danger and loss had created a sense of urgency to hold on to what they had and who they loved. She tried to enjoy every moment of the short walk to her cousin's home.

As Lydia entered the front door, a state of confusion seemed to reign at the Murray home, but she knew it was well under control. Lydia walked into the parlor and Claire, in a black day dress and apron, stopped for a quick kiss on the cheek, energy and purpose exuding from her.

"Thank goodness you're here. Help Cecil arrange the parlor. I must see to the rest of the food," Claire said as she turned toward the kitchen. She looked back over her shoulder and gave Lydia a dazzling smile.

Cecil was directing two men who were moving some of the larger pieces of furniture out to the other parts of the house. The vacant parlor would be used for dancing later that night. Family and friends were lining up chairs on either side of the room.

"I'm not as helpless as she thinks I am," Cecil said as he hugged Lydia.

"Oh, I know. This is her favorite event. What would Christmas Eve or Las Posadas be without her party?" Lydia replied with a smile as Cecil handed her a large bunch of fresh pine boughs for decorating.

"I'll leave the windowsills up to you since you know how she likes them done," he said.

Lydia found the candlesticks and placed one in each of the windows around the room and then laid the fresh pine boughs around them. The heady aroma surrounded her, and she deeply breathed in the sharp, familiar smell. She closed her eyes for a moment and could see the candles lit and the room full of people laughing and dancing, swirling to the music. She opened her eyes, smiling at her own thoughts. She reached for the mistletoe and, adjusting herself on a small ladder, carefully hung it from the viga nearest the front door.

Lydia gave one last look at the parlor, which was nearly finished, and turned her attention to the dining room. Knowing exactly where the linen was kept in the ancient armoire, she pulled out the lace tablecloth and unfolded it over the length of the dining table. Cecil walked in and took hold of the other end of the cloth.

"Claire has agreed to leave for Madrid the day after Christmas with Violet and her mother." Cecil was looking directly at Lydia who was absorbed in smoothing out the wrinkles on the tablecloth. He moved closer to her. "Lydia, it would mean so much to us if you would..." She raised her hand to stop him.

"I would do almost anything for Claire or you, but I can't do this, and I don't want you to ask me. It will be comforting to know they are safe and sound." Cecil nodded his head, respecting her choice. "Now, let's find that wife of yours and see if there are any other orders she has for us before I leave to get dressed for the party."

*   *   *

Lydia and Alita walked home at a fast pace. Even though she had spent the entire afternoon helping her cousin, Lydia was filled with energy and anticipation for the night's events. They made their way upstairs, and Alita checked on her mistress' bath that had already been filled with hot water from the kitchen. Lydia slipped off her dress and undergarments.

She walked to the large brass tub sitting in the middle of the room. The bath was steamy and fragrant with oils. She stepped gracefully into the water, letting it surround her. Her whole body relaxed, and she let out a satisfied sigh.

The events of the day paraded across her mind. She was glad she had been so busy; it had kept her from thinking about all the predicaments this war had caused, such as Claire's decision to leave. Lydia wondered for a moment if she should go with her, away from the impending danger. Everything inside her said no. She was determined to see this through. For a moment, she wondered if her decision had anything to do with Eli.

She took the bar of scented soap and let it slide like silk over her skin. She washed her slender legs and arms and finally picked up a cup and poured water over her long hair. It didn't take long for her to work up a luxurious lather which she eventually rinsed. The water was becoming cold, so she stood and reached for a thick towel to dry herself.

For a moment, her thoughts turned back to the war. *Not tonight*, she told herself. After all, it was Christmas Eve, and she was going to share a wonderful night with family and friends. For some, it may be the last Christmas they would spend together.

With that thought, she poured all her energy into her preparation. As she combed through her hair, she decided tonight would be one of fantasy for her. *I will pretend I am not engaged to Carlos, that Claire is not leaving, that there is no war, and no one is in any danger*, she thought to herself.

Her mood brightened as she smoothed oil over her body before slipping into her robe. The fire burned brightly in her room and chased away any chill. Lydia's dress had been ready for days, a rich apricot velvet with simple lines and dark brown lace trim. She was pleased at how much the color enhanced her own as she held it up to her and twirled around in her bare feet.

Alita entered the room and smiled at her mistress, who was acting like the young girl she had once been. Outside, darkness began to fall across the small town as everyone prepared for the special evening. This night, with its magic, would be a celebration of life.

*   *   *

Manuel pulled his stopwatch out of his pocket and looked up at the staircase. Eduardo, standing next to him, pulled his gloves on, waiting impatiently for his sister.

"Lydia," Manuel called. "We will be late for church. Are you ready?" She didn't answer, but they could hear her petticoats rustle as she came down the staircase.

"You both look very handsome," she said as her father held her woolen wrap for her.

"And you, Lydia, look like a flower that has just bloomed," Eduardo said.

Lydia exchanged a look with her father. All of a sudden, her brother seemed so mature.

"Merry Christmas," she said and leaned over to kiss Eduardo's cheek tenderly before they made their way to the door.

The stars glistened in the sky above. Light-hearted greetings and Christmas wishes among friends and neighbors were exchanged as they made their way to the church. The joyful sound of the bell rang into the night, and everyone moved in its direction. Las Posadas had been taking place for the last eight days, and after mass tonight, there would be the final and most elaborate celebration at Claire's home. They filed into the candlelit church, kneeling as they entered the pews.

After the service, there was a sense of gaiety as the group made their way to Claire and Cecil's home. The young man and woman, portraying Mary and Joseph and their quest for a night's lodging so the Christ Child could be born, led the procession. They stopped at several residences, asking for shelter, and were laughingly sent away.

Upon their arrival at the Murray home, Mary and Joseph asked,

"Is there room for us here?" The front door was opened wide by the cheerful couple, and the already assembled crowd standing behind them let out a resounding "Yes!"

The large living room glowed with candles, and music from a guitarist and two fiddle players filled the air with a nostalgic Christmas song. The atmosphere was charged with light and energy.

Lydia looked around the room, wondering if Eli had arrived.

*   *   *

I thought this day would never end, Eli thought to himself as he brushed Coal's dark coat. The work was mindless and just what he needed after a long day of training with his men.

"They put in a good day's work today," he said out loud to Coal. "But we need more time and that seems to be a luxury we don't have." He made sure Coal was bedded down and walked towards the main building.

The soldiers had already had dinner and were sitting contently by the fire in the mess hall. Some of the women in town had prepared a feast of tamales, beans, and tortillas to celebrate Christmas Eve.

"We're headed to the saloon to drink up some holiday cheer. Join us, Lieutenant, there are some fine-looking women in this town," Davis said.

Eli smiled at him. "I know that Private. You men stay out of trouble." Davis winked and nodded. "We'll start drills early tomorrow," Eli said. As he was walking away, he turned back to the group of men and said, "Merry Christmas."

All day long, Eli's thoughts had drifted to tonight's gathering. He had been surprised when Manuel had extended the invitation. They had worked closely together the last few days and now shared a mutual respect. He smiled to himself as he poured water into the porcelain basin. He began washing his face before shaving. What was it about Lydia that made him have these feelings?

He had never wanted to be near a woman so badly before. "She is beautiful and spirited and I may just have a chance with her," he said out loud as he pulled on his best shirt and finally his uniform pants and dark blue double-breasted coat.

The night seemed special as he stepped into the darkness. He could feel the magic as he walked, and he recognized his own joy. He was overcome with a new sense of confidence that hurried his steps.

The Murray house seemed to shimmer in the moonlight. The frosty layer on the outside reflected the glow of the moon and stars. The noises of life, music, laughter, and conservation drifted towards him. As he approached the front door, he exchanged greetings with a small group of men tending to the luminaria, a small bonfire built to welcome the Christ Child.

Eli knocked soundly on the door, and Claire opened it with a smile. "I don't believe we've met, Señor. I am Mrs. Murray. Merry Christmas and welcome to our home."

Eli removed his hat and took her hand, a genuine smile falling across his face. "I am Lieutenant Colonel Eli Stevens. Thank you for having me."

She opened the door further. "Please, come in out of the cold, Señor Stevens. Follow me and I will get you something to eat and drink."

They made their way through the crowded hall and into the main part of the house. All along the way, she briefly introduced Eli to the townspeople as Señor Stevens, ignoring his military rank. He was greeted warmly.

The large dining room table was piled high with steaming tamales, pork roasts, beans, red and green chile, tortillas, and posole—a slow-cooked stew with corn and meat—along with desserts that included fruit-filled empanadas and biscochitos.

Claire picked up a white plate and handed it to Eli. "Please, help yourself. The women in town have been cooking all month long for this night," she said with a smile.

Filling his plate high with dishes he had never even heard of before, he found a place against the wall and began eating. The warm, exotic food tasted wonderful, and he hadn't realized how hungry he was.

Two elderly women approached him, and knowing he was not

from the area, asked about where he was born and raised. "I was born in the eastern part of the States," he said. "But my family moved to the Colorado Territory when I was just a young child. I consider this part of the country home."

"Well, we are certainly glad to have you here and Merry Christmas to you and yours," one of the ladies said as they both made their way to another group of people.

Home, Eli thought. He imagined what his mother and brother were doing right at this moment. They were probably knee-deep in snow on the ranch and enjoying a warm fire and good food. He missed them and promised himself he would write to his mother the next day.

*   *   *

The musicians gathered close to the piano and began tuning their violins and guitars, sending soft notes across the crowded rooms. Lydia stood with a small group of young women in the doorway with her eyes and cheeks glowing. She was ready to dance.

Dressed all in black, including a stiff bonnet and lace gloves she refused to remove, the age-old Aunt Docinea joined the group of young women. She was squarely built, very proper, and considered herself a keeper of the old ways and traditions. A pillar of the community, no one really knew how old she was, and she still had a sharp tongue. She was often consulted on the propriety of marriage proposals, as was the case with Lydia and Carlos.

Lydia glanced at the old woman and noticed her thin lips pierced together in a stern, disapproving line, and her small, round, beady, ever-seeing eyes looking out from her weathered and wrinkled face. She always wore black, as a symbol of her constant state of mourning for a husband she had lost many years before.

All the young women greeted her with respect. Lydia kissed her cheek and wished her a Merry Christmas in Spanish. "Buenos noches, Tía Docinea. Feliz Navidad."

"Lydia, you look lovely this evening. But I have not seen Carlos, is he with you?" she asked.

"No, Tía, he is not here," Lydia replied and offered no further explanation to the nosey old woman.

But she pressed on. "I have not heard a word about wedding plans."

Lydia sighed. "It is difficult to say when we can get married, given the war. We will have to wait and see."

The old woman's questions seemed to open the topic for conversation, and Lydia was besieged with comments and opinions from the other young ladies about her situation. "Can't you get married before the war comes here?" one young woman asked. Many were in the same circumstances, with promises of marriage from young men who would soon be off to fight the war. Lydia did not answer the question and instead, turned her attention to the musicians who had started to play.

"Well, I think your father would be able to have some sort of small ceremony before too long," said Docinea directly to Lydia. "It is only proper your marriage is secured quickly."

Eduardo, standing close by, put his glass down on the fireplace mantel and stepped in close to Lydia's side. "Tía," he said as he kissed the old woman's hand, "you look beautiful as always." The comment from such a young man made the old woman blush. "My sister and I have had such little time together since my return, and this is one of my favorite songs." He offered his arm to Lydia. "If you will excuse us." They headed towards the dance floor.

Lydia's eyes were glittering with amusement, and they shared a knowing smile as they turned to one another to join in the festive dance. "Thank you for saving me. I didn't know what to tell them." She looked up at her brother.

Eduardo approached the subject lightly as he drew his sister towards him. "I have been wanting to ask you, but I wasn't sure how." He paused. "This all happened while I was gone, and I want to know if you are happy about this marriage." The look on her face told him all he needed to know. "Shall I speak to Father?"

"Not tonight, Eduardo, there is wonder and happiness here. Just dance with me," she said, and only the sound of the music filled the space between them.

As she twirled around Eduardo, Lydia sensed Eli in the room. She glanced at the crowd over Eduardo's shoulder and saw him. He looked directly into her eyes and smiled deeply, showing his dimples. She could feel the color rise in her cheeks as she looked away during a turn. Somehow, knowing he was there made her excited and afraid. She finished her dance, never doubting that he would wait for her. The attraction between them was strong and vibrant, and they both drank of it like a deep, rich wine fulfilling their souls.

She left Eduardo's arms and walked towards Eli, holding her colorful fan up to her face so that only her shining eyes were visible. She could feel her heart pound and her hands shake, and she hoped her voice would be normal when she spoke.

She gave him her hand. "Señor Stevens, thank you so much for coming and Merry Christmas." Her voice did not quiver, and she breathed a sigh of relief.

Curious, Eduardo had followed her and stepped up to them. "Lieutenant Stevens," he said with enthusiasm as he shook his hand.

"Please, call me Eli." Eduardo nodded.

Lydia stood very close to Eli. He was taller, but they fit well together, and she felt drawn to his side. There was an awkward moment of silence, then they all began to speak at once.

Laughing, Eduardo said, "I will go and get some punch, I'll be right back." Lydia barely noticed he had gone.

"Are you enjoying the party?" she asked Eli.

"Oh yes, very much, Lydia." His voice was deep and resounding, and it was almost impossible for her to look right into his eyes.

"You look lovely this evening, Lydia."

She looked up, glowing with delight. "And you look very handsome in your uniform."

Eduardo returned with their drinks, and they spoke of the weather and the holiday. They were young and gay, and the war seemed a million miles away.

"Eli, come with me and I will introduce you to some of my family and friends," Lydia said.

They moved through the large group with ease. The townspeople knew the men from Colorado had come to help them fight the war and they were grateful. Eli was slightly embarrassed by all the thanks but was gracious in return. He felt comfortable and welcome, especially when they met up with Claire.

"Señor, have you eaten?" And even though he nodded and placed his hand satisfyingly on his stomach, she insisted, "You must have more, there is so much food and the music will start again soon. You must have energy to dance." She had a mischievous twinkle in her eye as she glanced at Lydia.

"Would you like something more to drink?" he asked Lydia, and she nodded. "Then, I will be right back."

He touched her hand before he turned to go but immediately turned back when a loud burst of music filled the room and people began to clap. Everyone gathered around as a young couple took the dance floor. Twirling and moving to the lively chords was contagious and soon, many other couples were dancing.

Eli stood close to Lydia and felt her body swaying to the music. He was about to ask her to dance when Eduardo swung around from her side and took her out. Eli could tell by her frown that she was scolding Eduardo, but then her face broke into a radiant smile, and she looked right at Eli as she picked up her skirts. Eli could not take his eyes from her as she moved with grace and ease and became part of the song.

The music was lively, and her hips swayed from side to side as she raised her arms above her head. Occasionally, her eyes would meet Eli's and he could see the passion burning within her as she turned and pounded the wooden floor with the heel and toe of her shoe. A thin film of sweat glistened on her face and shoulders, and strands of hair came loose from their pins, giving her a wild, sensual look. Her eye caught Eli's after a turn, and she did not break the stare. Her lips were parted as she took in a great breath of air. He could only imagine how she would feel in his arms.

The music ended and Eli watched as she quickly left the room. He had to keep himself from darting after her as Claire brought a group of young ladies to introduce to him. Eli was cordial, but Claire noticed he could barely follow the conversation and was anxiously looking past them all to the door. Suspecting this had to do with Lydia, Claire excused herself to find her cousin.

Lydia waved her fan quickly over her face, letting the cool air wash over her. She closed her eyes and willed her heart to stop beating so fast. As she looked in the mirror at Claire's dressing table, she saw her skin was glowing a rosy pink, which she knew was more from her feelings than the dancing.

She sat up straight in the chair and blew the breath out of her lungs. Her breathing became normal, and she began working her loose curls back into place. She picked up the powder puff and dabbed her shoulders delicately. Her mind was racing. Everything about him was perfect—his smile, his broad shoulders, and the way he looked at her. She was so busy thinking about him, she did not hear the bedroom door open and close.

"Why are you hiding in here?" Claire asked.

Lydia jumped and her eyes were round with surprise.

"I am not hiding," she said indignantly. "I'm just freshening up."

Claire pulled a chair close to Lydia and sat down with her hands folded in her lap. Leaning in, she asked, "Does this have anything to do with that handsome young soldier who is only waiting for the moment you walk back into the room?"

"He is?" Lydia asked with delight.

Claire nodded her head and smiled, but Lydia cast her eyes down. She took one of Claire's hands. "I am getting married, and I am not supposed to feel this way about someone else, am I? I can't embarrass my family. I won't."

Claire's voice was soft and gentle. "Love only happens for some. It is a gift, a gift that will last a lifetime. All I can say is, you must listen to the words in your own heart, not what everyone else is saying. Now, let's go back and enjoy this wonderful evening. Who knows what will happen tomorrow." The two women stood and hugged and walked out into the parlor together.

Composed and calm, Lydia and Claire joined the party. Eli had been patiently waiting with a cup of punch in his hand and handed it to Lydia.

She smiled. "Thank you."

Many people had left and so the room was much quieter as the music softly played.

"What a wonderful gathering this has turned out to be," Eli said as he turned to Lydia. "And the only thing left to do is dance."

He took Lydia's hand and led her to the middle of the parlor. They stood close to one another, and Lydia drew in a light, ragged breath as he stared deeply into her eyes. She hardly felt his arm go around her waist or his hand pick up hers. They started moving to the music.

They never spoke and concentrated only on one another. Conversations and laughter floated around them unheard; they were both caught up in the moment of being so physically close.

The song finished and Lydia thanked Eli for the dance while still holding his hand. As she turned to move off the floor, her father was at her side.

"It's time to go, my dear," Manuel said softly, and she looked up at him with clear and innocent eyes.

"Yes Papa. I'll get my wrap."

Manuel was not sure if his instincts were correct, but he could sense the strong emotions flowing between the two young people. As Lydia walked away, he motioned for Eli to walk with him towards the front door.

"I hope you have enjoyed this evening," he said to Eli.

"Yes sir, I have and thank you for inviting me. I don't think I have ever spent a Christmas Eve like this."

Manuel smiled and stopped walking as he turned to Eli. "Lieutenant," he said. "Lydia and Eduardo mean the world to me. Since their mother died, I have devoted myself to them and their well-being." Eli nodded in understanding.

"I want you to know that Lydia is engaged and will marry after the war," Manuel said.

Eli felt like he had been kicked in the stomach.

When he found his voice, he said, "Please give my thanks to Claire and Cecil. I must be going."

He found his hat and left, entering the cold, dark night alone.

≡ 9 ≡

Time seemed to be an enemy for Lydia over the following days. The holidays had come and gone and, with them, any peace. The community was responding to the inevitable danger that awaited. Anxiety was like a thick fog mixing in with the winter air surrounding them.

Lydia spent much of her time at the store. She would wake up early and make sure a hearty breakfast was prepared for Eduardo and her father, who continued to train the New Mexico Volunteers before they headed south towards the Confederate army. Once she arrived at the store, her days were filled with customers and orders and trying to help friends and neighbors make ends meet. The war had caused many of the routine shipments by stagecoach to cease, since the operators were fearful of getting caught in a battle zone.

This morning, as she flipped the closed sign to open, she saw Sister Cathleen from the Loretto convent waiting outside with an empty basket.

"Ah, good morning, Sister, please come in. We don't have much, as you can see, but we want to provide what we can," Lydia said.

"Oh, Lydia, we are beginning to run out of our reserves of food. I have very little money to pay you, but I promise we will make things right after the war ends." The sister was ringing her small, capable hands.

Lydia noticed her black habit had been mended many times and made a mental note to try and find some new black cloth.

"I never imagined we would be in this position. We are doing our best with the orphaned children placed in our care. We are in constant prayer and already preparing to aid with nursing for any soldier who suffers from an injury. We have consolidated the children into two rooms and have prepared all other rooms for any long-term care that may be needed."

"We all appreciate your efforts, Sister," said Lydia. "It is heartening to know you and Sister Teresa will be there to help if needed. I know medical supplies are being collected and will be delivered to the convent as Dr. Porter requested. Let's look at your list and see how we can help."

Her father and Ramon had stored up on staples such as flour, sugar, and canned goods for the past few months in anticipation of possible scarcities. Lydia was able to give some items to Sister Cathleen along with some dried beef from her own home she had brought to the store.

"You come back when you need to. If I am not here, Ramon will know what to do. The whole community is trying to conserve and share food and other resources so we can make it through the next few months," Lydia said as she wrapped her arms around the appreciative sister.

"We will keep you and your family in our daily prayers," Sister Cathleen said with genuine thanks as she headed toward the door.

Lydia spoke the same reassuring words each day to many of the women she had known all her life. She became very good at calming their fears and comforting them, even though she continually struggled with her own feelings.

"What do you think will happen to us? We hear rumors the rebel army burns houses and kills the people, do you think that is true?" an older woman with a dark shawl wrapped around her head and shoulders asked as her wrinkled hand went across her head and chest in the sign of the cross, muttering a blessing under her breath.

Lydia placed the canned goods on the counter and patted the top of her weathered hand. "Do you think our men, our soldiers, would let anything like that happen to us? No, and don't listen to the gossip. I wish people had better things to do than scare us all with their talk. Take care now, Señora, and I will see you soon." Her voice was strong and convincing, but inside Lydia wasn't sure at all.

After a long day at the store, Lydia would go over the figures with her father. "You are doing such good work. But I worry it is too much for a young woman," he said on one occasion. Lydia assured him she could handle these tasks. "You are so busy with the troops, and I know that you and Eduardo will be leaving Santa Fe soon. It's something that I need to do. I feel like I am contributing," she said.

In the evenings, she would meet with a group of women at the church hall as they rolled bandages and prepared poultices and herbs to have ready for the troops to carry with them. It was mindless work for Lydia, and she enjoyed the endless chatter and fellowship among the women.

Aunt Docinea was part of the makeshift work group and kept the conversation lively with town gossip and her own opinions. The candles burned low on the table where the women worked, and Lydia's eyes strained to see as she mixed a batch of herbs.

"You look tired, Lydia," Docinea said. "You are doing too much, and I think you should have gone with your cousin instead of staying here. It is not right, a young unmarried woman left to the mercy of those savages."

Lydia looked up at her great aunt, her jaw firm and her eyes burning with defense. "I have every right to stay, Tía."

Docinea huffed with disapproval. "What does Carlos think of all this? As your future husband, he must be concerned about what you are doing."

The other women kept busy with their own small tasks, but all eyes and ears were on Lydia. "I have told him of my decision. I am not married to him yet."

Docinea made a disapproving clicking sound and let the conversation end. First thing the next morning, she would find Manuel and speak to him about the situation.

As Lydia and Alita made their way home, Lydia wondered if she should have left with Claire. She realized how much she missed her and called up the strong memory of Claire's departure.

*   *   *

Right after Christmas, final preparations were made for Claire's trip to Madrid. Lydia and Claire spent as much time as they could together. Lydia helped Claire pack for herself and Violet. They talked and laughed and shared their secrets, as they had done all their lives.

"This will all be over soon," Claire said as she folded the baby's nightdress and placed it in the small trunk while Lydia sorted through dresses and petticoats laid out on the small sofa. "We will be back before the spring; I just know it." She spoke loudly, not only to convince Lydia, but herself as well. "Come and sit down with me for a moment. There are a few things I want to tell you."

The two women moved to the edge of the bed to sit down. Claire was trying hard to be strong, but her shoulders began to quiver, and she began to weep. Lydia held her as the tears streamed down her face. Lydia stroked Claire's hair and face. They did not speak, they didn't have to, and words would not have mattered.

"I want you to watch out for Cecil if you can," Claire said between big gulps of air. "Please make sure he is well and that he stays well." Lydia nodded her head in agreement. "How am I going to manage without him and without you? I know it won't be for long, but I am so angry at these men for turning our lives upside down." Lydia could not conceal a small giggle.

The slightest bit of amusement glinted in Claire's teary eyes. "I have hidden everything. There is a small ledge just inside the well outside. I put all the valuables and my jewelry in gunny sacks and covered it with mud. If they ransack my house, there won't be anything to take." Both women smiled then laughed as they held one another tightly.

The next morning, there were no tears or laughter, only goodbyes. They hugged one another then held each other's hand.

Claire whispered in Lydia's ear, "Please take good care of yourself. I wish I could stay, but I must protect my child. A piece of my heart stays though."

"And a piece of mine goes with you," Lydia said as Claire finally stepped into the stagecoach.

Lydia and Cecil had stood together and waved until they couldn't see the carriage any longer.

*   *   *

As she and Alita came closer to home, Lydia placed her hand on the pocket of her dress which held the note she had received from her cousin just that afternoon. Lydia had read it so many times already that she had memorized the contents.

My Dearest Lydia,

We have arrived safely in Madrid after a long and very bumpy ride. I had forgotten what a poor traveler my mother is, and I had to listen to her every complaint as though each was brand new. We are settled in with my grandparents and the house is very lovely. The weather, so far, is most agreeable for me and Violet, who was no trouble at all during our journey. I am deeply concerned for your safety and want you to write to me as soon as anything happens there. I am worried more for you than for Cecil, at least he gets to carry a gun.

Love always, Claire

Lydia pushed open the front door to her home and stepped inside. She never knew if her father would be there but was pleasantly surprised to find him in front of a warm fire in the parlor. She removed her wrap, scarf, and gloves and joined him.

Manuel looked up at her and was about to speak when she stopped him by saying, "Please don't tell me how tired I look or how I shouldn't be here. I just want to sit with you and enjoy the fire."

He nodded, and she curled up at his feet with her head resting against his leg. He stroked her hair as they sat in silence. He was aware of her fast pace during the day, knowing his own days were filled with preparations for war. He knew her anxiety and restlessness came from many things but didn't know all that was going on inside of her head.

As she gazed into the fire, exhaustion overtook her body and she relaxed. She closed her eyes and her thoughts drifted to Eli. She had memorized everything about him. The way he walked, how his hands moved when he spoke, the shape of his face, and the lines of his jaw; she even knew the exact shade of his eyes, a deep rich brown that held the slightest specks of gold. She felt he was a part of her, but she wasn't sure why or what she should do with these feelings. She had not seen him since the party on Christmas Eve, and she craved his physical presence much like a starving person craves nourishment.

She desperately tried to keep everything deep inside, locked away so her emotions would never see the light of day and become reality. She was confused about him and wondered if he was feeling the same. Had he felt the pull, the same intense attraction? She was not sure and thought she might never know.

Exhausted at night, she would think of his face and his voice before she closed her eyes to sleep. Sometimes, in the early morning hours, she was not able to sleep, and she would wrap herself in a soft woolen blanket and sit in her chair. She allowed herself this time to imagine a life with him. Each of them sharing the joy and pain and knowing she could love him forever.

She was suddenly very tired and rose to her feet. She leaned over and kissed her father goodnight. He watched as she walked slowly up the staircase to her room.

The store was particularly busy the next day. The townspeople were stocking up on any and all food items they could get, and the word was out a delivery was expected later that day. Lydia was not sure this was true since they had not received a shipment for quite some time, but she also kept the hope alive.

Manuel stopped by to check on Lydia in the middle of the day, and she greeted him with a warm smile as she looked up from behind the counter. She had just wrapped up the last of the items for a woman with her child.

"I can't believe how much you have grown, Miguel," Lydia said as she handed the young boy a piece of hard candy. "I put an extra pound of flour in your order, Señora Vigil. I don't know how long our supply will last and don't worry about paying us right away. I know your husband is training too." They exchanged an understanding glance and gratitude spilled from the woman's eyes.

Just then, a wagon pulled up to the entrance of the store. The driver was tired and dusty and in moments, he was surrounded by people, including Manuel, asking questions and anxious for any news about the Confederate army.

"Well," the driver began in a slow drawl, "I don't know much about their exact location, but I hear they are about to head north, ready and willing to take this territory." Gasps came from the women and the men nodded their heads in a mutual understanding. "If I were you, I would leave this God-forsaken place and move to higher ground, get as far away as you can from them," he said. "I hear they are vicious."

Manuel supervised Ramon while he unloaded the precious supplies. He picked up a large brown package tied with sturdy string and addressed to Lydia. He took it back into the store and laid it carefully on the counter as he called her name.

Lydia came out from the back room and looked at the package with surprise. "That's funny, I don't remember ordering anything. Maybe it's from Claire."

She found a knife and cut through the string with one stroke. As she tore through the paper and opened the box, yards and yards of white silky material spilled over the counter.

A note fell to the floor, and Manuel reached down for it and read it aloud.

My Dear Lydia,

I have taken the liberty of selecting the material for your wedding dress. It is the highest quality, and I know you will look lovely when you wear this to become my wife.

Your fiancé, Carlos Aragon

Lydia looked right into her father's eyes, and he saw a spark of anger that made all her features tense.

"How dare he," she said as she grabbed the note from her father's hand and tore it into shreds. "How dare he even think he will have that much control over me. I will pick my own material as I wish," she said loudly, looking at her father. "Anyone else would let me have control of my own life." She wrapped the material in the discarded paper and shoved it underneath the counter, then she went back to supervising the shelving of the new supplies.

Manuel, disconcerted, left the store and made his way to head-quarters by walking through the plaza, which was quiet and deserted. He was worried about Lydia's reaction and was wrapped up in his own thoughts when Docinea stepped up next to him and asked for a moment of his time.

"Good afternoon, Manuel," she said with sweetness dripping from her lips. "I wonder if you have a moment. It's about your daughter, Lydia, and my own fear for her safety."

Manuel stopped dead in his tracks as he looked directly at the old woman. "What would you like to know, Docinea?" he asked with reservation. They moved to a secluded spot underneath an oak tree.

"I am wondering if you have made any arrangements for her departure. She is a young and very beautiful woman and could easily come to harm if the Confederates come here. She should have gone with Claire, but I understand she was very determined to stay here. You must not allow it, and the next best place is the Aragon ranch in Chama. I am making my own plans to leave this town," she said smugly and tightened her black shawl around her shoulders. "As her father and her guardian, you must be sure she is safe," she said indignantly.

Manuel knew she was right, but he didn't admit it to her and wanted to be rid of the over-bearing woman.

"Thank you, Docinea," he said with false charm. "As always, you are right, and I will do everything I can to keep Lydia safe." He tipped his hat, dismissing her.

"Good day," she said and nodded to him. Her lips pursed together in a small line of satisfaction as she watched him walk away.

* * *

The Indian boy, wrapped in a fur vest and deerskin leggings, moved cautiously through the thicket of pine trees and chamisa bushes. His soft moccasins made barely any noise on the frozen ground. He had been tracking a deer all morning and was not about to let it get away.

He moved quietly and had the deer in range to strike a blow with his bow and arrow. His hands shook slightly as he aimed expertly at the animal, which was scanning the trees for any sign of danger, ears alert.

The young boy readjusted his stance and felt a clump of dirt beneath his feet shift, causing him to lose his balance. The deer caught sight of the boy in the corner of her eye and leapt away to freedom. His arrow sailed through the air and fell to the ground, missing the animal altogether.

The boy dropped his bow in frustration and exhaustion. He was not sure he had the stamina to go on chasing the deer, and he sat on a large rock to rest for a few moments. He pulled a piece of dry meat from his pouch and bit off a large chunk.

He looked down towards the mound of dirt he had stood on and noticed that it was fresh, not frozen solid. Curious, he knelt and began removing the branches and brushes strewn over the top of a large area of disturbed soil.

With that finished, he removed a small hatchet from his belt and pounded the ground, loosening the remaining soil. Eventually, the boy could see a small piece of dark blue wool. He knew instantly this was the uniform of a Union soldier, and even though the stench was powerful, he worked to uncover the body. There might be gold or something of value in the man's pocket.

Rivera's body was frozen solid from the exposure to the cold. Dried blood and dirt covered his face and chest. The boy searched Rivera's pockets for anything of value. Finding nothing, he kicked the body in disgust and began to cover it back up with the branches.

Pausing for a moment, the boy decided he should take this information to the soldiers in Santa Fe. Maybe they would find the information worth something and give him a reward.

* * *

Eli knew this was going to be a difficult sale. The old Mexican man ran his hand across the silky coat of the dark brown horse. Eli had already spent most of the gold coins the Colonel had given him. It had been a very long day, traveling from ranch to ranch, trying to gather horses for the men. Many of the owners had grudgingly parted with some of their livestock. But others, like this old man, saw it as an opportunity to make money, probably enough to feed his family through the rest of the winter.

The young soldier who had accompanied Eli was a local and possessed a bright smile and friendly disposition. He greeted everyone by their first names and had been quite persuasive. So far, they had acquired ten horses, not counting the one they were now negotiating for. Eli listened as the two spoke in Spanish and could tell from the old man's vigorous pleas that he would not let this horse go for little money.

"Well, Lieutenant, he says this is the only horse they have and the only way to get into town. But he'll sell her."

Eli reached into his pocket and pulled out what was left of the gold. "Not much left," he said to the young soldier.

The old man leaned over and counted the coin. He was pleased with the amount and turned the lead rope over to Eli.

Back on their horses, with the new horses tethered behind, they headed back towards Santa Fe. They were riding on the upper north side, and they could see the whole city. It was a beautiful place, with the rolling hills, the evergreens, and the golden brush that dotted the landscape.

Eli had been quiet and pensive all morning, and the young soldier, after being ignored many times, understood his mood and left him to his own thoughts. The clouds were gathering near the mountain and Eli wondered if they would bring more snow. Dark and gloomy, they reflected his own mood.

How could I have been so foolish? he thought to himself once again. *How did I let myself feel like this?* was the recurring thought in his mind. He remembered walking back from Claire's on Christmas Eve.

Spoken for. He'd kept repeating the words to himself. Why hadn't he asked Lydia if she was available? How could he believe that such a beautiful and intelligent young woman would not be engaged?

He had promised himself to stay away from her. He couldn't afford the feelings she caused in him. He tried to forget her sparkling eyes and the beauty in her smile. But it was impossible; thoughts of her continued to creep into his mind.

As the sun slipped behind the mountain range, they arrived at headquarters. Eli was immediately summoned to see Colonel Canby.

A young Indian boy was sitting by the fire as Eli entered the room. A translator was speaking to him in a calm voice and the boy was responding in a language that Eli did not understand. He knew from the look on the Colonel's face something was wrong.

"There's been trouble, just as we feared. I am certain Private Rivera was killed shortly after he left. I've dispatched two men to follow the young boy to the site and, hopefully, they will bring his body back and we will know for certain."

For the next three hours, Eli paced the hallways inside the building. Rivera had not gotten far at all, and certainly not all the way to Colonel Riley in the Colorado Territory.

Impatient, he decided to saddle up Coal and ride out on his own. He knew the path he had taken when arriving in Santa Fe and thought Rivera would have gone out the same way. As Eli made his way to the stables, he saw the two soldiers come into the gate with a blanket-covered body flung on the back of one of the horses.

Without saying a word, he followed them to the stables. Once inside, Eli removed the covering and looked right into the frozen eyes of the young soldier. He covered the body and asked one of the soldiers to check with the priest about a gravesite.

Eli walked slowly back to the Colonel's office.

"It's Rivera. I've decided I'll go back to Colorado this time. We can't take any more chances. The Confederates are getting closer each day."

Colonel Canby sighed and nodded in agreement. He did not want to lose Eli but knew the successful completion of this task could be the difference in maintaining the Union's occupation of the area.

"I will need you here for the next few days. I will send a tracker from Carson's unit, one who knows the territory well. He can get to Colorado quickly and then you can meet up with the troops in Taos and lead them back. My plan is to move all the troops to Fort Craig."

*   *   *

Word slowly spread among the officers that Eli was leaving for Taos soon. Manuel had not seen Eli since Christmas Eve and never realized the impact of his words that night. He just assumed Eli was as busy as everyone else. On his way home, Manuel had a thought about how he might protect Lydia.

During dinner that evening, he noticed the fatigue in her face and tried to coax her to eat a little more as she picked at the food on her plate. "Rations are getting scarce, my dear. You must eat more; you are too thin."

But Lydia only wrinkled her nose and looked away from her food. "Papa, I would rather rest well than eat well. At least then, I can forget about all this war nonsense, even if it is only for a little while." She stood, kissed her father and her brother on the cheek, and made her way upstairs.

Left alone at the dinner table, the two men talked about the volunteers and how soon they would be leaving.

"I have been thinking, Eduardo," Manuel began slowly and leaned back into his chair. He knew if he could not convince Eduardo, he would never convince his daughter.

"I want Lydia away from here. The Confederate soldiers are already on their way. I don't want any harm to come to her and I don't know if we can protect her. At the beginning, I thought we could, but now, we can hardly tell what's going to happen next."

Eduardo adjusted his position, feeling the weight of the decision they were about to make. "Where can she go?" he asked. "There are no more stagecoaches coming in or out."

Manuel rested both hands on the table, certain he had made the right choice. "I want her to go to Carlos' ranch in Chama, to the north."

Eduardo challenged his father. "I know she will refuse to go, with many good reasons. They are not married, she does not know him well and only remembers his mother from her early childhood."

Manuel acknowledged what his son was saying. "I know she won't like being there, but she will be safe, far away from the battles. You must help me convince her that this is the right thing to do."

"What do you think Carlos will say?" Eduardo asked.

"He will be pleased and go along with this decision. I trust he has her best interest in mind. He wouldn't want any harm to come to his bride to be," Manuel said.

Eduardo shook his head. "She is not going to like this, Papa. She is going to fight you every step of the way."

Manuel sighed. "Fight us, Eduardo. She is going to have to fight us."

*　*　*

Lydia woke up in an anxious mood the next day. She was still tired as she hadn't slept well. Her head ached and she was especially sensitive to the cold drafts sailing throughout the cracks and crevices of the old house. She dressed especially warm with extra wool stockings and her dark blue wool skirt, which was her thickest. After pulling on her blouse, she wrapped a heavy woolen shawl around her shoulders and secured each end inside her leather belt—but she was still shivering.

Before going downstairs, she lit a candle to a small statue of St. Jude, the saint of the impossible. The small hand-crafted santo had resided on her dresser in her room since she was a small child, and his rough, wooden face was comforting.

Kneeling, she made the sign of the cross across her face and chest and prayed silently that those she loved would be safe this day. She rose and was about to make her way out of the door when she saw Alita about to blow out the candle.

She touched Alita's hand and said, "No. I will blow this out later. Don't worry, I won't forget." Alita understood; the prayer belonged to Lydia.

Downstairs, she was pleased to find her father and brother at the breakfast table.

"I am so glad you are still here," she said. "It seems like I am always having my meals alone these days and that is not something I enjoy. I'll check on breakfast," she said.

In the steamy kitchen, she poured herself a hot cup of coffee and merely held it in her hands for warmth. She watched as the cook finished up the eggs, red chile, and tortillas and heaped them on plates. Lydia followed her into the dining room. Luckily, they still had plenty of chickens producing eggs.

"You look better this morning, my dear," her father commented.

"I think it must be the food and company," she said as she sat down at the table.

After the plates were cleared, Eduardo rose and said, "Papa, I will see you at the training ground." He stopped and kissed Lydia on the top of her head.

Lydia moved her chair back and rose to get ready to leave for the store.

"Sit down for a moment. I would like to speak to you," her father said. He knew he had to say this in just the right way.

He cleared his throat and looked at her. "I have a proposition for you, Lydia." She turned to him and placed her hands on the table. "It is my wish that you go to stay at Carlos' ranch until the Confederate army is safely away from here."

She looked right back at her father and calmly and precisely said, "No, I will not leave you and Eduardo." Her back straightened and she folded her arms in front of her, braced for his response.

"You must, I promised your mother I would always look after you and care for you. Our troops will be leaving in the next few days, and if I am fighting in a war, I won't be able to do that," he said. "And neither will Eduardo."

She opened her mouth to speak, and he held his hand up to silence her. "I know how strong-headed and stubborn you are, Lydia, but now is not the time. Your safety is all that matters to me."

She could see the emotion in his eyes and hear it in the strain of his voice. She had moved her hands to her lap, and they were tightly laced together. She looked down at them. In her heart she knew it was for the best and her father would worry so much less if he knew she was safe.

"All right, Papa," she said, looking up with a sigh. "I will go, but only for you."

Her father's shoulders relaxed and for the first time in a long time, he smiled. "You will see this will be a good thing. Now, you must start packing for your trip," he said.

As she reluctantly rose from the table, she asked, "Will Eduardo be riding with me?"

"No. I am going to ask Lieutenant Stevens to take you on his way up north," he said.

≡ 10 ≡

In the early light of dawn, Eli rode the short distance from Union headquarters to the Sena home. Straight backed and rigid in his saddle, his face was frozen in a frown and a deep ridge had settled between his eyebrows. He steeled himself to see Lydia. As he pulled up to the stable, Manuel, in a wool coat and heavy gloves, was adjusting the saddle on Lydia's horse, Sadie, a palomino.

Eli nodded to Manuel. "Is she ready?" he asked tersely just as Lydia came through the front door and started towards her horse. She was bundled from head to toe in a long black wool skirt, leather boots, and a wool coat closed with a leather belt. Her hair was secured in a tight bun, and she had a wide-brimmed hat on her head, tied under her chin. She unconsciously placed her right hand to her waistband to feel the heaviness of the revolver her father had given her that she wore underneath her coat.

Lydia stopped at Eli's horse and smiled warmly at him, offering him her gloved hand.

"Good day, Miss Sena," Eli said coldly with a hard look in his eyes as he held her hand momentarily. "We need to get moving. It is a long ride to get you to your fiancé."

She suddenly realized he was angry either because he was burdened with her or because she was engaged, or both. She turned her head away and moved to her father's side.

Manuel wrapped her protectively in his arms and kissed her cheek. "Be safe, my dear," he said with a voice that cracked with emotion. She stood in his arms for a few minutes and touched his face.

"Please be careful, Papa. I love you and I will see you very soon," she said.

With that, he helped her into her saddle.

Manuel reached up and shook Eli's hand. "Thank you," he said with genuine gratitude, and he watched them leave the stable to the main road.

As they neared the edge of town, Eli asked gruffly, "How well do you ride?"

Lydia looked squarely at him. "Probably better than you," she yelled as she yanked Sadie's reins and galloped off down the icy road.

Eli cursed under his breath as he motioned Coal to move faster. Lydia had gained a long lead in a short period of time, and he pushed hard to catch up to her.

Lydia was familiar with the path, and she turned her horse expertly on to the trail off the main road. She could hear Eli behind her, and she rode faster.

Eli lost his bearings momentarily on the small, unmarked trail, but he eventually caught up to her. He ran Coal right up alongside Sadie and grabbed hold of her reins. She shot him a dirty look and tried to take them back. He slowed down both horses, which were breathing heavily after their gallop.

Eli's own breath was heavy with anger. "Don't do that again, Lydia," he said with frustration.

Lydia stopped her horse and looked right at him. "You cannot give me orders. I am not a soldier in your army. I can get there by myself. I don't need you to protect me, and if you agree, I will find my own way there."

"Agree to let you travel alone? In the middle of a war?" he asked, exasperated. "This is a task I didn't ask for and I shouldn't be taking you with me. Let's get a few things straight. You'll do what I tell you. I'm in charge of this expedition. I don't want to do this anymore than you. I have a mission to complete and a war to fight, and both are far more important than being your nursemaid."

As the words came out of his mouth, he knew he had crossed a line. She glared at him and turned her horse back towards the trail. Coal fell in step right behind Sadie.

Lydia was tempted to look back at the city. From much experience, she knew the view from where they rode was beautiful, showing off the soft curves of the adobe structures surrounded by the gentle hills, all lit by the warm glow of the early morning winter sun. The dim light would be barely touching the walls of the buildings and the majestic church steeple, making them a shimmering reflection against the remaining darkness. She closed her eyes for a moment and imagined how it looked, since her pride would not let her turn back and say goodbye.

Eli's mood was quiet and sullen. He told himself he was angry at her simply because she was there, but he knew it was much more than that. He was even angrier at himself for not controlling his own emotions. The path ahead became wider, and he nudged Coal forward with his knees and pulled ahead of Lydia, anxious to take the lead and quicken the pace.

The fresh winter air and prominent scent of pine eventually softened both their moods. After about an hour or so, they arrived at an abandoned house and Sadie instinctively moved towards the barely standing wooden fence.

Eli took the opportunity to break the silence. "Your horse has been limping. I need to check her shoe," he said. "She might have a stone caught."

They both dismounted, and while Eli carefully lifted Sadie's front hoof, Lydia walked to the front of the partially burned-out house surrounded by thick piñon trees and gray, rounded sage brush.

The structure was ancient looking, but the adobe edges on top of the foundation were still visible. A weathervane, worn from years of exposure to the elements, sat at the top of the partial structure, having been spared by the fire. It twirled effortlessly in the light wind. The front door was the color of ash, white-washed from years of wind, snow, sun, and rain, and yet, all that only seemed to add to its character and wisdom. She picked up a rusty spoon and brushed the dirt away from it with her gloved hand.

"Interesting place," Eli said, coming over to stand next to her. "What happened?"

"Who knows, Señor, perhaps it was Indians or illness. It has been this way as long as I can remember. Claire and I used to come out here and play sometimes. Someday, I am going to buy it and restore it. Someday, I will raise my children here," she said, then immediately regretted sharing that wish with him.

"We better get moving," Eli said uncomfortably, not wanting to discuss that part of her life. "We have a lot of ground to cover, and you are going to have to keep up."

They rode the rest of the day without speaking, which relieved him on some level; he felt fatigued from the day's emotions. *It's unbelievable*, he thought to himself. *I can command a whole unit of men, but give me this one woman to watch and it's almost too much.*

Eli spotted an alcove protected on one side by large boulders and on the other by tall pine trees and barren, twisted oaks with enormous trunks and gangly branches. He called back to Lydia, "Let's make camp for the night" and pointed to the spot. She nodded and moved in front of him, directing Sadie in that direction.

The long day's ride, along with the cold weather, had been uncomfortable for Lydia and she was ready to get off her horse. She felt good as both feet hit the ground, and after she tied the horse's reins to a tree, she was able to fully stretch her arms and legs.

Eli moved Coal behind her and easily dismounted. He began removing his saddle bags and bed roll, intending to remove the saddle. Lydia did the same, moving her belongings to a large boulder. He watched in case he could help her, knowing how heavy a saddle could be—and knowing she would not ask for his help. She reached under her horse and unbuckled the leather straps. Eli was immediately at her side, pulling the saddle up and over the horse.

Lydia lowered her eyes for a moment. He was so close she could smell his rugged scent. She felt a blush rise to her cheeks, but she was determined not to let him see.

"I have been riding since I was a young girl and know very well how to care for a horse," she said to his back as he laid the saddle on a rock.

"Suit yourself," he replied.

By the time Lydia had wiped down, watered, and fed Sadie a few oats, she was ready to crawl into her bed roll; but she knew they must eat. Alita had packed a stew in Lydia's knapsack with fresh tortillas. As soon as Eli had a small fire burning, she placed the stew in two tin bowls over the flames to warm. Then she sat on a fallen log close to the fire.

Night was closing around them quickly. Eli made a quick check of the parameter of the camp. They were well hidden, and the alcove would provide some protection from the harsh, cold wind and, more importantly, from intruders.

Without a word, Lydia moved the bowls and laid the tortillas to warm on a stone by the fire. She handed a bowl and tortilla to Eli who squatted by the warmth of the fire. He ate with gusto, famished from the day's ride and the emotional tension. Lydia finished eating and set her bowl down, pulling her shawl tighter around her shoulders.

The wind picked up slightly and began sailing through the tops of the majestic pine trees. Darkness fell quietly around them, and Eli knew it was time to bed down. He picked up their bowls and spoons and walked to the nearby stream to rinse them.

Lydia was busy laying out her bed roll when he returned. He placed the bowls and spoons in his saddle bags near Coal. The wind carried a cold bite and he longed to be warm. Eli kept his eye on Lydia from where he stood, reasoning that it was only for her protection.

Kneeling on her bed roll near the fire, Lydia removed her hat and began to pull the pins out to loosen her hair. It fell like a piece of silk down her back and shoulders. She pulled her hairbrush out of her knapsack and began pulling it through the thick strands.

He was caught in the moment. She was so beautiful. He noticed how the firelight reflected fiery red accents in her hair. Engrossed in her own thoughts, she seemed unaware of Eli at first, but then realized he was staring and looked directly into his eyes. He was embarrassed and looked away as he made his way towards the fire, bed roll in hand.

"You'd better get some rest," he said, roughness rounding his voice.

She ignored him, tied her hair back, slipped off her boots, and wrapped herself up in her wool blanket then slid into her bed roll. She turned her back to him and the fire, gazing out at the now blackened landscape.

Eli adjusted himself on top of his bed roll and placed his rifle next to him. He put both of his hands under the back of his head and gazed at the stars.

Damn her, he thought to himself and yet he knew he didn't mean it. He was angry at himself for feeling the way he did about her and would do anything to protect her.

Lydia felt safe knowing he was near, and she relaxed. Exhaustion finally took over and they both fell into a deep sleep.

She woke right before a dawn that promised a glorious sun and made her way to the stream to freshen up. Her father had taken her and Eduardo out on camping trips many times, to check cattle and to hunt. She felt secure and confident as the cold morning air awakened her senses, and she dismissed the winter chill of the water as she dipped a handkerchief in to wash her hands and face.

The sun was just breaking above the mountains, and small pieces of light made the snow on the ground sparkle like diamonds. A soft, chilly wind blew, and her skin had goose bumps as she pulled off her heavy coat. She unbuttoned her blouse and pulled it down around her shoulders and to her waist, splashing some of the cold water to her neck and arms. No one to bother her, no one to tell her what to do— the moment was freeing and exhilarating.

Eli stirred and then was fully awake in an instant. He looked over and, seeing she was gone, jolted out of his bed roll and grabbed his rifle. He cautiously stepped around the camp, desperate to find her. His heart was pounding because he knew of the dangers that could be lurking in the wilderness.

What if someone has taken her? he thought. *I should have better guarded the camp*. He cursed himself as he made his way down the small path. He called her name softly, not wanting to give himself away. There was no answer as he made his way to the stream, pushing aside the foliage on either side of him.

He finally came upon her at the water's edge. Her hair hung long and loose around her shoulders and graceful arms, and the sun's rays touched the strands and her skin, creating an incandescent glow. He caught his breath at the sight of her firm, round breasts.

He took a deep breath and stood straight, knowing she had not seen him yet. "What are you doing," he yelled to her.

She looked up, startled for a moment, her eyes round with fear until she locked her gaze with Eli. The fear slid into anger as he made his way to her.

She pulled up her blouse to cover her chest, used her shawl to dry her arms and her face, then stepped firmly to the bank. Facing him, she stood her ground for a moment.

"I needed some fresh water," she said defiantly as she grabbed her coat and began walking right past him.

He grabbed her arm as she brushed by, anger and relief spilling out of him. He turned her to face him, pulling her close.

"You can't go off on your own here. This is not a game. You could be killed or taken by Indians or Confederates. I was crazy enough to promise your father I would get you safely to your groom, and I fully intend to do that, with you all in one piece."

She stared at him coldly for a moment and then pulled her arm out of his grasp. She took a step back from him, wanting to slap him across the face. "Don't think for a moment, Señor, that I want to be on this trip with you. Had I been able to, I would have stayed and helped protect my home. This journey is as much a burden to me as it is to you."

They stared at each other for a moment.

"I suggest we get going," she said hotly and turned and walked with sure and determined steps back to the camp. Lydia was very close to tears, and she knew in her heart that he had never felt the same way she did.

Eli followed her back to camp. They did not speak to one another as they packed up but moved efficiently to get their gear back on their horses. They mounted and fell into a solid gallop on the trail. Eli was riding closely behind her, his gun ready at his hand.

He chastised himself for being so blunt, but he also knew it was for the best. He was delivering her to another man, her fiancé. He would probably never see her again. Watching her as she rode in front of him, he thought, *I need to keep reminding myself she's taken.*

As they traveled further north, the weather turned bitter cold and there was an increase in the snow on the ground, making it more difficult for the horses to maneuver the path. They rode for several hours, and Lydia never once complained or asked to get down from her horse.

Eli rode up to her on the trail. "Lydia," he said, and she looked over to him. "We need to stop and eat and water the horses."

She simply nodded and let him lead the way to a small clearing by the stream. Dismounting, he used the butt of his gun to break the ice that had formed, allowing the horses to drink the frigid water. He took a handful of it himself and washed his face, then filled their canteens.

Lydia had come down from her horse and moved into a small grove of trees. She knew Eli was vigilantly watching so she quickly relieved herself and adjusted her clothing. Her muscles were beginning to ache, and she took a moment to stretch her arms and legs.

Eli tied both horses to a nearby tree, allowing them some rest. Lydia took a long drink from her canteen and pulled the collar of her coat more closely around her neck, tucking it tighter into her leather belt. She opened her saddle bag and carefully unwrapped two tortillas and some dried jerky.

"You ride better than many men I know," Eli said, trying to break the silence that had built up between them.

Lydia handed him the food with a look of frustration and disbelief on her face. She huffed and walked away to find a secluded spot to eat her food. He grimaced before taking a bite.

They soon got back on the trail, doing their best to shield themselves from the frigid air carried by a bitter wind. Eli let Lydia ride behind him since he now trusted she could keep up and would stay close by.

Lydia noticed how sore her rear, her back, and her shoulders had become. She glared at Eli's back and thought to herself, *How arrogant he is. I grew up here and know the way better than he does.* She sat up straighter in her saddle and squared her shoulders.

Eli could feel the negative thoughts aimed directly at his back and wondered what she was thinking.

They were both startled by a loud crack in the brush. Eli stopped his horse abruptly, turned back to Lydia with his gloved hand up and a hard look in his eyes, and motioned her to come up next to him. He pulled out his long-barreled rifle and they both waited.

The only noise was the wind sailing through the tops of the pines. Eli looked from side to side, his gun ready. He turned his head quickly at the sound of a footstep in the snow.

The tall Indian appeared from behind the trees, his manner commanding respect. His hair fell down his back with crow feathers attached near his face. His buckskin shirt, pants, and moccasins were worn soft from wear, and a large silver concho belt around his waist reflected the sunlight. Strands of bright turquoise, blue lapis, red corral, and white albacore hung around his neck. He was pulling a black stallion stacked with pelts.

Lydia thought he looked regal in this setting among the pines and the white snow and nodded to him respectfully.

The Indian held his hand up to Eli in a gesture of peace. Eli put the gun back into his side saddle and slowly dismounted his horse. He looked up to Lydia as he handed her Coal's reins.

"Do you have a gun?" he asked her softly. She nodded and placed her hand on her right side. "Stay right here. I'll be back." She nodded, and Eli walked over to the Indian.

They spoke for several minutes. The Indian knew some English and said his name was Yas. After pointing to Eli's uniform, the man informed him that he should be careful. Yas knew there were white men in the area planning to help the Confederate soldiers when they arrived.

To make sure he understood what Yas was telling him, Eli asked,

"Do these white men have guns and supplies ready for the Confederate soldiers?"

Yas nodded.

Eli asked, "Do you know where?"

Yas shook his head no. Then he looked over to Lydia and asked Eli about her. Eli understood the basic meaning and sternly said, "No!" Yas asked another question, and Eli's voice raised in another emphatic "No!" as he shook his head and hands for emphasis.

Lydia could see both men and could hear small parts of the conversation. She could tell they were talking about her and wondered what they were saying. Eli finally walked back to her with a concerned look on his face.

"We better move on, night will be here soon," he said, pulling his gloves back on.

She handed the reins to him, and he mounted Coal quickly. They both watched Yas walk away leading his horse. Lydia looked over at Eli, and he nodded to her to get in front of him.

He was now riding much closer to her, making even her horse uncomfortable. She looked back at him with a puzzled look and saw he was looking and listening in all directions.

"Señor," she began, but he put his finger to his lips to silence her.

They rode like this for at least two hours. Finally, feeling he had created enough distance, Eli stopped them to let the horses drink from a stream.

Lydia got down from her horse and started to walk away to get some space between them to relieve herself.

Eli said sharply, "Lydia, you must stay close by me. You can't wander off alone."

"Why?" she asked defiantly.

"That Indian back there wanted to trade for you, that's why. I have a feeling he is following us."

Lydia was surprised and began looking around. She turned back to Eli, remembering something from her childhood. "He had crow feathers in his hair. There is an old Indian legend about the crow," she said. "When the Snow Spirit took the warmth from the Indians, they sent the Rainbow Crow to ask the Creator to make it warm again. The Rainbow Crow sang beautifully to get the Creator's attention, and the Creator thrust a stick into the Sun. The stick started burning and the Creator handed it to Rainbow Crow to take back to the people. He flew as fast as he could, but the fire from the stick burned all his feathers, and the smoke damaged his voice. So, crows are forever black with a hoarse cry—but, in the right light, their feathers still hold the beautiful colors of a rainbow."

"That's a wonderful story, Lydia, but we need to find a safe place to stay the night. I don't want to run into him again," Eli said.

He decided they would head to Sutton's ranch, recalling how accommodating Sutton had been to him and his men on their way down from the Colorado Territory. They rode hard the rest of the afternoon, and by the time they reached the ranch, darkness was rapidly descending. As they approached the house, Eli felt relief.

Sutton came out to greet them. "Lieutenant, I am glad you stopped here." He caught sight of Lydia. "I didn't realize you have a young woman with you. Welcome to my home. I am Thomas Sutton."

"Hello, Señor Sutton. I am Señorita Sena, and I thank you for your hospitality."

The older gentleman helped Lydia down from her horse. He was moved by her slenderness and the deep blue color of her eyes. She reminded him of his late wife.

"We'd be much obliged, and if it is not too much trouble, I'd like the lady to sleep in a warm bed," Eli said.

"No trouble at all," Sutton replied.

Lydia entered the large entryway of the hacienda, impressed by the furnishings and the considerable number of books on the shelfs. Sutton called out and Leena, a middle-aged Hispanic woman, appeared wiping her hands on a dish towel tucked into her apron. She smiled broadly at the sight of Lydia and, with a confirmed look at Sutton, led her up the stairs to a large, warm bedroom.

"We will run a bath for you, Señorita," Leena said as she began pulling towels and soap from a hand-carved armoire. "I will be back with hot water for the tub. Just rest for a little while," she said kindly and pointed to the brass bed covered with a colorful quilt.

Lydia sat down on the soft bed and ran her hand over the bedspread. She had been riding for only two days, but it felt like an eternity. She didn't realize how exhausted she felt or how much her muscles ached until she removed her riding boots and coat and lay down across the bed, allowing herself to enjoy the comfort. She could hear Leena bustling around the room, and in a heartbeat, she was drifting off to sleep.

Downstairs, the men sat across from one another in Sutton's study. He had poured stiff whiskey, and Eli savored the rich taste of it, letting out a sigh. He described the incident with the Indian to Sutton.

"He won't bother you here," Sutton said. "Although, they have been very restless with all the comings and goings of men and equipment. I just don't think they understand this war. Hell, sometimes I don't even understand." Eli nodded in agreement.

They discussed strategy and troop movement. Eli trusted Sutton, but he didn't want to give away any pertinent information. He finally asked Sutton if he knew anything more about the civilians' plans to side with the South.

"I did have a young man ride through not too long ago," Sutton said. "He stayed the night in the barn with his horse, and the next morning he told me he was heading to Santa Fe to join up with the Union army. He said it was the only way he could forgive himself for what he had done. He wasn't specific, but he did confirm he had been a part of a group who believed the South would overtake the territory soon and said he'd committed some horrible undertakings to make sure that happened. He never gave me his name, but I could tell he was remorseful."

Eli knew Sutton would have shared any and all information he might have come across. "I will try to find him when I return, but the information he gave to you is helpful and I will make sure the Colonel is aware."

Sutton nodded in agreement and said, "Let me show you to your room. I am sure you could use some rest before dinner."

After Leena woke her and Lydia indulged in a hot bath, she could smell the delicious aroma of dinner. She changed into a simple brown dress and placed her hair up, thinking to herself, *We are at war, but surely a young lady should still try to look nice.* She made her way downstairs.

Sutton greeted her at the bottom of the stairs. "You look lovely, my dear," he said, and he took her arm to lead her to a chair.

Eli was standing at the table. He felt much better after changing his own clothes and cleaning up, and he thought Lydia looked refreshed and glowing and some of her vibrancy had returned.

They all sat down and began eating the delicious roasted lamb with potatoes.

Sutton asked, "Señorita, you are from Santa Fe?"

"Yes," she replied. "And please call me Lydia." She went on to tell him of her father and brother.

Sutton mentioned that he might have met her father a few years back. He was charmed by her, remembering how he had enjoyed the company of his wife before she died. "Are you going back to Colorado to be with family?" he asked Lydia.

"No, Señor," she said. "I won't be going that far."

Eli knew Sutton was curious about her and said, "I am taking her to her fiancé's ranch, close to Chama. Her father thought she would be much safer there."

"And what do you think about that, Lydia?" Sutton asked innocently.

She was surprised, most men didn't ask for a woman's opinion about their own destiny. "I don't want to go there. I would have rather stayed and helped when the Confederates come. I am not afraid."

Sutton exchanged a smile with Eli, openly admiring her courage. "Well, I am certain that you would give them a run for their money if you ever get a chance to encounter them. But I understand your father's concerns, and your protection is what is most important."

After dinner, they sat in the parlor as the fire burned brightly, and for a while, they all forgot why they had come together. Lydia watched Eli through eyes veiled by her long lashes, but she felt relaxed and warm. Her mood towards him softened, and for the first time, she realized how difficult this situation must be for him. Not only was she an excess burden in this critical time, but if he had any feelings at all for her, he wouldn't be pleased about taking her to another man. She shook her head as the reality set in.

They needed to get an early start in the morning, and Sutton finally stood. "I surely miss the company of young ones," he said. "I can't tell you how pleasant this evening has been." He extended his hand to Lydia to help her up from her chair. "You both get a good night's rest," he said. "You have at least two days of riding left to get where you are going."

Lydia held Sutton's hand in hers. "You have been very kind and gracious. Thank you."

"I'll see you to your room," Eli said. He stood so close he could smell the sweetness in her hair.

As they climbed the stairs he said, "Lydia, I am sorry for yelling at you today, for being so rough. I just don't want anyone or anything to harm you."

She turned to him and said, "I understand what you are doing." She lifted her hand and placed it on his arm. She could hear his heartbeat and the sound of his breathing.

They stood in the dark hallway, each struggling with their own desires and barely able to look in each other's eyes. Eli barely brushed against her as he reached over to open the bedroom door, and they both felt the attraction between them.

Not knowing whether he could maintain his composure, Eli abruptly ended the encounter. "Sleep well, Lydia. We have an early morning."

"Good night, Eli," she said and walked into the room, closing the door behind her.

He smiled—it was the first time she had called him by his first name.

≡ 11 ≡

The wind howled without mercy the next morning and thick clouds hung in the sky. Lydia was awake early, before the sun came up. She had slept well, due to exhaustion, but felt achy and worn. She knew, though, they had to go on. The closer they came to the Aragon ranch, the more she wanted to turn and run away. She couldn't face the idea of being near Carlos, much less marrying him. She washed her face and brushed her hair before loosely pinning it up. She could feel her resentment and anger spill over, and she let out a cry when her hair pin jabbed too close to her scalp.

Leena had delivered a silver tray with a pot of coffee, eggs, and toast and was busy laying out Lydia's clean riding garments. At Lydia's cry, she looked up, startled. "I am fine," Lydia said with a forced smile. She thanked the housekeeper as she pulled on her clothes and sat down to eat a bit of eggs and toast. When she finished, she packed up her few items in her knapsack, pulled her coat and hat on, and made her way downstairs.

Looking out the front window, she saw Eli outside saddling both the horses.

Sutton pulled on his wool coat and walked outside to help Eli. He wanted to make sure their horses were in good shape. The wind cut right through him as he checked each of the horse's shoes to make sure they were on properly and not loose.

"Take these oats with you," he told Eli as he strapped the bag on to Lydia's saddle. "It will give them more energy, especially after a day like today. If you're ready, I'll get Lydia." Eli nodded in response.

Sutton made his way back into the house. Lydia was thumbing through one of his books in the parlor. Sutton was generally a quiet man, keeping a lot of things to himself, but since the death of his son, he'd felt more compelled to speak up.

"Miss Lydia," Sutton said. "I think the Lieutenant is about ready to leave. I wanted to tell you how nice it has been to have you here, even if it was just overnight. I forget sometimes what a lonely old man I am," he said with a melancholy smile.

Lydia walked to him. "Señor," she said softly while reaching for his hand, "I want to thank you again for your hospitality. Maybe after the war we can return to see you."

"I'd like that," he said, and they walked outside together.

Eli had both horses waiting and helped Lydia up to her saddle. Then he turned and shook Sutton's hand. "This seems to be an oasis for me. Thank you once again."

Sutton nodded. "Be careful. Lydia, remember, you are in the best of hands."

They started off and the old man watched until the sight of them faded away.

The path was mountainous and the two rode along without speaking. Lydia had wrapped her blanket around her shoulders and the back of her head to keep the wind off. Thick, dark clouds hung on the sky, and the wind whipped the freezing air around the vast and barren landscape only to gather strength to lash against the two riders.

About midday, Eli thought they should stop and make camp, but a voice in his head told him to go further. If the snow came, and the wind was promising it would, they would need a cave or some type of covered shelter to spend the night.

As the day wore on, Lydia could hardly sit upright in her saddle. Every movement sent pain through her aching body and head. She wanted to stop, but she knew they had to keep moving. She tried to think of pleasant things to keep her mind off how she felt, and thinking about how Eli was right behind her was enough to comfort her.

Sadie slowed down, and Eli came up next to her. "Lydia, do we need to stop?" he asked with concern in his voice. She looked over at him, and he realized by the look in her eyes that something was not right.

He took her reins, and they stopped at the next clearing. He slid easily from his saddle and reached up for Lydia. She almost fell into his arms. She was limp, and Eli could feel she had a burning fever. He was frightened by her condition. She looked up at him with glazed eyes and buried her head in his chest.

"Lydia," he said softly against the wailing wind, and he brushed her hair from her face.

He looked around in all directions. The clearing they were in would never give them enough protection through the night.

Snowflakes had begun to fall, but before they could touch the ground, they were swept up by the gusts that blew all around them. The gray, ominous sky held an immense certainty of a bitter storm.

He checked Lydia's coat to make sure it was wrapped around her tightly and gave her water from his canteen. He pulled his own woolen blanket from his bed roll and wrapped it securely around her.

He easily pushed her up on Coal and sat her in his saddle. He then tied Sadie's reins to his own. He got into Coal's saddle behind Lydia, and she leaned into him as both his arms went securely around her. Eli could feel her shivering, and after adjusting her weight against him, he held her tightly to try to keep her warm.

Lydia's head was pounding with pain, and the fever was raging through her body. All she could do was lean against Eli. She trusted him completely and knew he would take care of her. She closed her eyes and tried to sleep.

Eli wished they had stayed at Sutton's ranch. The snow was falling faster, and he could feel Coal begin to step cautiously on the slippery trail. Eli's only concern was for Lydia and finding a comfortable place for her.

I shouldn't have pushed her so hard, he thought to himself. *I wish she had said something to me about how she was feeling.*

He tightened his hold around her and leaned his head to her ear. "I'm going to find a place to stop soon. You just rest, and I'll make sure we are all right through the night."

She nodded her head and whispered, "Thank you."

The blowing snow had turned into a blizzard with thick, bulky snowflakes falling in a blinding whirl around them. The sky was growing darker, and Eli knew the night would come quickly. He brushed the snow from the blanket covering Lydia.

Coal was having some trouble navigating the slippery road. Eli pushed forward. He knew he couldn't stop on this unprotected road where he might not survive, much less Lydia.

The muscles in his back were stiff from holding her up these last many hours, and the cold had begun to seep into his body. It was difficult to see very far in front of him. He tried to remember, when he'd come to Santa Fe from the Colorado Territory, if there were any homes or ranches nearby, but they had pushed through so quickly, he couldn't recall. The conditions of the storm left him with little sense of direction, but he thought they were getting close to a small village called El Rito.

Lydia moved, and Eli knew she was trying to get comfortable. He stopped for a moment and gave her a sip of water from his canteen.

He scanned the foothills and the flat mesas that were almost covered in snow. He could hear a pack of wolves howling in the distance. To the north, he thought he saw a light, just a glimmer and, taking a harder look, saw there was a light. Eli quickly moved Coal in that direction.

He hoped the light was from a house and not just a campfire, but even that would have been a welcome sight. It seemed to take hours to get there, but eventually he was able to see an adobe home nestled in the foothills.

Thank God, he thought to himself as he pushed towards it and, hopefully, a warm welcome.

They crossed a small bridge suspended over a stream to get to the house. He wasn't sure what to expect from the adobe's occupants, so he gently moved Lydia forward to rest on Coal's neck. He dismounted quickly so as to not disturb her position.

He walked up to the thick wooden door that had been batted down tightly and knocked with a gloved hand. He began shivering himself and waited only a few moments before pounding on the door.

A man's voice asked angrily, "Que quieres? Who are you and what do you want?"

Eli responded, "I am Lieutenant Colonel Eli Stevens of the Union army. I am escorting a young woman from Santa Fe to Chama. She is ill and I need help."

Eli could hear the bolt being removed from the inside. He hurried to get Lydia and took her gently down from the horse, carrying her to the door.

A short, dark-skinned man with gray hair and sharp, intense eyes was waiting, holding a lantern and a knife. He was wearing a cotton shirt and home-spun pants. He looked at Eli suspiciously and indicated for him to open the blanket covering Lydia before letting them enter.

Holding her gently, Eli put her feet and legs down on the ground and pulled the thick blanket away from her face. She was drenched with sweat. Her color was bright from the fever, but her skin felt cold and clammy. Seeing what Eli had said about her was true, the man motioned for Eli to follow him, and he quickly scooped up Lydia and followed the man into the house and down a dark hallway.

The old man stopped at the opening to a large room to the right. Eli moved past him and stepped into the room. A fire burned brightly from a small fireplace in the center. Eli could feel the warmth and took a deep breath, still holding Lydia in his arms. He could see small children settled in the chairs by the fire, looking at him with curiosity.

A pretty, young woman with dark hair and gray eyes came from inside an adjoining room, adjusting the tie of a white apron that covered her skirt. She quickly assessed the situation. "Bring her in here so I can tend to her," she said as she motioned with her hand towards a room down the hall.

Eli walked through the doorway into a large bedroom. A thick, feather mattress and inviting quilts covered the bed, and the headboard was made from local pine carved into intricate circular patterns. He laid Lydia down on the bed and carefully pulled away the blankets and her thick wool coat. The young woman did not speak again, but her hands were busy checking for signs of a specific illness in Lydia. They both worked to remove Lydia's layers of clothing, leaving her only in her shift which was moist from her sweat. Eli noticed several jars of various herbs on the dresser.

"Señor," the young woman said, "I will put her in a fresh gown. You can take your coat off and warm up in the sala."

"Thank you," Eli said as he extended his hand to her.

Ignoring his hand, she said, "My name is Lupe Martinez. The man who let you in tonight is my father-in-law. My husband left with a group of men only a few days ago to join in the war. Now go, Señor, join my father and children so I can help this young lady."

"Her name is Lydia, and I am Eli," he said.

"Lydia," she repeated and turned to change Lydia's shift to one of her own as Eli left the room.

The old man sat in front of the fire with a pipe in his mouth. He barely looked up when Eli entered, a look of distrust passing over his face. Four children, ranging in ages from about three to twelve years of age, were scattered through the room: two were quietly reading and the other two played with wooden toys on the floor. They all looked up at Eli as he joined them but did not make a sound. Eli noticed they all had the same dark eyes, black hair, and facial features. The youngest, a girl with long braids trailing down her back and coddling a corn-husk doll, smiled shyly at Eli, showing him her small, white teeth.

Eli felt uncomfortable, especially when the old man did not offer him a seat. The oldest child, a boy, jumped up from his seat and offered to take Eli's coat.

"Thank you," Eli said.

"Can I get you some coffee, Señor?"

"Yes, that would be good."

Silence filled the room as the rest of the children looked at Eli with interest but turned away whenever he made eye contact. Eli glanced around the room and noticed the furniture was well-made by hand

and the floors were well kept. A clock on the mantle ticked the minutes away, and Eli saw a beautiful hope chest with delicate rose carvings standing in the corner of the room. Eli assumed the family made their living by cattle ranching and farming.

He could tell the house, which seemed ancient, had been added to by each generation and knew the older man was the current patriarch. He imagined this family had strategically chosen this isolated location to protect them from Indian raids and other possible threats.

The children had all moved together to the floor and were playing with a top, each trying their hand at making it spin. The youngest boy eventually became bored, and they all giggled as they started wrestling. The noise was a relief to Eli's jagged nerves.

The oldest boy finally returned with a full cup of coffee and handed it to Eli. He sat right next to Eli, and the youngest girl climbed into the boy's lap. The boy said, "My name is Jessie. My grandfather doesn't speak very much English." Eli nodded and sipped his coffee, appreciating the warmth as the chill in his bones began to recede.

"Our father left a few days ago," Jessie said. "He went to fight in the war." The boy looked at Eli with wide eyes. "He's going to be okay, isn't he, Señor? I hope he comes back soon."

Eli struggled for a response. He knew these brave, untrained men were in for a fight against the more experienced Texas troops and didn't know how they would fare.

"Is your father good with his gun?" Eli asked, and Jessie nodded enthusiastically.

"He will be fine then," Eli assured the young boy. "I'm certain he will do his best to win the war so he can get back here to you." Jessie smiled at Eli's words.

Eli kept looking at the door to the bedroom and wondered how Lydia was doing. Finally, Lupe stepped out and gently closed the door.

She spoke to her father-in-law. "Por favor, yo quiero mas madera."

As the grandfather was getting his coat and hat on to gather more wood from the pile outside, Eli stood and followed Lupe into the bedroom where Lydia was tucked in under several blankets.

"She seems comfortable right now, and I have given her some

herbs to help ease the fever," Lupe said. Eli sat on the edge of the bed and gently took Lydia's hand.

"She is quite ill, Señor. We will have to hope her fever breaks quickly. I can't find any symptoms of cholera or smallpox, so we'll have to wait and see."

Eli moved closer to Lydia and gently touched her face. He could feel the heat rising from her skin. Her eyes were closed, and she seemed to be sleeping, even though her breathing was shallow and labored.

"The herbs I gave her will help clear the congestion in her lungs and allow her to rest." Lupe put her hand on Eli's shoulder. "You must rest too, Señor. Come and I will get you something to eat and show you a place you can sleep."

"No ma'am. If it's okay, I will stay here with Lydia. By the way, please call me Eli and thank you for opening your home to us. Can I bother you for a chair?" She nodded and left the room.

He leaned down and whispered, "Lydia, we're in a nice, comfortable house. You are going to be fine now, just rest… just rest." He didn't even know if she heard him.

The door opened. It was Lupe returning with a tray of food and her father-in-law behind her carrying an armful of wood for the fire. Jessie followed, carrying a simple wooden chair. Lupe set the tray down on the bureau and motioned to her son to place the chair next to the bed. The old man placed the wood near the grate and made sure there were enough logs in the fireplace for the next few hours.

"Señor, you must eat, you need your strength." Lupe could see the exhaustion in Eli's eyes and noticed the shadow of his beard creeping over his face.

"I'm fine," he said brusquely.

"I am going to put my children to bed. I will return and we can make your bed up in the sala."

Eli nodded to her, and when she left the room, he moved the chair closer to the bed. Sitting down, he took hold of Lydia's hand again—the only thing he could think to do to comfort her. He thought about how she had ridden the last few days, longer and harder than most men, and she never once complained. He missed seeing the light in her eyes and her smile, even though she hadn't shared that with him very much these last days.

He rubbed his thumb lightly across her hand, and she moaned softly. As he continued rubbing her hand, her moans grew louder. The herbs had taken her into a deep sleep, but it was not restful. Her body was fighting the infection, and her mind was tormented.

Lydia was dreaming she was riding her horse, and it seemed endless as she flew through the forest, her horse's feet barely touching the ground. She could feel the wind on her face and blowing through her hair flowing freely down her back. Her hair occasionally blew into her face, obstructing her line of sight. She could hear hoofs beating the ground behind her, but when she looked back, she saw nothing. Why was she running? From whom? Something told her to stop. She did and turned her horse around to face this thing head on. She could see a dark shadow on a black horse coming towards her. She waited. As it came closer, she saw the rider's face was masked with sheer gossamer floating all around him. At first, she thought it was Eli and reached her hands up to move the veil away from his face. Recognition flooded her senses. Carlos smiled wickedly before he grabbed her wrists. She screamed.

Lydia's head turned from side to side and her moans grew louder. She called out to him, "Eli…" and he tightened his grip on her hand.

"I'm here, Lydia, I'll always be here," he said as he brushed the hair back from her forehead. "Shhh, it's okay now, rest."

Lupe knocked on the door and came back into the room. "Señor, I will be happy to watch Lydia while you take some rest in the other room. I am going to give her another dose of the herbs."

"No, I'll stay here with her."

Lupe moved to the bed and touched Lydia's face. She had brought a small cup filled with a steamy brew that filled the room with its pungent aroma. She moved Lydia's head forward so she could drink.

They sat in silence for a while, listening to the wind blow outside and the house creaking as it settled in for the night. There was a sense of closeness and trust between the two as they watched Lydia together.

"You must miss your husband," Eli said. "Your son told me he left several days ago to join the Union army."

"Oh yes," Lupe replied wistfully. "I pray he returns to us safely. His father is very angry about this war. He doesn't understand why we are involved. That's why my husband waited so long to leave; he didn't want to hurt his father. But he did depart, and they did not say goodbye," she said, shaking her head.

"My sister is married to Colonel Carson, do you know of him?" Lupe asked.

"Yes, I met him in Santa Fe. He's a very rugged soldier, and we are lucky he is on our side," Eli said.

She nodded in agreement. "He and my sister have eight children. This war needs to end quickly so we can all get back to our lives."

"You must love her very much," Lupe said as she looked at Lydia.

"She is not mine to love. I am taking her to her fiancé's ranch so she will be safe."

"I am sorry, Señor. I can tell by the way you look at her she should be yours."

Lupe finally stood up. "I will rest in the other room, but I will check on her soon."

Eli nodded, and when the door closed, he sat down in the chair and laid his head on the bed, still holding Lydia's hand, and made himself as comfortable as possible. Eli relaxed finally and slipped into a deep sleep surrounded by the darkness of the night.

Eli woke suddenly. It was early morning, and Lupe was wiping Lydia with a cloth dipped in a bowl of warm water. She smiled at Eli. "She is better. Her fever is lower."

Lydia opened her eyes, and Lupe talked soothingly to her about where she was and about Eli's vigilance as the morning sun poured into the room. Lydia turned to look at Eli and felt a flush of relief. She felt weak and tired, her body drained, and she was very thirsty. Lupe handed her a glass of water and she took a sip. Then she turned her head and closed her eyes.

"She will rest more, Señor, and you will have some breakfast and clean up."

Around midday, Lydia was sitting up in bed sipping broth from a cup held by Lupe when Eli knocked and opened the door. He had eaten breakfast and had rested for a while, knowing she was on the mend.

"Eli," she said weakly. "I am better. Thank you for finding this place."

He moved closer to the bed. "Yes, we were fortunate. We were caught in the snowstorm. Just rest Lydia. We will leave when you are ready."

"I am feeling better, and I can be ready soon. I know you need to get back to the war, and I don't want to hold you up any longer," she said.

Eli turned to Lupe for direction. "She is better, her fever has subsided, but she is weak. If you leave, she should only ride for a short distance."

He nodded his head and looked into Lydia's eyes for any remaining sign of illness. "If you are sure, I will get the horses ready, and we can get back on the road."

Eli had the horses saddled and packed. Lydia had dressed with Lupe's help and had pulled on her wool coat. Eli wrapped her in a blanket and set her in front of him once again.

He offered his hand to Lupe as her father-in-law and the children gathered outside to see them off. "We won't forget your kindness, ma'am," he said and mounted his horse.

Before Eli turned to the road ahead, he saluted the young boy Jessie, whose whole face broke into a smile.

The sun was brilliant and bounced across the thick, white layers of snow that had yet to melt. The sudden storm had passed as quickly as it had come. The temperature was not bitter cold, but Eli could see his breath. He knew if they could get a few more hours in, they would be that much closer to their destination. He was torn about leaving her at the ranch in Chama but knew, with some internal conflict, she would be much safer with Carlos than in Santa Fe.

Lupe had told Eli of a deserted cabin several hours ride away. They used it for hunting, and it would be perfect to keep Lydia out of the cold weather that night.

Lydia felt warm as she leaned back into Eli's chest. His arms circled around her, and occasionally, he would wrap his entire arm around her waist and secure her even closer to him.

Moving at a slower pace, Eli was moved by the beauty surrounding him and the expansive vista he could see from their vantage point at the top of a pass. The air was crisp, and the light wind tossed the snowflakes from tree branches, catching the sunshine and sparkling before falling to the ground.

He was much more relaxed. Lydia was feeling better, and his anxiety, worry, and fear dissipated. He was glad to continue their journey. He breathed a sigh of relief knowing she could have been extremely ill and that he might have had to leave her, or worse, lose her to death. The thought caused him to pull her closer to him. He could detect the faint aroma of flowers from her hair.

The hours went by quickly, and finally, the abandoned cabin was in sight.

≡ 12 ≡

The log cabin stood on a ridge overlooking a sweeping canyon filled with fragrant pine trees and soaring aspens that had lost their leaves to the winter. There was stillness in the air, a calm after the storm. Eli left Lydia to sit on Coal while he checked the entrance. He pushed hard on the rustic wooden door, and it eventually gave way.

There was a musty smell inside, but it was relatively clean and free of any animals or debris. Eli knew it had been used by the Martinez family in the fall when hunting game would have been plentiful. There was a bed with a cast iron frame and a stone fireplace meant to warm the entire room. A bearskin rug took up much of the floor space. Three mismatched chairs stood around an ancient wooden table, and a long shelf filled with pots, pans, and metal plates and cups lined the wall. The walls were cast in a golden glow from the sunlight pouring in through the small glass window. Eli thought it would be perfect for the night, and he went back outside for Lydia.

He reached up for her, and she gently fell into his arms. She still felt weak and shaky but stood firmly, and while holding onto her arm, Eli led her inside the cabin. He helped her onto the bed.

"I'll get the rest of our supplies," he said.

She ran her hand over the handmade quilt, admiring the assorted colors and patterns. Eli returned quickly and laid out both bed rolls across the bed. Lydia stood to take her coat off and felt a wave of dizziness, so she quickly sat back down on the edge of the bed.

"Why don't you lie down, and I will get a fire going so we can warm up," he said.

Eli foraged for firewood in the forest surrounding the cabin, and soon there was a fire roaring in the fireplace, casting a welcome radiance of warmth throughout the cabin.

Eli stoked the logs and looked over to Lydia who was leaning back on a pillow. She cast a sleepy glance towards him. "You should get comfortable. We will be here for the night. Do you need help getting undressed?" he asked innocently.

Lydia blushed slightly. "I think I can manage," she said. "But thank you."

"All right then. I'll see to the horses," he replied. "Yell if you need me," he said with a deep smile.

Lydia removed her plain black wool dress and unlaced her boots. She kept her woolen stockings on. Only in her light chemise, she shivered. She unpinned her hair from its bun, shook it out and got right back into the bed, slipping under the blankets and the bed rolls.

After unsaddling and stabling the horses in a makeshift stall near the cabin, Eli brought the food supplies inside. He opened the small package of an herbal mixture that Lupe had provided for Lydia to help her recover and placed it on the table.

Eli had filled a cast iron pot with snow, and he now slipped it over a rod that was built into the fireplace. He knew a stream must be nearby, but he was anxious about getting Lydia's tea ready. When the water was warm, he transferred some into a cup and carefully measured the aromatic mixture, following Lupe's instructions.

He had removed his hat and coat and had rolled up the sleeves of his white shirt. Lydia watched him, admiring his nurturing streak and his strong physique as he was busy with the tea. They were comfortable in each other's presence and didn't feel the need to speak.

He brought the cup to her and held it to her lips while sitting on the edge of the bed. "Be sure you drink it all," he said with concern.

"Lupe said this will help you immensely."

Lydia looked at him over the edge of the cup, and he could see the tiniest smile in her eyes. His heart turned over.

Making sure she was finished, he took the cup and pulled the blankets up around her. "Now rest, Lydia," he said. "And that's an order. I'll be right here if you need me."

Eli burrowed through his duffle bag for his leather-bound *Great Expectations* by Charles Dickens. His mother had saved up and sent away for the book before he'd left the ranch. The leather bore some scars from Eli's travels, and many of the pages were turned at the corners to mark a favorite spot.

He pulled up a chair and asked, "Would you like me to read to you?" Lydia nodded.

In his deep voice, Eli began to read about Pip who worked as an apprentice in a forge but dared to dream of being a gentleman. Lydia, feeling comfortable, safe, and warm, nestled back into the pillows and blankets and stretched her long legs out on the bed. She could not take her eyes from Eli as he continued reading in a soothing manner. The herbs were once again taking effect, and Lydia could not resist their sleep seduction. Her mind became hazy.

"Eli," she said softly. He looked up, hearing her whisper, and looked into her deep blue eyes. "Thank you for taking care of me," she said. He smiled, and she drifted into a sweet, restful sleep.

He was content for a time to simply listen to her even breathing and enjoy the fire. He had almost left her at the Martinez home. It would have been easy to have Lupe's father-in-law take her the rest of the way to the Aragon ranch in his wagon. But Eli could have never let her go like that. He kept telling himself it was because of the promise he made to her father, but he knew better—it had only to do with his feelings for her.

He got up from his chair and quietly walked to the bed. Her hair fell across the pillows and her arm lay across the layer of blankets. He leaned over and placed his hand on her cheek to check her temperature. She felt cool and normal.

Thank God, he thought to himself. *She is on the mend.*

Eli tucked her slender arm inside the covers. The room was warm from the fire, and he decided to get enough wood to last through the night and into the next day, if need be. He pulled his heavy uniform coat on and stepped outside.

Eli breathed in the fresh, crisp air deeply. There was just enough light from the moon to see by. He felt as though he could finally relax from the tension he had been carrying with him. He gathered a few large pieces of wood and then retrieved the ax tucked away in a corner of the porch. He set a piece of wood on a stump and swung heavily downward. Tiny splinters of wood flew in every direction as the pieces broke away. It felt good to engage in strenuous physical activity.

Eli kept turning his head toward the cabin, just to make sure it was not disturbed by anyone or anything. He continued to split the wood and, as it had been lately, his thoughts returned to Lydia.

How can I take her to another man? he thought to himself as he tore mightily into a log. *How can I leave her there for him when I know she should be with me?* He had no answers for these questions that had been circling in his mind since Lydia's father had asked Eli to accompany her.

He didn't know if Lydia understood how much he cared for her and decided he couldn't tell her, as much as he needed to. It could only hurt her. She had an obligation, and Eli did not think her meticulous father would allow her to break that obligation.

Eli split up the last log with excess energy. He leaned down and began picking up the pieces of wood and stacking them on his arms. He said out loud, if only to himself, "I don't know what will happen. I only know I love Lydia, and even if I can never have her, she will be in my heart forever."

He opened the cabin door slowly so he wouldn't disturb her. He glanced over and saw she was still sleeping soundly. After he quietly placed the wood near the fireplace, he decided to warm the food prepared and packed by Lupe.

The fire burned brightly and soon the lamb stew was sending hearty scents through the small cabin. Eli lit the candles he found on the shelf, and they cast a warm, flickering light across the room.

The smells and sounds woke Lydia from her sleep. She opened her eyes slowly and was met with the sight of Eli leaning near the fire. The highlights in his hair were like flecks of gold, and she could see the hair on his chest through the opening of his shirt. The muscles in his arms stood out against the tight cotton fabric of his shirt.

She did not move but only tried to memorize every part of his face. He sensed she was awake, and he turned to her. Their eyes met and held for a few moments.

"How do you feel?" he asked with concern in his voice.

She took an inventory of her own body. She was weak but rested. "I feel well, better, much better," she said.

"Good," he said. "Would you like something to eat? I've warmed some stew."

Lydia enthusiastically replied, "Yes, I am starving," and she sat up against the pillow. Eli brought two bowls and spoons, handed one of each to her, and sat again in the chair near the bed.

She was blowing on her meal and at the same time was trying to eat as fast as she could.

"We are going to have to get on the road again in the morning," Eli said. She nodded, but then a small tear spilled from the corner of her eye, and she lowered her bowl to her lap.

"Lydia," he said as he placed his spoon back into his bowl and looked right at her. "Do you want to go to the Aragon ranch? Or more importantly, do you want to marry Carlos? Are you doing this for you or are you doing this for your father?"

Lydia wiped her eyes and turned to look at him. "At first, I agreed because I wanted to obey my father, especially with the war. I have tried to see his viewpoint, but the more I think about this, the more I understand I do not have any feelings for Carlos, and probably never will. In some way, he frightens me. Do you think it's fair, a life without love?" she asked innocently, choking back a sob.

Eli waited a moment before responding. "I only know love between two people makes all the difference when it came to raising children, building a life together, and growing old together. I witnessed that kind of love between my own parents."

"I thought I would never be forced to get married," Lydia said with a sigh. "I was led to believe I would find the man I loved and make the decision for myself. What can I do, especially now with the war?"

"I am not sure," he said. "Let me get you there safely and then, when this war is finished, you can speak to your father and tell him how you feel." She was looking up at him with wide eyes full of sincerity and trust.

He placed a hand on her arm for a moment, then he stood up to clear the bowls. He was glad she had finished her stew.

After he rinsed the bowls, he turned to her and said, "I'm going to check the horses." He wanted to give her a few minutes to herself. He pulled his uniform coat on and placed his holster around his waist.

As soon as the door closed, Lydia slowly raised herself from the bed. She poured some water from the canteen into one of the bowls and rinsed her face and neck, using a clean cloth to dry off. She pulled her brush from inside her knapsack and brushed the tangles from her hair.

She felt rejuvenated, and a sense of excitement caught in her chest. The thought kept running through her mind that she and Eli were completely alone. She pulled a clean shift and shawl from her bag. She changed quickly and got back into bed, pulling the shawl loosely around her shoulders.

Eli returned and closed the door behind him. She turned to him, and an unspoken understanding passed between them. He removed his coat and walked towards her, sat down, and reached for the book he had left on the bed.

"The fire feels good," he said, trying to ease the nervousness that was palatable in the room.

Lydia adjusted her position and her shawl slipped away from her shoulders. Eli stretched from his chair and reached over to place it back around her. Lydia put her hand on top of his and looked directly into his eyes with a smoldering desire in hers. Her lips separated as though she needed to say something, but the words did not come. Her breathing was shallow and quick.

Eli moved her hand to his lips, grazing her fingertips across his mouth. She shifted to be closer to him and the shawl fell away completely. He moved from the chair to the bed, not letting go of her hand. His mouth lightly caressed the inside of her wrist, and she moaned. He could feel her pulse beating. Eli was desperate to hold her against him and kiss her full, beautiful lips.

Passion for him was emanating through Lydia's mind and body. It was an awakening within her, and she felt so alive, every part of her tingled with excitement and yearned for his touch. She closed her eyes, lost in her own desire.

"Lydia," he said her name softly, and it sounded melodic to her.

She moved closer to him where he sat on the edge of the bed. Her chemise was a light, thin cotton gown clinging to her body. Eli could see her chest rise and fall with each breath and her breasts outlined by the fabric. Her hair fell around her in a silky cloud. He caught both her hands in his own and held them tightly.

"Lydia, are you sure this is what you want?" he asked, his voice filled with emotion but still controlled.

"Yes," she moaned and looked straight into his eyes. She could not find the words to tell him how she felt. She would rather have stopped breathing than not have him near her.

He pulled her up gently as he stood, and they embraced. Their bodies molded together, and he held her tightly against him. Her head rested on his chest, and he kissed the top of her hair, her fragrance filling his lungs and making his body pulsate with desire.

She turned her face up to him, her lips quivering with anticipation. He leaned down and placed his mouth on hers. An intense feeling traveled through each of their bodies like an electric current. Neither one was prepared for its strength. Their kisses became more passionate and filled with the promise of satisfaction.

Without hesitation, Eli pulled away from Lydia and swept her up in his arms. He carried her to the bearskin before the fire and laid her down with care. Her eyes were smoldering as he lay down next to her. His hand slipped behind her neck, and he brought her mouth to his.

The fire blazed, casting a reflection of their shadows on the wall. It was difficult to distinguish one from the other as their bodies joined together.

Lydia could feel how strong he was, yet she was amazed at Eli's gentle touch. She moaned with pleasure as his hand moved down her shoulders and arms.

She pulled away and stood, and for a moment, he thought she had changed her mind. But, in one swift and graceful motion, she untied the strings holding her chemise, her eyes never leaving Eli's as the garment fell in a puddle around her feet.

Her hair hung wildly around her and the light from the fire and the candles made her skin incandescent. Her passion caused color to rise high on her cheeks. Eli was shaken by her beauty.

He pulled her gently to him as he knelt and allowed his mouth to explore the soft flesh of her stomach. Her arms instinctively went around his neck, and her fingers played with the hair on the nape of his neck. Eli's mouth moved to her breasts and nipples, and feeling his warm breath and moist desire, she moaned with pleasure.

Eli pulled away and stood, unbuttoning his shirt while Lydia's hands explored his chest. She brushed the shirt from his shoulders and his arms. He drew her to him once again and kissed her hard on the mouth so she could feel his need for her. Then, holding her at arm's length, he kicked off his boots and removed his pants. She wrapped her arms around him, and he pulled her down gently onto the rug.

Her hands traveled lightly across his hard body, carrying the soft whisper of what was to come. His beard was rough, and she moaned deeply in her throat as he kissed her neck and breasts.

"I think I fell in love with you the minute I first saw you," he whispered as he moved her so she was beneath him.

Lydia's hands explored his back, shoulders, and chest, then shyly down to touch his manhood where she felt his desire for her in its intensity and firmness. His hands ran softly along her thighs and legs that felt as soft as rose petals.

She was lost in their desire as he kissed her, moving his hand longingly between her legs and feeling her moist readiness, he entered her as gently as he could.

She instinctively moved with him and ignored the first wave of pain that gave way to pleasure. They moved together in rhythm, touching and stroking one another as their passion and desire engulfed them.

Eli kissed her deeply as he exploded inside her. She wrapped her legs around him, pulling him even closer as she felt her own pleasurable rush move through her.

Eventually, he moved to her side and secured his arm underneath her head. He wanted to look at her and marvel at what they had found together. Her hands danced delicately across his chest, and she gazed at him with a smile. Her hair spread across his arm in a tangled mess. They were content and fulfilled.

The fresh sweat from their lovemaking clinging on their bodies, his hand rubbed her shoulder up and down.

"I love you, Lydia," he said, and she leaned close to kiss him on the lips.

He stood and reached for her hand to help her stand. They both moved to the bed and pulled the covers up around them. As he moved to her side, he could feel her body relax. Soon her breathing was deep and rhythmic, and he felt his own eyes closing as they both fell into a deep, satisfied sleep.

Eli woke at the sound of movement and quickly opened his eyes. It took a moment for his sight to adjust, and when he saw Lydia, he was filled with emotion. She was stoking the fire, making the flames come back to life. She had her chemise on and her long woolen leggings. Her hair was loose and hung down around her.

Eli lay naked in bed, tangled in the blankets, and watched her. He was caught up in feelings of love and desire.

She turned to him, catching his eye, and smiled broadly, knowing she had found an absolute and complete bond with Eli.

"Good morning," she said.

He smiled back at her, pulled the covers away, and stood up. Lydia stared in amazement at the sight of him. She had not seen him completely the night before as they were washed only in candle and firelight. He pulled his arms above his head and stretched, his muscles flexing, and Lydia admired the contour of his chest and back. He realized she was staring at him and brought his arms down as they both burst into nervous laughter.

"I hope you like what you see," he said.

She put her finger to her lip. "Oh yes, Eli, I do," she said, her eyes dancing with amusement and a hint of excitement.

He walked over to her and took her in his arms. As she leaned her head back to meet his mouth with her own, her need for him radiated through every fiber within her. She was taken aback at the instant desire, having never felt this before. She was still learning and gauging the depth of her own sensuousness and the fulfillment of her needs.

She felt so alive, as though she had waited so long for this. Her soul had been asleep and was now awake only to him.

His hands easily pulled her chemise from her shoulders and slid it down. He pulled her stockings down and explored her silky thighs with light touches. She pulled him up and closer so she could feel his chest against her breasts. Her mouth traveled first to his neck, then his chest, leaving a trail of light kisses.

He was overcome by his need for her, but he wanted the moment to last forever. He went down on his knees and kissed the soft skin of her stomach and then the tender inside of her thighs. They explored one another greedily in the early morning light, without hesitation, basking in their delight.

She pushed him onto his back on the bearskin rug and lowered herself over him, feeling him slide deep inside her. She held his hands and looked with love into his eyes as she moved against him, with ever increasing intensity. The heat spread across their bodies as their passion simultaneously reached a peak. Lydia collapsed down on Eli's chest, their sweat mingling as their breathing returned to a normal pace.

Lydia leaned down and kissed Eli. "Mi amor, yo siempre te adoraré," she whispered to him as she laid her head on his chest.

The early morning sun poured in and covered their bodies like a blanket of gold. Both could have stayed locked in this embrace forever. But both knew their journey must continue.

Finally, Lydia raised her head. "I am faint from hunger," she said lightheartedly.

"We must take care of that," Eli said and kissed her one long last time before getting up and pulling on his shirt and pants.

Lydia pulled her chemise and stockings back on and pulled her shawl around her for warmth. They fried bacon over the fire in a cast iron pan and then warmed some tortillas. They both ate slowly as they sat next to one another at the table, enjoying each other's company in silence.

Eli used water from the canteen to rinse the dishes. She wiped them with a cloth she then hung to dry. He went outside to tend to the horses and gather some snow to put out the fire.

When he returned, Lydia had pulled her black wool dress from a hook on the wall and was getting dressed. She moved slowly as she was in no hurry to leave. He helped her tie the laces on the back of her corset and watched as she pulled her dress over her head, adjusting it as it fell over her body. She stepped into her boots and tied them. Then she washed her face and neck with water and brushed her hair.

Eli placed the herbs and food carefully back into the saddle bag while watching Lydia braid her hair. She used a sliver of mirror wedged on the shelf to pin the braid up. Despite the many pins, curls escaped from all directions. Smiling, he moved behind her and wrapped his arms around her waist.

"Your hair is unruly but spectacular," he said.

A small laugh escaped from her throat, and she leaned back into him. As he pulled away, she tucked the last pin in her hair and reached for her knapsack to pack away the rest of her belongings.

Without speaking, they both knew it was time to leave. Eli rolled up their blankets, while Lydia tenderly straightened the bed and put the quilt in place.

He noticed the pensive look on her face and walked to where she stood. Taking her by the shoulders he looked in her eyes. "Lydia, I want you to know what happened between us has deep meaning for me. I will not let him marry you, but under the circumstances, I must take you to the ranch for safety. I will speak to your father as soon as I get back to Santa Fe. I want you to know I will make sure we are together when all this is over. It is my promise to you." She leaned her head on his chest as his arms held her tightly.

"No, not yet," she said. "I don't want my father to worry about me. I will write to him soon and explain everything. This must be our secret for now." She looked up at him with pleading eyes.

Eli reluctantly nodded. "I won't say anything to him, not until we are through the battles ahead."

She pulled on her coat, buckled the leather belt around her waist, and placed her hat on her head. She gathered her knapsack in her hand but stood at the front door, not wanting to push it open, knowing where they were going. She turned her head and looked to Eli for strength, and he finally opened it for her.

The whole world looked different to Lydia as she stepped outside. Everything had changed.

≡ 13 ≡

Armstrong waited in the shadows until the soldiers at the fort in Santa Fe had gone to sleep. He casually walked past the guard at the gate, who nodded at Armstrong. It wasn't unusual to see soldiers coming and going; the fort was alive with activity at all hours.

Armstrong pulled his coat tighter around his neck. He stopped and carefully pulled out the cigarette he had rolled earlier, striking a match on the old adobe wall of a now vacant building. Armstrong passed a man and a woman walking arm in arm; they were nameless and faceless to him—he had his mind on his own future.

Anxiety filled his thoughts. He had experienced a moment of regret when he'd killed Rivera and taken the note from him. He hadn't had a chance to share that information with Carlos but hoped his new information would be much more useful.

He was getting closer to the inn where he was to meet, for the first time, the old Indian that Carlos had told him about, and he began to walk faster. He stopped across the street from the inn and inhaled his cigarette deeply as the cold night air settled around him. He could see through the large, plate glass window that the elaborate lobby was empty—because of the war. Normally, the inn was frequented by those traveling through to California or traders who were selling supplies.

Armstrong slipped across the street and walked towards the stable at the back of the inn. Moving cautiously, he crept through the shadows and came to the darkened corrals. He could see the horses' breath.

He was on high alert and looked around for the old man. He walked from stall to stall, being careful not to disturb the horses. Frustrated, he turned to make his way back to the entrance and almost ran into a slightly built man huddled against a stable door. The man was wearing a large cowboy hat decorated by strands of beads around the brim and was wrapped in a colorful blanket.

The old Indian stood his ground and did not move. Armstrong made note of the layers of wrinkles set deeply in the man's face that showed no emotion, only contempt. Armstrong pulled a note from the inside of his coat and handed it to the Indian, feeling sure this was the right person. For good measure, he reached into his pocket and pulled out a three-dollar gold piece and pressed it into the man's hand. "This is for Aragon," Armstrong said. "Make sure he gets it." The man nodded, stood, and was gone, disappearing into the shadows of the stables in the blink of an eye.

Armstrong made his way back to headquarters, stumbling as he crossed the dark street. He hoped the note would help Carlos' efforts to stop the Union. Armstrong knew troops from the Colorado Territory were on their way, and all the men would be leaving for Fort Craig in the next day or so. He thought to himself, *I hope this gamble pays off for me.*

* * *

Lydia and Eli rode side-by-side on the well-established road to Chama. The road was lined with sprawling cottonwood trees with their snarled, bare branches dormant and quiet. Eli knew the Aragon ranch was only about three hours away. They were traveling at a moderate pace, each with their own worries, and neither wanting this trip to end.

Eli's mind had been working at a fast pace. He knew he had to get to Taos quickly, hoping the troops from Colorado would be waiting there. He knew lives were depending on him. He was torn. Even though his head told him he should get Lydia to the ranch and get on to Taos, his heart overruled.

Reaching his gloved hand over to Lydia's, he squeezed it tightly. She looked over at him, and even though the hat she wore covered much of her face, he could see her slight smile. Eli detected the small fatigue lines around her eyes which only confirmed his decision.

He stopped his horse and Lydia, somewhat surprised, did the same. He motioned her to follow him as he moved off the main road to a well-worn trail he had spotted hidden among the trees. Lydia stayed close behind, not quite sure where they were going, but trusting Eli's decision.

Eli stopped at a secluded clearing shielded by a rock formation. He jumped down from Coal and helped Lydia off Sadie. She slid easily into his arms, her hat falling to her back, and he held her for a long moment.

She closed her eyes and leaned her head on his chest, wanting to remember how he felt against her and the way his arms folded around her and shielded her against the world. She knew the reality outside of their relationship was close by, and all day long her thoughts had been about saying goodbye to him.

He pulled her face up to his with a hand under her chin.

"We are going to stay the night right here, Lydia," he said. "I think you are exhausted from the ride, and you must rest."

She hoped he was saying this more from his need to be with her rather than her need for rest, and the look of devotion and love in his eyes answered her question. She closed her eyes, and he kissed her eyelids softly.

"I'll get a fire started. Take a seat," he said, pointing to a fallen log. "This won't take long."

Lydia needed a moment to get control of her array of emotions, and she walked toward the edge of a nearby stream that held patches of ice. She pulled her coat tighter around herself and wrapped her arms against her chest.

The crystal-clear water ran quickly past her, and she felt it was her own life rushing by. Her heart was filled with love for Eli, and yet she knew their time together would end soon. Tears welled up in her eyes. For a moment, she felt like giving in to the overwhelming grief within her soul. Then she straightened her spine. She could not let him see her like this. She would not make it worse for him. She had tasted and felt the magnitude of love in his arms and, although she may never have a life with him, the piece she carried in her memory would last forever. It was bittersweet, but she knew she wouldn't have changed anything. To know him was to know love, and her life seemed dry and desolate until now.

She raised a hand to wipe a single tear falling down her face. She had him for a little while longer and thought to herself, *I will not waste this time*. She composed herself and turned toward the campsite.

As she came into view, Eli looked up from the fire. "There you are, my love. I was about to send a search party," he said with a grin.

Eli had unsaddled both horses that were now tied close by. He had unpacked the saddle bags, and their bed rolls were already laid out by the fire, side-by-side.

She walked over and sat next to him on a big stump. The fire was small but felt good against her hands. She leaned her head on Eli's shoulder.

He breathed in deeply and caught her scent of flowers with the smells of their day's ride mixed in.

They sat together, watching as the sun cast long shadows through the trees and surrounding hilltops. They were completely content being next to one another. There was so much to say; their minds and hearts were full, and the words were waiting and yearning to come from their lips. But neither spoke. They held each other's hand and gazed into the fire now burning brightly against the impending nightfall.

As the sun went down, Lydia stood and stretched. "Would you like something to eat, Eli? You must be hungry."

"No," he said as he stood up, "I'm not hungry. I'll make a pot of coffee and that will be enough for me."

She nodded; she wasn't hungry either. All her body's energy was focused on him. She sat back down by the fire and watched him pour water from his canteen into a pot that he placed over the fire. When it was boiling, he measured some coffee paste from his Union rations and placed it into the pot so the coffee could simmer.

"That will be ready in just a few minutes," Eli said as he stood and wrapped a blanket around her shoulders. "You can't afford to catch a chill." He sat behind her as she scooted forward and wrapped his legs and arms around her.

She wondered what it would be like to grow old with him, to spend her whole life loving him. These next few hours together might have to sustain her.

"Lydia," he whispered in her ear. "I will love you for the rest of my life. I will never let go of you now that I have found you." Those were the words she wanted and needed to hear. "Come with me now. I will find a place for you to stay until the war is over."

She turned around to look into his eyes and touch the strong line of his chin with her hand. "Mi amor, we have no choice right now. I must go to his ranch. Everything must seem normal. I will write to my father as soon as I get there and hope I can reason with him. Besides, getting through this war safely is the most important thing for both of us."

"Then, I will come for you after the war is over," he said firmly.

Lydia smiled at him and brushed her lips softly to his. He captured hers for a long, deep kiss. She turned back around and snuggled even closer to him, leaning deeper into his chest.

"Tell me what you were like when you were a little boy," she said.

"I was adventurous, and my parents scolded me often," he said, chuckling. "I always had my younger brother in tow. He wanted to go everywhere with me and so I learned to look after him early on," he said with a smile. "When we came to Colorado from Pennsylvania, we used to run and play like wild Indians. There is so much open space there and the mountains are so beautiful. The sky is so wide and blue.

"My family started a sheep and cattle ranch in the San Luis Valley. We worked very hard to get it going and then my father died. We were so afraid we would all be killed by the Ute Indians, but my father died of a fever in the middle of a very cold, hard winter. My brother and mother are still there. I never saw eye-to-eye with my stepfather about how to run the ranch, so I left, and I haven't been back since."

His eyes turn misty. "I'd like to take you there someday, Lydia. I'd like you to see how beautiful it is. I'd like you to meet my mother. She is a lovely woman, inside and out, and I know she would care for you as much as I do."

Lydia turned to him and placed her hand tenderly on his face. She stood, pulled the coffee from the fire, then sat down next to him, catching his hand in hers and placing it on her lap.

"What about you?" he asked. "What were you like?"

"Oh," she said with chuckle, "I was a little adventurous myself. Papa was always worrying about me. He had his hands full with the store, the cattle, the land, the house, and me and Eduardo," she said. "Alita was wonderful and watched over me very well, but sometimes Claire and I would run off to play in the arroyos or we would ride our horses far beyond the places we were allowed to go. I had a lovely childhood filled with love and attention, even though I'll always wonder about and miss my mother. I know the heartache and pain there is from losing a parent. I didn't realize, though, until I got older, what a vacancy is left in our lives after they depart." Eli nodded in agreement.

A vast array of stars glistened in the night sky, and the full moon was bright and glowing. "We'd better rest," Eli said. They both stood, and Eli went to get more wood to add to the fire while Lydia shook out their bed rolls and blankets.

They lay right next to another, as close as they could get with their clothes between them. Eli buried his face in her hair and said, "Tomorrow is going to be the hardest thing I have ever had to do."

She nodded, unable to answer.

Feeling desperate, he tried again. "I'll take you to Colorado. You can stay at Fort Garland until the war is over and I return."

Lydia turned and looked into his eyes. "I made a promise and so did you. If anything, we are both honorable and I want to believe, despite our circumstances, this will all work out. I am so amazed at how quickly I had feelings for you. There is still so much we need to learn about one another, and we need time to examine our own feelings and their truth," she said.

"For me, it all feels so right, as though we were destined to be together," she continued. "There is an old saying I want to share with you, and I never really understood the meaning of it until now. 'El amor es como el agua que no se seca.'" Eli looked at her with a question in his eyes. "In English it means, love is like water that never dries up. True love lasts forever." With that, she leaned into him and kissed him deeply.

They held one another and looked up at the night sky. A shooting star blazed across the heavens and seemed to evaporate just above them. Lydia thought it was a good sign, and she closed her eyes and made a wish. She was pinning all her hopes on that wish.

The dawn came quickly, and waking early, they saddled up and gathered their belongings.

"I want you to take this," Eli said after reaching into his coat pocket. "It is my father's gold watch. It always helped me keep track of time. I used to hold it up to my ear when I was little, whenever I missed my father. Take care of it for me, Lydia, so I can come back for it. And for you."

She held the pocket watch tight in her gloved hand and reached her arms up around his neck to kiss him. "I have nothing to give you, expect my heart."

He folded her into his arms. "That's more than enough. I'll take good care of it."

* * *

Carlos looked out from the front window of the Aragon home. He was growing more impatient by the minute and turned his gaze to the room where he was sitting. He was surrounded by shelves filled with glazed Indian pots, oak furniture, and comfortable chairs covered in thick fabric that sat upon large rugs.

A young maid entered and carefully placed a tray with coffee on the table before him. She waited for a moment with her head down, afraid to ask him if he needed anything else and even more afraid to look him in the eye. "Usted puede ir," he said roughly in Spanish, directing her to leave. The girl quickly made her way out of the room, almost bumping into Mr. Aragon, who walked in slowly with his cane and made his way to his favorite chair.

Carlos stood and helped his father to sit. This was the only person he loved and felt a need to show compassion and protection.

"Stop being so hard with the help, Carlos," Mr. Aragon chided. "We will probably lose her too."

Carlos sat in the large comfortable chair across from his father, and they drank their morning coffee from China cups. The only sound was the old clock on the mantle ticking away the minutes. Carlos had not shared the information he had received in a letter from Manuel with his father. *Let him be surprised*, he thought to himself. *It will be a good distraction to have my fiancé at the ranch.*

Knowing when Lydia and her escort had left Santa Fe and how long it was taking them to arrive was causing Carlos some concern. He decided he would ride out after breakfast to intercept them. He was pleased she was coming and hoped for a quiet wedding ceremony while she was here. Things had worked out even better than he had planned.

"You are quiet this morning," his father said. "What are you thinking about?"

Carlos ignored the question. "Let's have breakfast served. I have many things to do today."

*   *   *

Eli and Lydia were a short distance from the Aragon ranch. They had passed a large open space containing hundreds of head of cattle in a winter pasture, and they were getting close to the turn-off to the sprawling ranch house. A large windmill ahead spun around and around, and Lydia could feel the same spinning in her stomach. She was fearful of what waited for her. Her instincts told her to leave with Eli, but her love and loyalty to her father kept her moving along the path Manuel had chosen for her.

Eli rode alongside her, looking straight ahead. He looked tall and strong on Coal, and he wore his uniform well and with pride.

He looked over at her and his dark brown eyes said, *Let's run away together.* But their horses picked up their pace, sensing their destination was near.

*   *   *

"Someone is coming, Señor Aragon, a soldier," said the ranch hand as he burst into the dining room with his hat in his hand and his breath drawn. "And he has a woman with him."

Mr. Aragon looked up at Carlos with surprise as he placed his fork down near a plateful of eggs, bacon, and buttered bread. Carlos simply wiped his mouth with his napkin and stood up from the dining room table.

"How far away are they?" he asked the ranch hand.

"Only about a mile, Señor. They should be here very soon." Carlos nodded at him, which meant he was dismissed from the room.

Carlos took one last sip from his coffee, and before his father could speak, he said, "It is Lydia. She will be staying here until the war is over."

His father nodded with a pleased, but confused, look on his face. He asked, "But why didn't they send for you? Why is she traveling with a soldier?"

"I don't know, Father, but I will find out," Carlos said as he walked out of the room.

*   *   *

Lydia and Eli rode to the front of the adobe house surrounded by mature cottonwood, elm, and oak trees. Carlos opened the elegantly carved front door and stepped outside to the front porch that circled the whole east side of the sprawling home.

"Lydia," he called to her loudly as he came down the steps.

Eli noticed the tense lines around his eyes and mouth.

"I am very delighted to see you, my dear," Carlos said as he helped Lydia down from her horse.

"Papa thought I should be here, just until the danger settles from the war," she said.

Eli got down from Coal and held Sadie's reins. He held himself back from tearing Lydia away from Carlos' grasp. He took an overall measure of the man and was momentarily impressed by his physique and his confidence.

"This is Lieutenant Colonel Eli Stevens, with the United States Army. He was kind enough to accompany me here," Lydia said as she gestured towards Eli.

Eli simply nodded at Carlos, and did not offer his hand.

"Thank you for bringing her here," Carlos said. He pulled Lydia close to him and took the reins from Eli's hands. "She is very precious to me."

Eli let the comment brush past him. He was only concerned with Lydia and her safety. He felt uneasy about Carlos and realized this man truly thought Lydia was his possession.

"She was very ill during our journey," Eli said as Carlos guided her up the stairs to the porch. "She will need to rest and eat something."

Carlos paused and looked at Lydia. "You do look thin," he said. Carlos turned to Eli. "Don't worry. She is home now and will receive the best of care. You should get on your way. There is a war underway."

A revulsion and overwhelming sense of protectiveness struck Eli to his core. He placed his hand on his revolver and exchanged a look with Lydia.

"Take care of yourself, Lydia," Eli said, and with that, he mounted Coal, turned, and rode away.

*   *   *

Carlos took Lydia's arm and led her inside the house. She was limp, like a rag doll, and all she could do was nod when Carlos asked if she would like to rest. He led her upstairs to a room and, once inside, Carlos kept talking, but she turned away, half listening, her heart breaking at being separated from Eli. The door closed as Carlos left the room, promising to send a maid to help her undress.

She moved quickly to the window. She could still see Eli riding away from her. She pressed her hand up against the glass and her forehead touched it as her head bent. Great tears spilled from her eyes as she whispered his name.

≡ 14 ≡

The next few days had gone by quickly for Eli. He'd arrived in Taos three days after leaving Lydia and was relieved Colonel Riley had already sent several infantries of men, who were waiting for him and ready to leave for the New Mexico Territory. Eli led the company consisting of regular soldiers, miners, and frontiersmen to Santa Fe in record time.

The morning after he arrived in Santa Fe, Eli was to join a meeting between Colonel Canby, Manuel, and a large group of other highly ranked men who would study a map of the territories secured to the wall and discuss the advance of the Confederate forces.

While he was waiting for the others to arrive, Canby reached for an envelope on his desk and unfolded the letter he had received from Washington. He'd sent several letters to President Lincoln expressing his concern of a Confederate win in New Mexico. What he had received in exchange was an empty promise of 5,000 troops that had never materialized. He held the letter and looked out his window. He knew the men and equipment he had would have to be enough for now. He turned at a knock at the door and placed the letter back in the envelope and in his desk.

"Lieutenant Colonel Stevens, I am pleased you made it back," Canby said with a look of concern and relief as the men entered.

"Thank you, Colonel. I have brought a hundred men, some on horses, and all very well-supplied for right now," Eli said. Canby nodded in appreciation as Eli took his seat.

"We know there are over three thousand Confederates, and we are not sure of their heavy artillery," Canby said as he stood before a map. "We do have scouts in place, and they have reported the three regiments have been traveling from San Antonio the last two months to Fort Thorn, and there they wait."

"I suspect they are recuperating and waiting for any stragglers that may have fallen behind," Canby continued. He turned from the map and placed his hands resolutely on his desk. "My plan is to move all Union troops to Fort Craig at once. We should be in full force by the end of January. We will spend the next day readying to travel. Most of Colonel Carson's men are currently stationed in Albuquerque. I sent word this morning that he and his men should collect supplies and be ready to join us as we make our way through."

"I will dispatch a few men to gather any extra food supplies the community can spare," said Manuel.

"How about your men, Stevens?" Canby asked.

"We are ready," Eli replied. "Colonel Riley has committed more reinforcements if we need them. Although, he predicts we can defeat the Confederates at Fort Craig."

"We will do everything we can to make that happen. That is all for now," Canby said as he nodded to the group, signaling the meeting was over. The men stood and filed out of the room.

Eli waited behind. "Colonel, I have news of a recent recruit who may have information about ranchers helping the Confederates. Can you provide a list of those who recently joined?"

"Yes, I will have my aide get that to you," Canby said. Eli nodded his thanks and left Canby's office.

As Eli walked down the hallway, Manuel, who had been waiting, stopped him with an outstretched hand. Eli noticed the anxious look on Lydia's father's face.

"Lydia is well?" he asked Eli.

"She was fine when I left her at the Aragon ranch," Eli said. The words were almost too painful for him to express. "Have you had any word from her?" Eli asked.

Her father shook his head. "I am not surprised though," he said. "There is very little regular communication taking place. People are nervous about the troops moving in and some are confused about their allegiance and who they can trust."

"Tell me, Eli," Manuel said as his voice cracked with emotion, "was she happy to be there, did she feel safe?"

Eli paused, knowing the truth, but unable to say the words to her father because of his promise to Lydia. "I don't know if she was happy, sir," he said. "I only know, when I left her, she was well."

*   *   *

General Sibley and three Confederate regiments were making their way to Fort Craig. The weather had been freezing cold with snow and sleet bombarding them every day since they had started their movement towards the New Mexico Territory. Each small town they passed through gave them the opportunity to leave behind critically ill men, exhausted from the cold and the hardship of the march, in the hands of the residents. Sibley was surprised at their generosity in caring for his men, since his army had taken any food supplies that were available.

He pulled his gray coat more tightly around his girth and looked at the men surrounding him. *They are a tough lot, and together we will get this done*, he thought to himself and smiled. He pulled the sliver flask from his pocket and took a long, hard drink. The late afternoon shadows were beginning to creep up on the crusted snow, and Sibley, noticing an area covered by a bank of tall trees, lifted his left hand, the sign for the troops to stop and make camp for the night.

A young soldier who was riding directly behind him stopped and quickly dismounted. He moved to the General's side and offered assistance. He was specifically assigned this task and many others related to Sibley's frequent overindulgence of spirits.

A group of soldiers began pitching tents, and Colonel Thomas

Green, a seasoned war veteran and former Texas congressman with broad shoulders and solemn demeanor, approached General Sibley. Sibley knew Green was confident in his own skill and had an enthusiastic belief in the South's determination to win this war.

"We will make camp here for the night," Sibley ordered. "We should be there soon, but just to be sure, I would like you to lead your regiment ahead. We can make it there faster if we break into groups." Green nodded and looked pleased with the decision.

"Let's get this battle out of the way, Colonel, so we can move on to greener pastures, as they say," Sibley said with a grin.

*   *   *

The Union troops moved quickly to the outskirts of Santa Fe and kept up a swift pace as they traveled through the snow-laden landscape towards Albuquerque.

Once there, the troops were joined on the main road by Colonel Kit Carson who led half of the 1st New Mexico Volunteer Regiment. This group was made up of citizens who had joined the Union army to fight for their homes and loved ones. They carried their own weapons and rode their own horses. They were boisterous and their arrival sent a stir of excitement through the entire army.

As dusk approached on the third day, the men noticed lights flickering in the distance. As they got closer, the fort seemed to rise from the earth. Fort Craig, the largest and most strategic fort in the western region was mainly used by the United States Army during Indian uprisings as were most of the forts in the territory. The fort held two enormous adobe buildings, which were surrounded by a wall that had openings carved out for the cannons.

Fort Craig was full, with nearly 4,000 men, and many were forced to make camp outside the walls. Colonel Canby, Eli, Carson, and the other high-ranking officials made their way inside the gates, climbed down from their horses, and entered the main building which contained their quarters and a central meeting area.

They were greeted by Captain Piño, a slim and wiry young man with dark hair and a rugged demeanor. "Colonel, we have word Colonel Green is on his way here. He was spotted about twenty miles out. Sibley's men are not with him."

"Thank you, Captain. We may be in for a long wait, but it will give us time to plan our defense. Show us where we can bunk, and I will need to have some space to work," Canby said.

*   *   *

Colonel Green had been marching his troops at a feverish pace towards Fort Craig. He was leading the 5th Texas Calvary Regiment, which consisted of nearly 1,000 men along with a group of artillery fighters.

Green turned to his captain. "Let's make camp here," he said, looking through his spyglass and barely making out the outline of the fort. "We'll wait here for General Sibley. Send out some scouts to watch for the rest of our troops. They shouldn't be too far behind."

Within a few days, Sibley and the rest of his 2,500-man brigade had joined Green, setting up camp fifteen miles south of Fort Craig. The Confederate leaders understood they could not attack the massive fort head-on. For the next three days, Sibley ordered his troops into a line about a mile from the fort, hoping to draw the Union forces into a fight. But Canby chose not to attack.

Late on the night of the third day of trying to draw out the enemy, Colonel Green was sitting with General Sibley in his tent. "We need to bypass the fort. Make them come to us. We can cross the Rio Grande here to the eastern side," Green said, pointing at a map. "We'll have the high ground and can then move all the troops back to the western side at the Valverde ford, where the river is shallow enough to be crossed on foot. The battle will be here, and we will have cut their communications to Santa Fe. If there is no battle, we will have bypassed the Union forces and we can keep moving."

The General studied the map. "We are very low on provisions, only enough for a few days," he said. "Get the men ready, Colonel, and let's proceed with your plan."

The Confederate army crossed the river in the early hours of the next morning. Through the day and night, the men climbed to the top of a rugged mountain that was covered with sand and deep ravines, leaving them at a higher elevation than the men at Fort Craig and hidden from sight of the Union soldiers.

*   *   *

A Union scout brought word to Colonel Canby the Confederate forces were on the move to Valverde. "They are headed in that direction, and I heard one of their artillery men shout, 'On to Valverde,'" the young scout said.

In response, Canby sent 720 men, including infantry, cavalry, and artillery under the command of Colonel Roberts, across the river to try to block the enemy's northern movement and hold the crossing. Knowing the cannons would slow the progress of the men, Roberts ordered Major Duncan and his cavalry to move ahead and secure the area on the western side of the Valverde ford to prevent the Confederates from crossing the Rio Grande.

Canby also ordered the New Mexico volunteers and the troops from Colorado to watch the Confederate's movements, threaten their formation from either side or the rear, and interfere with their movement.

Eli tightened the straps on Coal's saddle, checked his ammunition, and placed his hand on his secured gun in the leather holster on his right side. Climbing up on his horse, he yelled an order to his captain to have the Colorado company form a line behind the troops moving out.

Manuel and Eduardo were at the entrance of the fort, and as Eli passed, he nodded his head in a solemn greeting. He knew they would be heading to the river crossing shortly.

*   *   *

When the Confederate troops arrived at Valverde ford, they realized Union forces were blocking them from crossing. While waiting for reinforcements, the Confederates took cover behind a riverbank.

In the meantime, the Union artillery had arrived and remained on the western bank.

The battle stayed a stalemate until noon, when Canby and the rest of the Union forces arrived. He ordered the calvary and infantry to cross the river to the eastern bank, leaving the New Mexico forces on the western bank.

*   *   *

General Sibley, who had been overseeing the battleground from a high vantage point, was not sure the Confederates could win. He sent word to Colonel Green to come to him.

"This battle is about to start," Sibley said as he took a drink from his flask. "Since this was your idea, I am turning control of the troops over to you. I will be watching from here."

Colonel Green saluted with resolution and rode his horse back to the battleground where he immediately authorized a lancer company to attempt a charge on the Union extreme right.

*   *   *

Eli steadied his men as forty Confederate soldiers with sharp lancers came at them at full force. Eli shouted out, "We are not going to lose this day!" The men waited until the lancers were close enough and released their rifle fire simultaneously, killing or wounding the entire group of Confederate soldiers.

By the late afternoon, and after intense fighting, the Union had the advantage. Colonel Canby ordered the companies to move to his right. However, this repositioning weakened the center of the Union line and the battery on Canby's left.

Colonel Green ordered an attack on the Union right with a battalion. This attack was met with frontal fire and a flank attack from the 1st New Mexico Volunteers. Leading his men, Manuel was shot in the shoulder and was thrown from his horse. Eduardo watched his father fall but could not assist him as the battle carried him away.

Green then ordered the Confederate right under Lieutenant Colonel Scurry to charge the Union center and the battery on the left. Scurry's 750 men attacked in three successive waves.

The Union army countered with a cavalry charge, but the main Confederate force pressed Canby's left flank and broke the Union battle line. The confrontation soon turned into a panic-stricken retreat of both Union regulars and volunteers.

Knowing he could not win the battle, Colonel Canby sent a white flag to Colonel Green to give the Union survivors time to collect the dead and wounded. General Sibley agreed to the truce, allowing Canby to reorganize his men and order a retreat to Fort Craig.

Left in possession of the battlefield and the road northward to Santa Fe, the Confederates had however suffered substantial casualties of soldiers, horses, and mules. Sibley decided to abandon his attempt to capture Fort Craig, thus ceding the battlefield back to Union control. The Confederates instead continued northwards towards Albuquerque and Santa Fe, where they hoped to capture much-needed supplies.

*   *   *

The Union troops had also suffered losses, with over 400 Union men killed, wounded, captured, deserted, or missing. Canby knew, as he sat in his office at Fort Craig, that this battle had been a victory for the South and his failing had cleared the way for Sibley to move on to Albuquerque and then to Santa Fe and further west.

He acknowledged a knock at the door. "Come in," he said.

Eli entered with a stack of papers in hand. "Good evening, sir," he said. "This is the list of the dead, wounded, and missing. I wanted you to know that Captain Manuel Sena is among the missing."

The Colonel accepted the stack from Eli and began thumbing through the names and ranks of his officers. "We need to regroup," he said, looking up at Eli through tired eyes. "I'll need you to get your men ready for immediate departure to Fort Union. That will be the last stop for Sibley before he moves on to Colorado and California. We must defeat him there."

≡ 15 ≡

The darkness of the room was broken only by a fire burning in the stone fireplace. Lydia opened her eyelids, but they felt heavy and swollen, and her tongue felt thick in her mouth. *It must be either early morning or late afternoon*, she thought to herself. She couldn't tell since the heavy curtains were drawn. Gloom seemed to hang in every corner of the room.

She pulled herself upright on the bed and leaned against the pillows, trying to recall the events of the last few days. After cleaning up and resting the day she'd arrived, she had shared dinner with Carlos and his father that evening.

Carlos had asked her incessantly about her illness and what had transpired on her journey there. She had finally answered him defiantly. "I resent your tone, Carlos," she said, glaring at him and his father. "I do not plan to stay here any longer than I must, and I will be writing to my father to learn when I can return home. I do not want to get married." With that, she threw her napkin down on her plate and slowly made her way up the staircase to her room.

She had found sympathy in the young maid, Rosa, who had been attending her. As she helped Lydia undress, Rosa had warned her. "Please be cautious, mistress. I want you to know they have been administering something to Señora Aragon for a very long time, after she disagreed with them, to keep her quiet."

Taking heed, Lydia stayed in her bedroom for the next several days, claiming she was ill. A tray had been left at her door with a sound knock for breakfast, lunch, and dinner. Rosa, who checked on her each day, was always nervous and afraid to answer any of Lydia's questions.

Over time, it had become harder to concentrate and get out of bed, and finally, she had been unable to rise, overwhelmed with exhaustion. After that, she only remembered drinking small and constant amounts of water or tea administered by Carlos.

Lydia tried to move her body. Her muscles were weighted down, and she panicked for a minute. *Could I be ill again?* she thought. But the feeling was different, as though she was simply drained.

Her first impulse was to lie her head back down and sleep, but something inside her, a voice or a feeling, told her to rise and move around. She sat on the edge of the bed and shook her head from side-to-side, trying to get rid of the haze and fog that clung to her.

Hanging on to the nightstand, she stood up slowly and for a moment felt like she might fall over. She steadied herself, demanding that her body respond to her requests, but the feeling of sluggishness was overpowering. She collapsed back down on the bed, only to close her eyes once again and fall into a deep, dreamless sleep.

*   *   *

Many hours later, the maid cautiously opened the door to Lydia's room to see her still sleeping. Rosa smoothed the covers over her and brushed her curls back with her hand. "I hate him," she said under her breath, knowing Carlos had put laudanum in Lydia's tea. An old trick he'd learned from his father. Lydia's breathing seemed normal, and Rosa turned to leave. She would prepare a small meal for Lydia and bring it up herself.

Rosa gasped with fright as she turned and saw Carlos approaching the bed. She had not heard the bedroom door open.

Without looking at her, he asked, "Is she still asleep?"

"Si Señor," Rosa said with her eyes cast downward.

"Good," he murmured, and Rosa turned and hurriedly left the room, not wanting to know what might happen next.

Carlos crept silently to the edge of Lydia's bed. *How beautiful she is,* he thought to himself. Ignoring her statement from dinner, he was determined they would marry, and soon. He could feel his desire for her as he watched her chest rise and fall and, in the dim light, was aware of the outline of her breast against the blanket. His own breath became quick as he moved closer to her.

His large hand hovered over her body. He smiled with anticipation. Taking Lydia under normal circumstances would be a challenge, he knew. She would fight him, which would be pleasurable, but this, her helplessness, was very inviting. His fingers brushed lightly over her breast. Lydia did not respond. Aroused, his other hand moved to her thighs. He planned to keep her at his ranch as his wife and felt there was no harm in this exploratory endeavor.

Lydia's eyes flew open, a look of horror on her face as she realized what was happening.

Carlos was calm as he removed his hand and spoke soothingly. "Mi amor, I am glad you are awake and feeling better. How was your rest?" he asked as though everything was normal. "We are hoping you have not relapsed from your illness."

Lydia sat up and pulled her knees up close to her chest. Anger boiled in her eyes, changing their color to a dark blue.

"Don't ever touch me again," she said, her teeth gritted with determination. "Or I will kill you."

The words hung between them for a moment, and Carlos' eyes locked with hers in a challenge. He was the first to look away.

"Would you like something to eat?" he asked. "I can have Rosa prepare something for you now."

"No!" she screamed at him. "I don't want anything from you, and I won't drink anything either. You put something in my tea, didn't you?" she yelled. "Didn't you?"

"Calm down, Lydia," Carlos said.

Lydia pulled the covers away and got out of the bed on the opposite side. She grabbed the vase from the nightstand and held it up, ready to throw it at him.

"You have not been yourself since you arrived," he said with false concern. "Of course I did not give you anything. You are only exhausted from your illness and the trip."

Lydia was shaking her head no. "You cannot hold me here against my will."

"Lydia, get a hold of yourself," Carlos said calmly. "Your father agreed to our marriage and placed you in my care. I will not allow you to leave. You don't know what you are doing or what you are saying. Now, put the vase down."

"No, not until you leave," she said. "Get out and stay away from me."

As he turned to leave, she threw the vase, barely missing him. He muttered under his breath, closing the door behind him.

Lydia was shaking from anger and shock. She huddled in a corner of the room. *I must leave. I have to get out of this place, back to Eli*, she thought. "Eli," she whispered, and as his name lingered on her lips, tears escaped from the corners of her eyes.

She realized she had to get up and find a way to escape.

Lydia placed a chair up against the door so no one could come in. She felt alone and vulnerable and needed the time to think clearly. It would take time for the drug's effects to be gone from her mind and body. She splashed frigid water against her face and chest, determined to overcome the exhaustion.

Lydia changed into a warm wool dress; the black seemed to suit her mood as she pulled the woolen shawl around her shoulders tightly.

She paced the small room, trying to decide how and when she could leave. Anxiously, she sat down at the writing table. With pen in hand, she looked into the fire. Who could she write to? Eli, her father, Eduardo, Claire? Who could help her? Feelings of despair came over her and she put down the pen, realizing she could only rely on herself.

There was a soft knock at the door, and Lydia knew it was Rosa. She stood at the doorway, ready to move the chair, but first asked, "Are you alone, Rosa?"

"Si Señorita," Rosa replied. Lydia moved the chair and opened the door.

Rosa carried in a tray with an elaborate dinner of roasted meat, potatoes, wine, coffee, and steamed fruit for dessert. The sight of it made Lydia's stomach turn. The drug could be in anything, and she couldn't take the chance.

"Rosa, please take it back. I'm not hungry," she said sternly.

"Señorita, there is nothing in this food. I prepared it myself," Rosa said. "You must eat."

Lydia looked at her. "I can't take that chance. I know you are trying to help me, but he could have had someone else drop it into any dish. This is exactly what they have done to Señora Aragon, isn't it?" Rosa did not look into Lydia's eyes but nodded as she began to shake and cry uncontrollably. Lydia put her arms around her, but she had no words to offer.

Rosa pulled a letter out from her apron pocket. "Señor Aragon gave me permission to give this to you."

Lydia could see her father's handwriting on the outside of the envelope. She took it and held it to her chest, as though it was a part of him.

"Thank you, Rosa, you may go now," she said, and she closed the door solidly behind her and replaced the chair.

Lydia sat down on the bed to read the letter and could tell the envelope had been opened. This made her furious, but she was thankful the correspondence had found its way to her. She could almost hear her father's voice as she read.

My Dearest Daughter,

I hope you are doing well. The house is not the same without you. Nothing seems to be as it once was. Your brother and I are well. I am glad you are not here as the Confederates head this way. Many are concerned about our small town and whether she will survive if they attack. I think she will be just fine.

Remember to be strong, my dear. You are like your mother, determined and stubborn.

I will write to you soon. You are always in my thoughts. Please thank Carlos and Señor Aragon for their hospitality on my behalf.

> *Take care, my dear Lydia.*
> *Your Father, Manuel*

Lydia read the letter many times before folding it up and putting it in her dress pocket. "I am trying very hard to be strong, Papa," she said, if only to herself.

The night became late, and Lydia was afraid to fall asleep in the event Carlos might return to her room. Changing back into her night-gown for comfort, she sat down to write a letter to her father. She did not tell him how difficult her situation was, only that she missed him and Eduardo. She couldn't even tell them about her trip with Eli.

She was restless and hungry, and she decided to find something to eat and drink. Pulling her shawl around her, she left the bedroom. It felt good to be out of the confining, dark chamber. Her head was finally clear from the drug, and she moved quietly down the stairs, her bare feet making little noise. She clung to the side of the walls, staying in the shadows.

She had an idea of where the kitchen was, and her steps and move-ments were cautious and controlled. She was almost at the main hall-way, but she failed to see the low, wooden storage chest and walked right into it. She put her hand over her mouth as pain shot up from her shin, and she sat down on the chest to recover for a moment.

She heard laughter coming from the parlor next to her. Her heart was thumping in her chest and adrenaline was racing through her, but she did not panic. She was tired of being afraid, and so she gathered herself and leaned back into the darkness near the wall. She waited, and soon the voices were clear.

"You know I have always loved you, Savina," Carlos said, his voice soft with liquor.

Savina laughed and the sound floated across the room. "You don't know the first thing about love," she said. "Besides, you must marry your beautiful bride-to-be."

"Yes," Carlos said. "She is beautiful, and her father is very rich. We are going to be married in two days at the church in the village. Every-thing has been arranged. Did you know that once a woman is married, it is nearly impossible to end that marriage? Will you come?" he asked.

"Yes, my love," Savina said. "I will come."

Lydia could hear their soft, shared laughter in between long kisses.

She could imagine their heads together and their bodies leaning close to one another.

"You know, Savina, I will always want you," Carlos said.

Lydia heard Savina moan in response and then there was a long silence. Lydia was about to move on down the hall when she heard Savina ask, "What about the war, aren't you afraid it may come here?"

Carlos snorted. "The war will be over in New Mexico very soon."

"How would you know?" Savina asked.

"For many months, my dear, I have been gathering men, supplies, and information for the Confederates. I even have a group of men who have been stealing and rebranding cattle from various ranches for the Southern cause. Right now, we know exactly where and what the Union army is doing. I have made sure of that. They will suffer great losses."

"You can't be serious, Carlos," Savina said. "Why would you do something like that?"

"For the money. I will be a very wealthy man when the Confederates reach the gold fields and overthrow this sham of a government, and," he continued, his voice growing stronger, "I will have a powerful position when the dust settles. I will have my lovely wife, who has a very prominent blood line. She will bear my children, and I will have you as my beautiful and passionate mistress. Now, let us finish what we started. I can wait no longer. Come upstairs with me."

Lydia moved quickly and quietly down the hallway and crouched down in the shadows behind the staircase. She waited until she heard Carlos' bedroom door close.

Alone in the darkness, she decided to return to Santa Fe at once, to warn everyone about Carlos' actions and to escape his forced marriage.

She quietly went back upstairs to pack her knapsack. She brushed her tangled hair and pulled it back into a ponytail. It was a pleasure to pull on her riding habit and her boots, knowing she would soon be gone from this house and a man she despised. She had hidden her father's gun from the Aragons, and she now placed it in her belt. She lovingly held Eli's pocket watch for a moment then placed it in her pocket—its weight and significance giving her comfort and strength.

She went downstairs and silently found her way to the kitchen. She would need food for a few days, and water. Lydia's mind was racing, and she didn't notice someone had entered the kitchen after her. Lydia gasped when she looked up and saw Rosa, who was looking at her with wide eyes in her night shift and a shawl. Lydia held her hand to Rosa's lips and her eyes were pleading. "Por favor," she whispered.

Rosa's hands became busy as she helped Lydia load her bag with dried meat and bread. She made Lydia wait, and when she returned, she carried a bundle of old clothes and a full canteen of water.

Rosa whispered, "The clothes will make you look like a peasant. Be sure to put them on once you are away from here."

"Thank you, Rosa. I must warn them about Carlos," Lydia whispered.

"Yes, I know of the supplies. I have been with one of the ranch hands who even told me of the cattle they have stolen. Most of the supplies are hidden underneath the Aragon's barn," Rosa said softly. "You are very brave, Señorita Lydia."

Lydia hurried to the back door as Rosa unlocked it with a key around her neck.

"Thank you," Lydia said.

Rosa put her hand over Lydia's. "Vaya con Dios, Señorita."

Lydia ran to the stables, found Sadie, and grabbed her saddle, cinching it onto her horse. She put the bit in Sadie's mouth and led her away from the house, taking a route hidden by trees.

The night was bitter cold, but she didn't care. She was free and nothing would stop her from reuniting with Eli.

≡ 16 ≡

Eli and his troops had completed the over 200-mile journey from Fort Craig to Fort Union with orders to watch and harass the enemy. Except for a few skirmishes, there had not yet been another full-contact encounter with the Confederates.

The Union troops were in a state of shock after Valverde, but Eli used this to make them move faster and assured his men that the war was not over. Eli had received word from one of the Union's scouts that more reinforcements from the Colorado Territory were headed to Fort Union.

The fort had been built in 1851 by soldiers to protect the territory from Indian raids. It was on a wide, barren plain in the Mora Valley, and the buildings, constructed from adobe and pine vigas, were widely scattered.

As they made their way through the main gate and dismounted, Eli was greeted by Colonel Paul, who was in charge and had received orders to hold Fort Union until Canby could join them. Colonel Paul saluted and said, "Welcome, Lieutenant Colonel Stevens." He motioned to a soldier to take hold of Coal's reins.

Eli saluted in response. "Can you tell me where to direct my men?"

Paul pointed to a series of garrisons. Eli signaled to his commanding officer to have his men go in that direction.

"I've had word, Colonel," Eli said as they walked towards the main building. "A regiment is on their way from Colorado. They should arrive any day."

"Yes," Paul nodded. "We are aware. My orders are to have all the troops assemble here."

"Have you heard from Canby?" Eli asked as they entered the building. "Yes, he should arrive soon, and I'm certain the Confederates are headed this way as well."

Eli eventually joined his men to make sure they had food provisions for the evening and would have a good night's rest.

The next morning in the early light of day, Colonel John Slough, a loud and boisterous man, arrived with the Colorado regiments. He and Colonel Paul met behind closed doors, and in an impressively short period of time, Colonel Slough was overseeing Fort Union and all the troops there. Word spread quickly through the ranks that he'd led his courageous group of men over 400 miles in thirteen days in the cold, wintery weather.

Standing on the steps of the main building, Slough gathered all the men around him. "Soldiers," he said, "saddle up your horses and gather your gear. Be prepared to depart in the next few hours. We are going to find the Confederates instead of sitting here waiting. They will be frightened by the fire in our hearts and the strength in our step."

*   *   *

The night had been dark and lonely, but Lydia felt exhilarated. Whatever happened, she was determined to get to Eli. All the years she had spent on a horse gave her an advantage as she galloped off the Aragon property. She never really thought about the danger that could be in store for her. As the night wore on, she'd put many miles behind her. Sadie's steps were sure, and they stayed on the main road, never looking back. The further away Lydia got, the easier she breathed.

The sun came up and light poured over the countryside. She could feel the hunger pains in her stomach, and she desperately needed to stretch her legs. She turned Sadie's reins and pulled her off the road to a path leading to a secluded spot near a stream.

Lydia stepped down from her horse and leaned her head against Sadie as the horse took in long drinks from the stream. She knew she couldn't risk a fire, but she grabbed the dark skirt and simple white blouse Rosa had given her and quickly changed into them. She hid her old clothes under a chamisa bush by the stream, hoping they would not be found. She splashed the icy water from the stream on her face, filled her canteen, and bundled up in her heavy shawl.

Lydia pulled a loaf of bread and some dried meat from her saddle bag. She was ravenous and shoved the food into her mouth as quickly as she could chew. She made herself comfortable on the ground with her bed roll and tried to calculate the length of time it would take her to get back home. Her mind was sharp and clear, and she realized it would take her a few days. She would be cautious about resting, and she put her hand assuredly on the gun tucked inside the waist of her skirt and then on Eli's watch inside her pocket.

Lydia leaned her head back against the rough trunk of a pine tree, watching Sadie nosing through the snow to get to any dried grass left from the summer. She closed her eyes and imagined Eli's face, the strong line of his jaw and the deep brown in his eyes. She could feel his arms go around her and give her strength to continue. She hoped he was well, and that was as far as her hopes would go. She didn't know what would happen after the war, or if they would even both survive. But, for now, she knew she could give herself to him without reservation, with only love.

Her horse whinnied at her, and Lydia opened her eyes with a smile. "Our rest is over Sadie. Come, we have many miles to cover to get home."

*   *   *

Rosa busied herself with chores all morning long and into early afternoon. She was thankful Carlos had stayed in his room with Savina. She had left a breakfast tray for them both outside the bedroom door, and she could hear them faintly talking and laughing as she backed away quietly. Carlos would have expected this from her, and she knew a leisurely breakfast would provide more time for Lydia to cover ground.

At the kitchen table, her hand rubbed a silver candlestick with a soft rag over and over; the motion was soothing, and the silver glowed from her touch. Keeping her hands busy, though, did not stop her fearful thoughts. She knew Carlos would explode when he found out Lydia was gone. Rosa had contemplated hiding how much she knew, but she was terrified of Carlos, and she knew he would hurt her to get to the truth.

I don't deserve to be here, she thought to herself. Only to become a meaningless possession like Mrs. Aragon, beaten down by the empty house and empty hearts of her husband and son.

She rubbed the candlestick even harder. She had suffered much abuse from the Aragon men since she had arrived here at a young age. Her parents had been killed as they were making their way to California. One of the men leading the wagon train had sold her to the Aragons. She never knew if she had any other family members anywhere.

Her name was Rosemarie, but the Aragons had changed it to the Spanish version, Rosa. She had wanted to run away hundreds of times but was not sure where to go. She was always haunted by nightmares of her parents' deaths and so she never ventured too far away. She was safe here, in some respects, even though she was miserable.

She had become tall over the last couple of years, and she was trim and fit from the hard work. She pushed back a lock of her golden-colored hair from her delicately featured face before putting down the polishing cloth to begin preparing dinner. She stoked the fire and cut the beef, onions, potatoes, and garlic and set those in a large cauldron with water to slowly boil. She worked quietly as she measured out flour, lard, and water for tortillas. She knew this task would take a while.

She heard a hard, rapid knock at the front door. Her heart pounded. Could it be that Lydia had been caught? Rosa made the sign of the cross across her chest and moved to the edge of the kitchen so she could hear what was being said.

*   *   *

Carlos also heard the knock and finished adjusting his pants and buttoning his shirt while walking down the staircase and opening the door. Armstrong stood in front of him, looking a bit ragged from the long ride but with a wide grin on his face.

"I have some news for you," he said as he pushed past Carlos and made his way inside. Armstrong looked at the rich surroundings with appreciation.

Carlos closed the front door and looked around to see if any of the servants were nearby. He gestured to Armstrong to enter the library down the hall. Carlos took a seat behind the mahogany desk, and Armstrong sat in one of the burgundy-colored chairs placed to the side.

"There's been a battle at Valverde," he began anxiously. "We were matched up well and the Union fought hard, but the Colonel made a grave mistake when he moved all his troops to one line. The South came at us, wave after wave, and broke the line. The Union couldn't recover, and right before nightfall, Canby sent a white flag. They are all making their way to Fort Union."

Carlos nodded. "It's time to get our stockpile to the Confederates. I will need you to stay on and help me get the wagons loaded. Unless, of course, you wish to return to the Union army," he said sarcastically.

"No sir," Armstrong replied enthusiastically. "No siree. That's why I am here. I deserted and my plan is to help you."

Carlos smiled as he stood. "I will have some of the ranch hands join you in loading the supplies. The barn is just south of the house. I will meet you there shortly."

Carlos' mind was moving rapidly, going through all that needed to be done. But first, he would check on Lydia. He ran up the staircase and knocked on her bedroom door. When there was no response, he burst in only to find the bed empty and some of her belongings gone.

He cried out in a bellowing voice, "Lydia! Where is she? Lydia!"

He ran down the stairs to the kitchen. "Rosa," he said angrily. "Rosa, where is she?"

Rosa was wiping her hands on her apron as she turned around to face Carlos. His dark eyes bored into hers, like two bolts of lightning; his nostrils were flaring against his own breath, and his body shook. Her lips were trembling and unshed tears shone in her eyes, unprepared for the depth of his anger.

"Where is she, Rosa?" he asked again with a clenched jaw and tightened fists. The second she hesitated; he knew she had helped Lydia escape. He brought his fist down hard across her face, causing her to hit her head against the stove. Her warm blood spilled across the floor as she fell into unconsciousness.

Carlos went back upstairs. Savina had dressed in her lavish gown and had put her hair back in a black beaded net. She was on her way out the door. Carlos raised his arms above the doorway and asked, "Where do you think you're going?"

"Home, my darling. Your fiancé's escape and your escapades with the Yankees have nothing to do with me," she said icily as she pushed her way past him. "I don't want to be part of this messy situation." She looked back at him with a delicious smile. "But do send word for me when things calm down, and I will come and see you." With that, she turned and moved quickly down the stairs and out the front door where her horse and small carriage were waiting.

Anger was the only emotion Carlos could feel as he darted to his room to don his riding gear. He would oversee the loading of the supplies, and he would get the supplies to the Confederates. He would send Armstrong to check for Lydia in Santa Fe since he was sure she had returned home. Once Armstrong confirmed her location, Carlos would ride his fastest stallion and bring her back.

He would not allow Lydia to make a fool of him. He would track her down and marry her before the battles were finished. Then, he could have control over her, and she would belong to him. His gun and holster were laying across the dresser in his bedroom. He made sure the gun was loaded as he strapped it to his waist.

*   *   *

The next three days were grueling for Lydia and would have exhausted even the strongest of men, but she had managed to stay out of harm's way. The winter winds of March blew and spread their icy touch over her. She pulled the woolen shawl that covered her head and face even tighter around her. Lydia could feel the tired movements of her horse and knew that Sadie needed to rest. Night was again about to fall, and she must find a safe and warm place to rest, if only for a short time. She turned off the main road and finally came to a clearing; inside the clearing was a small area surrounded by large rocks and brush. *Here*, she thought. She let herself slide off her horse, unsaddled Sadie, and quickly gathered brush for a fire.

The small area was warm soon and well-hidden. Lydia spread out her bed roll and blanket. She moved Sadie in close and tied her securely to a nearby tree. She ate what was left of her food supplies and washed herself off in the nearby stream. She could feel that she was close to home, and she only wanted to rest for a bit then begin again. Lydia laid her head down, covered herself with the blanket, and closed her eyes.

* * *

The light from the moon was just enough to let him see where he was going. His steps were thick and clumsy, the brush and rocks crackling under his boots. He had been following her on horseback for many hours, and he knew she had stopped nearby. He had left his horse tied up near the main road.

Excitement overtook him. He didn't know who she was or how she got here, only that he had been fortunate enough to find her.

He could see where she was lying, and he moved cautiously. She had fallen into a deep sleep, her face partially covered with a blanket. He was just a few feet away from her, when her horse began neighing loudly and stomping its hoofs in warning.

Lydia woke suddenly and sensed the danger, but she stayed still. She could hear the rustling of the brush and knew someone was approaching. She slowly reached for her gun. Her hand slid around the cold metal of the handle, and as she pulled it from the waist of her skirt, her finger was ready on the trigger.

She listened as the intruder moved closer. She knew he was now standing above her as she could smell him. Her heart was beating wildly, and she thought he must be able to hear the sound.

He dropped to his knees with a hard grunt and turned Lydia from her side over to face him. "Let's see what we have here," he said roughly as his hand moved toward the blanket hiding her face.

She tightened her hold on the handgun. She could feel how close he was to her; his body heat was overwhelming. He pulled back on the covering, revealing her face, but Lydia kept her eyes closed, pretending to still be asleep.

"What a pretty little thing," he said with greed as he positioned himself on top of her.

She held herself still, not struggling, knowing he had to be extremely close for the bullet to kill him. As he leaned his body weight onto her, she pulled the trigger.

The sound of the gun was not as loud as she thought it would be. The bullet had entered his chest, and he slumped onto her. Lydia worked quickly to release her legs from under his body, avoiding looking at his face. Her breath came in waves, and she shuddered—there was so much blood.

She stood up and thought about what to do next. First, she would make certain he was dead. Placing her hand on the man's chest, she felt no breathing or heartbeat. In the moonlight, she could see the front of his gray uniform coat was dark with blood.

He was heavy, but Lydia pulled him away to a place thick with trees and brush. She covered his body with branches that she cut with her knife from the surrounding bushes. Returning to the clearing, she quickly gathered her bed roll and blankets stained with his blood and walked them to the stream where she shredded them with rage and shame, sending the small pieces down the river's path.

She glanced around at her surroundings, listening, watching for a sign of anyone else. She realized the man was probably an advance spy, and she wondered if there were more men with him or perhaps a regiment close by. Not waiting to find out, she saddled Sadie with speed and was riding at a full gallop within minutes.

"Almost home," she kept telling herself. "Almost home."

* * *

The house creaked and moaned, and Alita opened her eyes and thought for a moment it was morning, but the shadows were too dark. She sighed as she pulled her covers up around her and tried to go back to sleep. Prayers that had only been a part of her day now consumed her nights. Her heart ached for Lydia. She kept imagining where she was and hoping she was well.

Manuel and Eduardo had been gone for many days. Before he left, Manuel had urged Alita to stay with friends outside of town. She'd flatly refused; this was her home and the only family she had. She would be here, waiting to take care of them all once they returned.

The people of Santa Fe had become more and more anxious as they received reports of the Confederate troops coming closer. They had heard rumors the troops were gathering in Albuquerque, taking any and everything of value from the residents along the way. They would be in Santa Fe soon.

Most of the men were gone, fighting in a war the women did not understand. There were severe food and fuel shortages. Alita had offered her sitting services to a group of women with children, while they traveled to the outskirts of town each day in search of wood for the fires and anything they could use for food. Some of the younger boys had become experts in squirrel and rabbit hunting using sling shots. There were few guns left behind and ammunition was a very precious commodity. Most people were living on the last bits of vegetables and canned items from the fall harvest. Alita had learned only today that the Union quartermaster, the one in charge of all the supplies, had evacuated Santa Fe, along with 120 wagons filled with food, blankets, ammunition, and medical supplies—taking it all to Fort Union.

She wanted it all over so that life could go on, so she could have the ones she loved back with her. Her eyes closed once again, and she fell into a light sleep.

Suddenly, she woke again on hearing a rustling noise outside the house. At first, she thought the wind had picked up. Then she heard it again, and she knew someone had entered the rear courtyard. She remained calm as she gathered her shawl, wrapped it around her shoulders, and picked up the heavy, ancient sword that had belonged to Manuel's grandfather. She made her way hesitantly down the staircase.

She stopped when she heard a key enter the lock and knew it was someone with knowledge of the key hidden under the kitchen porch. She didn't know who, so she tried to stay quiet as she heard someone enter the house and move through the kitchen and into the parlor.

Alita cautiously and silently crept to the parlor and bravely entered the room holding the sword upright with both hands. A figure was standing at the fireplace, holding their hands out to capture the residual warmth from the hearth. Alita was not prepared for the sight of Lydia. Her eyes opened wide, and dropping the heavy sword to the floor with a crash, she went to Lydia and wrapped her in her arms.

"Alita," Lydia said her name softly and with love. "You don't know how happy I am to see you. I have missed you so." The two women pulled apart, and Lydia could see the tears glistening in her caregiver's eyes. Her heart was singing inside her, it was so good to be home, and nothing compared to the warm feelings that enveloped her. She had wanted to sit in her chair in the sala and just enjoy being home and safe for a moment.

Alita moved to light the main lamp, but Lydia stopped her. "No, I can't stay. I only stopped to learn where I can find Papa or Eduardo. Do you know where they are, or where they could be?"

Alita explained to Lydia in her own way that she'd heard they were all moving to Fort Union, many miles northeast of Santa Fe. Alita wanted Lydia to bathe and change her clothes. She wanted to feed her. But Lydia said, "No, not yet."

Alita followed her to the kitchen where Lydia gathered up some food and filled her canteen with water. She pulled a blanket and a bed roll, along with oats for Sadie, from the storage area near the kitchen.

Facing one another, Alita put both her hands on her mistress' face.

She could see the wild look in Lydia's eyes.

Lydia put her hand on top of Alita's. "I am so glad you cannot speak. This way, if anyone asks if you have seen me, you don't have to answer. I must go now and get word to them. I love you." She turned and closed the back door solidly behind her.

Alita wanted to follow her. She wrung her hands as she stood in the middle of the dark, deserted kitchen. She trusted Lydia and suddenly realized she was on her own path now. Her prayers went with her.

*   *   *

Lydia had decided to stay off the main road as she headed towards Fort Union, which meant she would have to go through Glorieta Pass to get there. She urged her tired horse into a gallop. She had to find Eli.

She heard them long before she saw them and was surprised she had run into the Union army so quickly. She had only been traveling for three days. The rhythmic sound of boots moving together on crusted snow mixed with the clatter of guns and swords brushing against saddles was difficult to miss. The horses' whinnied, frustrated at feeling penned in by soldiers on foot. The mules grunted under the weight of pulling the heavy cannons and wagons loaded with ammunition. Commands floated from one senior officer to the next, guiding the men in the same direction.

Lydia was far enough away so she would not be seen, but stayed close enough so she would not lose them. As late afternoon approached, she finally heard the command to halt. She dismounted and stealthily pulled Sadie towards the noise of the soldiers setting up camp. By the time she was close to the camp, the sun had gone down. She tied Sadie to a tree, grabbed the few food items from her saddle bag, and crept her way towards the campsite. She would be far less noticeable as a maid delivering food to a loved one. She pulled the shawl up around her head.

She saw the U.S. flag proudly displayed among a sea of dark blue uniforms. She hoped Eli was here. She had no way of knowing if he was with this group and gathered her wits together as she came closer.

All of Lydia's instincts came alive. There were hundreds of men milling around the fires, tending to the horses, cleaning guns, and setting up tents. Some sort of sanity reigned in this sea of confusion, and to her relief, not one soldier stopped her as she cautiously proceeded. She pulled the shawl close around her face and kept her gaze down to the ground.

Her breathing quickened as she walked through the camp. There were men everywhere, but none she recognized. She noticed too there were some women at the outskirts, cooking and tending to soldiers who were ill.

Lydia stood for a moment amidst all the activity and glanced about nervously, trying to get a sense of the direction she should head. A young soldier approached her. "You look lost," he said graciously. "Can I help you find someone?" He waited, not sure if she had heard or if she only spoke Spanish.

She hesitated, but she sensed kindness in him. Holding tighter to the food in front of her, she said, "I am looking for someone. I have a delivery for Lieutenant Colonel Stevens."

"Would you like me to take these to him?" the soldier asked, reaching for the food.

"No!" she cried. "I have to give it to him myself." She clutched the provisions to her chest.

"Follow me then."

Lydia walked behind him, clutching her shawl. She still felt vulnerable and did not want to draw any attention to herself. They came to a large tent with a young soldier standing guard outside.

"Seth," the young man said to the guard. "This woman is here to see Stevens. Is he here?"

Seth nodded. "I'll tell him. What is your name, Miss?"

Eli had overheard their conversation, and before she could answer, he snapped the front flap of the tent open. His eyes never left hers as he spoke. "Thank you, men, that will be all for now." She felt faint and exhausted as he moved towards her and took her arm. "Come inside," he said calmly.

A kerosene lamp burned brightly and lit up the inside of the tent. Eli stood close to her, and they both exhaled with relief. With steady and strong hands, he removed her shawl and held her face in both hands.

"I wasn't sure I would ever see you again," he said.

She melted against him, and they kissed one another deeply. For a moment, there was no war, no world outside of them.

Eli gently led her to the cot and sat down next to her. "How did you get here, are you hurt, where is your horse?" His questions came rapidly, his voice filled with admiration and relief.

She put her hand to his mouth. "Sadie is tied to a tree just south of the camp. I escaped Carlos' house after I overheard him say he is helping the Confederates, and there are probably others. They will do anything to win. They have money and supplies. Your enemy is just as much within," she said. "Once I learned what was planned, I had to warn you."

"I'll have warm water sent in so you can clean up. I'll have some food brought to you as well. I will track down Eduardo and," he paused, "we haven't had word yet from your father. We're not sure of his location."

She stood quickly. "Where is he, Eli?"

"We believe he was taken prisoner at Valverde. We don't know if he was wounded."

The news hit Lydia like a hammer, and she stood still, not speaking, with her hand on her stomach.

Eli stood and gathered her to him. He spoke softly. "I think he must be injured. We have scouts everywhere and we would know by now if he had been killed."

"Yes, yes," she nodded in disbelief. "I am sure he is fine."

"I'll be back shortly. Please get some rest. You are safe here," he said as he kissed her forehead.

She watched him grab his hat and leave the tent. Alone, and finally safe, she returned to the cot and broke down in tears, from exhaustion and a new-found pain that resonated in her bones. She could not sleep and clutched her shawl to her more tightly, opening and closing her hands over the gathered fabric. She was thankful when a soldier brought her a bowl of warm water.

Lydia felt at least clean after she finished washing up. She was anxious to see Eduardo and pulled the last strands of her hair into a braid down her back. Eli had borrowed a skirt and blouse from the women following the army and had one of them take them to Lydia. They were not a perfect fit and were tattered in places, but the clothing was clean and warm.

She heard the flap of the tent open and smiled broadly when she saw Eduardo. She stepped towards him, and they embraced each other warmly. She kept her hands on his arms as they looked at one another. He looked older to her now, more mature with longer hair and a short beard. His arms too felt fuller and more masculine.

They sat down on the small cot. "Tell me about Papa," she began. "What happened?"

"We were together when we started out from Fort Craig," he began. "We made it down to the bank of the river. We were guarding the opposite side of where the main battle occurred. Father was leading our regiment. There were many small encounters with the enemy. When the Colonel arrived, we were ordered to move to the center of the main line of troops. We tried to cross the river quickly, but we weren't even in place when the battle began. There was firing, shouting, screaming. Horses were killed, men were killed. I've never seen so much blood." He took a long breath and continued. "We fought back, and when they retreated, we chased them into the small hills behind us. Father was shot in the shoulder and was thrown from his horse. I watched him fall but could not reach him as I was struggling to keep firing at the enemy and stay on my own horse."

Lydia put her hand up to stop him for a moment while she wiped the tears from her eyes. "Go on," she said.

"Many soldiers were killed, and we were all surprised when we were ordered back to the fort. We didn't even know it was over. I kept yelling for Father, but I could not find him anywhere." He looked down at his hands. "I killed two men," he said with a crack in his voice. "Shot one right through the chest and the other in the head. It was not what I was expecting, Lydia," he said as he finally broke down into tears.

Lydia took both his hands in hers and held them tight. Tears streamed down her own face as she looked into the eyes of her older brother, who looked so young and tender in that moment.

"Eduardo," she said lovingly, "all of this is so difficult. I don't understand why it's happening, but I do know our father raised us to be brave and to fight for the people we love."

She pulled him close to her and they wrapped their arms around each other tightly, like the small children they once had been, each knowing their father may be in grave danger as a prisoner or had been killed in the battle.

"You are not alone, Eduardo," she said. "Our mother watches over us from heaven, and I know we will all be safe and together when this is over."

"I have missed you, Lydia," he said through his tears.

After a while, they both relaxed and Lydia was able to tell him the story about Carlos and her ride back to Santa Fe. She did not share her killing of the soldier.

"I can't believe you journeyed back alone. You could have been killed, Lydia, or worse," he scolded her.

"But I was not, Eduardo, and I was able to bring the information about Carlos, which should help," she said.

"I suppose now you won't be marrying him."

Lydia sighed and shook her head. "No, I won't, and I know father will understand when he returns."

The night was growing late, and Lydia put her hand to her mouth as she yawned.

"I think you need some good rest, hermanita," Eduardo said as he stood and kissed her on the top of the head. "I will stop by in the morning to check on you." He moved to the tent flaps.

He turned to her before he walked out. "You and Eli," he said. "Is there something I should know?"

She smiled. "Yes," she said. "I am in love with him."

*   *   *

Carlos and his men had made great progress towards Santa Fe by stopping only briefly to rest. They had left the cattle behind with two of his men and a friend who was sympathetic to their cause. He would send word when he met up with the Confederates. Carlos had stayed with the more valuable supplies of guns and ammunition in the wagons.

He had sent Armstrong ahead to Captain Sena's home to see if Lydia was there. He hoped that she had run home and that she would be easy to find.

He saw Armstrong riding toward him as they headed east from Santa Fe. Catching up to Carlos' horse, Armstrong delivered his news. "She's not there. I searched the whole house. There was just an old Indian woman who couldn't talk. Don't worry. We'll find her."

Carlos did not respond; he was only more determined to find the Confederate army he knew was near Glorieta Pass, deliver the supplies, and then deal with Lydia.

≡ 17 ≡

Eli and Lydia lay close together on the small cot. It was that time in the early morning when night reluctantly gives way to dawn. Neither one had slept. Colonel Slough had ordered the men to be ready to march to Bernal Springs early that morning.

They didn't speak, feeling the warmth from each other's bodies. Eli's hand lovingly caressed Lydia's hair and face as she lay against his chest. She closed her eyes and could feel his lungs fill with air with each breath. She reveled in his scent and his embrace. She imagined them in another place, far away from here. She sighed.

Eli's arms wrapped around her, and he drew her face up to his. They kissed one another deeply, and their eyes told the other how much they meant.

"I want you to know," he said in a deep voice, "you are everything to me, Lydia. Our time at the cabin seems like a lifetime ago. All I want is to get through this war because I plan to spend the rest of my life with you."

She kissed him lightly on his lips. "I will be here waiting for you."

She stretched her hand across his chest and lay her head on his shoulder; she breathed deeply and closed her eyes. They both knew their time together was limited, and they cherished the few precious moments they had left.

"For now, we must get going," Eli said as Lydia reluctantly stood. "It won't take long to get to Kozlowski's Ranch. The plan is to leave any wounded and those that are tending them there. You will need to brush up on your caretaking skills, my love."

"I will be ready and honored to help the soldiers who have been wounded."

Eli was buttoning up his coat and reached for a small pistol lying near his duffel bag. "I found this for you last night," he said as he handed it to her. "I want you to protect yourself in case something happens to me."

"I am not afraid to use this," Lydia said as she pulled open her saddle bag and showed him the revolver her father had given her.

"Good enough," he said appreciatively, and they found themselves smiling at one another.

"I would like to make you something to eat before you go," she said.

"I'll arrange to have some food sent. I am going to check on some things. You'll be all right?" he asked as he placed his hat on his head.

"I'll be fine," she said soothingly. "Come back and I'll have breakfast ready for you."

"I will," he said as he opened the flap to the tent.

After Eli left, Lydia began gathering her few items to place in her knapsack. Soon, a young soldier brought a few precious food supplies, including ham and fresh eggs. Lydia found a frying pan, pulled the shawl around her head and shoulders, and went outside to the small fire that was burning next to the tent.

She was apprehensive as she had not been out during the day since the morning she arrived. In the daylight, she realized she recognized many of the men who were soldiers and some of the women who were following behind, cooking and mending, washing clothes, and bandaging wounds. They walked through the camp now, checking small wounds, gathering clothes to be laundered or mended, and helping to cook breakfast.

It was a crisp, clear morning and a dense smell of the outdoors hung in the air. They were surrounded by a forest and steep hillsides covered in pine, juniper, and aspen trees and low-lying chamisa bushes. Glorieta Pass was part of the Santa Fe Trail and was located on the southern tip of the Sangre de Cristo Mountains. The land was pristine and largely uninhabited except for a few ranches scattered near the trail that served as resting places for the stagecoach travelers.

Lydia fried the ham and then the eggs. Eli did not return, so she ate her portion, covered Eli's, and used the remaining water in her canteen to clean up the dishes.

Eli's tent was in the center of the camp. The soldiers were soon packing up their gear and getting ready to move forward. There was a sense of purpose and reason to all the commotion.

Lydia felt restless with thoughts of her father's wellbeing and hoped he had survived. She had an urge to seek out Eduardo but did not know where he might be. She decided checking on Sadie would calm her.

*   *   *

Armstrong had been waiting and watching near the corral, blending in on the outskirts among the many soldiers near the horses. Carlos had sent him to track his own troops, in the hopes that Lydia might be with them. Carlos wanted her back and was willing to pay a good price for it, too.

Armstrong watched out of the corner of his eye as Lydia made her way cautiously to the horses. *She may have wrapped herself up to look like a maid*, Armstrong thought to himself, *but her walk and mannerisms give her away.*

He followed her, and luckily, there were no soldiers attending to the horses. Lydia spotted her horse and, standing at the temporary rail, called softly, making clicking sounds. The horse came to Lydia and buried its head against her.

Armstrong came up from behind and easily swept Lydia up in a firm hold. He put his hand over her mouth and pulled her back to a group of low-growing pine trees. She tried to scream, and she kicked and jabbed him with her fists and elbows. He cursed her under his breath. He hadn't imagined she would give him this much trouble.

Her shawl had fallen away, and by now, many of the horses were disturbed, snorting and bustling about the pen.

Eli seemed to come out of nowhere. "Take your hands off her, Armstrong," he said with a gun pointed at him. "Let her go or I will kill you."

Lydia bit the soft tissue of Armstrong's hand as hard as she could and slipped out of his hold. She ran behind Eli.

"Put your hands up, Armstrong," Eli said. "You're under arrest for desertion and assault."

Armstrong stepped away and began to cautiously make his way to his horse tied nearby. "This is not my war," he said indignantly. "And just so you know, you will not be on the winning side today, my friend."

He turned and ran, sensing Eli would not shoot him in the back. He jumped into the saddle and forced his horse into a gallop through the surrounding forest.

*　*　*

Eli took Lydia in his arms. "You need to be extremely careful, Lydia," he said as she looked up at him. "I am not sure why that happened, but we will get to the bottom of this. You will need to stay with the women for now. Can you find your way?" She nodded. "Good, I must get to the Colonel right away."

He walked purposefully towards Colonel Slough's tent and ran into Major Chivington.

"Sir, I have heard news that a rancher is delivering supplies, gold, and guns to the Confederates. There was also an attempt made to take one of the women by a deserter named Armstrong. Should I send a group after him?"

Chivington put his hand to his chin and thought for a moment. "We must focus on the task at hand, Stevens. I can't afford to send any other men out now. All my scouts have been dispatched. We can try to find them after we find the Confederates."

Eli understood but still worried about Lydia's safety.

*   *   *

Lydia gathered her belongings and saddled Sadie, pulling her to the part of the camp the women occupied. There were fifteen other women, ranging from young girls to elderly women. They were busy taking down their tents and preparing the wounded to follow the main army.

Lydia tied Sadie nearby and walked towards a few of the women who were cooking eggs and meat on the fire. One of the women recognized her. "Miss Lydia," the older woman said brightly. "It is a surprise to see you here. I won't even ask why, but we are thankful for your help."

Lydia was able to place the woman. "Mrs. Quintana, these are strange circumstances to see you, but please let me know what I can do."

She grabbed a white apron from a makeshift clothesline and handed it to Lydia. "You will need this. We will be right behind them and will set up the tents on the outskirts to help any that are wounded. You can help by breaking down the tents."

As Lydia donned the apron, she could hear the army starting to embark on their journey. She knew those she loved would not be far behind.

*   *   *

Colonel Slough ordered a 400-man unit to head towards Santa Fe under the command of Major Chivington to find the Confederates. Eli and Eduardo were among the men.

The following day, Major Chivington marched his army towards Glorieta Pass and descended into the canyon. "Lieutenant Colonel Stevens," Chivington yelled. "You move your men out first." Eli nodded and turned to give orders to his men.

Before long, the Union soldiers came face-to-face with the Confederates traveling on the same road. Chivington, not far behind Eli, yelled out, "Stevens, take your men further up the sides and when I give the command, commence firing."

Eli nodded and gave the signal to his men to climb up either side of the narrow pass. The fighting began and acrid smoke filled the air, with loud gunfire and shouts of determination from both sides. As the long shadows of dusk began to arrive, the Confederate troops withdrew for the night and traveled back to their camp.

The Union forces regrouped and accounted for all the men. Eli rode next to Chivington and could feel the surge of excitement from the troops traveling behind them. "By the grace of God, I believe we won this battle, Stevens," Chivington said as he made his way up the steep pass.

"Yes sir, we did," Eli responded. "We had them running scared."

"Tomorrow will be critical," Chivington said. "If their reinforcements come through, we will have to contend with a much larger and well-rested army. Let's get back and get the men settled, and we will meet with Colonel Slough."

In the early hours of the next morning, Colonel Slough was preparing his men for the upcoming battle. Spirits were high as the Union men packed their gear and prepared to march. He had decided he would take 800 men and artillery along the pass that led to Santa Fe.

The Confederates had not sat idle in the canyon. Lieutenant Colonel Scurry moved his troops through Glorieta Pass, heading east. As the morning wore on, the Confederates came head-to-head with the Union forces, and Scurry ordered his men into a battle line, setting up the artillery on top of a low, flat hill.

Colonel Slough raised his arm and his Union troops halted. Turning to his captain, he said, "Move all the men into a straight line, parallel to the enemy, and quickly." Slough quickly realized that his battle line would be much shorter due to a lack of men.

The battleground was an open field, covered with rocks, pine trees, and low-growing chamisa bushes. Eli ordered his Colorado regiment into the line. He could feel the high energy and fortitude in the voices and movement of the soldiers. They stood side-by-side, guns loaded and ready. Upon the command, both sides pummeled the other with bullets and cannon balls. Many were injured or killed as the fighting continued.

The Confederates, having the advantage of more troops, pushed their line forward, causing the Union line to step back. This allowed the Union men to reposition themselves in a more protected area of the battlefield.

Colonel Slough ordered Eli to have his men attack the Confederate line to the right. Eli signaled to his men and headed the charge. They were met by a Texas troop, and a viscous battle ensued. From his viewpoint, at the front of his troops, Eli could see many of his fellow Coloradans taken down by bullets as the Confederates flanked his side—but his men continued their assault.

As the battle raged on into the late afternoon, the Confederates were able to attack the Union front. The Union held the Confederates off until their artillery was pulled back. Slough ordered a retreat, knowing his men were exhausted and the wounded would need attending to.

Unknown to the soldiers during the battle, Chivington and his Union men, who had traveled along a mesa not far from the battle site, had discovered the Confederate supplies. Taken by surprise, he ordered his men to capture the soldiers guarding the wagons and cattle and had them burn all the supplies including ammunition, tents, gear, bed rolls, and most importantly, food.

As the wagons were burning, Chivington looked over the small group of men who had been captured, restrained and guarded by soldiers with guns ready. One, without a uniform, caught his attention. He dismounted his horse and approached the man who had his hands tied behind his back.

"You," he began. "What is your name?"

"Carlos Aragon," the man responded indignantly.

"Why are you here, Mr. Aragon?"

"I brought supplies for the Confederate troops. We are loyal to the Confederates," he responded with arrogance and spite, not knowing yet who had won the battle and thinking he would be rescued soon.

Chivington ordered some of his men to stay and oversee the destruction of all the supplies. "Line the prisoners up. We will head back to camp," Chivington told his captain.

* * *

The wounded Union soldiers were brought to the medical tents and Lydia, without hesitation, helped the ones she could. She cleaned and dressed their wounds and held their hands while the surgeons performed the horrendous stitching, cutting, and amputations. Lydia was pulled along as the doctor moved hurriedly from patient to patient.

Hours seem to have passed since the wounded started coming in, and the front of Lydia's apron and her blouse were stained with blood. She ran to the supply table for more bandages and passed a row of men lying on the ground and not moving. One was Eduardo.

Lydia walked towards him as if in a dream and knelt beside him, placing her face near his. She detected shallow breathing, and she moved the hair from his forehead and wiped the dirt from his face with her sleeve. She placed a cloth over the wound on his chest, and it was soon saturated with blood.

Eduardo never opened his eyes, and she knew nothing could be done. Lydia leaned closer to him and softly hummed a Spanish song to him.

"I love you, brother, and this world will never be the same without you," she said with tears streaming down her face.

His breathing was ragged and irregular. He drew one last breath and released it slowly. Lydia crumpled on top of his body, calling his name. Her heart seemed to break apart with each new breath she took. He could not be gone, after all they had been through together.

Seeing Lydia was overwhelmed by the shock, Mrs. Quintana led her away from Eduardo's body and the medical tent. Once outside, she tenderly wrapped her arms around Lydia.

"Cry, my dear, cry all you need to," she said soothingly as she held her.

Finally, Lydia found the strength to stand on her own. "That was my brother, my only brother. I can make no sense of what has happened," Lydia said desperately.

The woman grabbed her shoulders. "There is never any sense to war, my dear, only heartbreak and loss, especially for women."

Lydia nodded her head and, still in disbelief, made her way back to Eduardo's body. "I must be with him."

* * *

Eli had been back and forth and in and out of the fire line. He had watched some of his men fall, which had fueled his courage to continue fighting. He fought furiously amid the smoke and powder emanating from the gunshots and the cannon balls sailing across the battlefield ending in loud explosions. He had his head turned, yelling out orders to a group to advance, when he was hit by gunfire from one of the Confederate soldiers. The bullet tore mercilessly through the flesh of his chest.

His hand reached up to protect the wound, but he continued to shoot his gun, over and over, until he fell from Coal and landed heavily on the ground. His sight became blurry, and he looked around for someone to help him, pain searing through his body. He finally lost consciousness.

* * *

The battle finally ended, and the Union soldiers collected the wounded and dead still on the field, bringing them to the camp. Lydia had not left Eduardo's side. She was only half aware the battle was over. Troops began filing in, and she waited desperately for Eli so she could share her grief. The waiting seemed endless.

Lydia waited with bated breath, lost in her grief for Eduardo. It seemed like hours went by, and still, Eli had not returned.

She sensed it was him before she saw him. She said his name in a whisper. His wound had been bandaged and cleaned, and he was lying on a gurney carried by two young soldiers. Lydia closed her eyes and tried to fortify herself before she walked to him. They gently placed the gurney down at a corner of the medical tent.

She grabbed his hands first and felt that he was alive. She placed his hand to her lips.

"Mi amor," she whispered. "You cannot die, I won't let you. You must stay here with me." She leaned down to his face and kissed his cheek gently.

His eyes fluttered and opened, and with great strength, he squeezed her hand. The two men returned and reached for the gurney.

"Where are you taking him?" she asked anxiously.

"To Santa Fe," one replied. "They can treat him better there."

"Can I ride with you?" she asked anxiously. The young man nodded, and she removed her apron, preparing to gather her things to leave camp.

* * *

In her haste, Lydia had not noticed that her shawl had fallen from her head. Her hair hung in a braid down her back, and Carlos recognized her from a distance.

The Union soldiers had brought him along with the others Confederates who had been guarding the supplies. He had been arrested for treason. Only the muscles in his face had flinched when they shackled his hands together.

But he had found Lydia.

Carlos leaned over to the Union soldier guarding him and said, "That woman there," he pointed to Lydia, "she is my accomplice, my fiancé. She helped me with everything. She is as guilty as I am. Please advise your superiors before she gets away."

≡ **18** ≡

Lydia followed Eli's gurney as they proceeded to a wagon where a doctor was overseeing the loading of any he could not treat. Eli's breathing was shallow, and all the color was gone from his face.

"It took him a long time to fall," she heard one of the men say. "That bullet hit him, and he still stood, he kept right on fighting. I hope he pulls through."

Lydia was making her way among the soldiers to be next to Eli when she suddenly felt someone grab her arm from behind. She broke free of their grasp, unaware of how much strength she was exerting. The soldier grabbed her again and this time, held her tightly as she was forced to turn and face him.

"Take your hands off me," she cried loudly. "Who are you and what do you want? Can't you see Eli needs me?" she said desperately.

"You're under arrest, now don't make a scene. Just move slowly. Major Chivington would like to speak to you."

Lydia stomped her foot hard on his shin, and he automatically loosened his grasp. She broke free and ran towards the wagon.

The soldier easily caught up to her once again. "We would just like to talk to you. Maybe we can straighten this out," he said with a steel grasp on her upper arm. "Now don't try anything again, just come with me."

All Lydia could see, or feel, was Eli in pain, and perhaps close to death. Still in shock over the loss of Eduardo, and knowing she might lose Eli as well, she reached underneath her shawl to her waistband with her free hand and grabbed her gun.

She pulled it up to the soldier's chest. "I don't want to shoot you, but I will, unless you let me go. I must be with Eli," she said.

The soldier loosened his grip. Her own escape or safety never occurred to her. She turned to run to Eli. Two other soldiers had seen her pull out a gun and they ran after Lydia.

Once again, she was at Eli's side. She had just enough time to lean down and kiss his cheek and say, "I love you" before the two soldiers each grabbed one of her arms. The gun fell from her hand and tears began falling from her eyes. She didn't know what was happening or why.

"Please, please. Take good care of him," she pleaded as the soldiers escorted her to the Major's tent.

As they came near the entrance to the Major's tent, Carlos burst out of the flap enclosure in a cloud of anger and disgust. His hands were handcuffed behind his back, and he was held on either side by a guard. He glared at her.

"Do not be afraid to tell them what you know, my love," he said. "I have already given them information about your involvement."

A shadow of hatred crossed over Lydia's face. This was a matter of survival, she realized. Anything he had said would have been damaging to her.

She adjusted her blouse and skirt and, with permission from the soldiers who held her, she smoothed her hair with her hands. They had retrieved her shawl and she wrapped it tightly around her, one guard still gripping her arm. She swallowed hard and felt the dryness in her mouth.

The soldier walked her inside the tent. It had been a long day for Major Chivington. The battle had been grueling. Many of his men had been injured or killed, and he was not sure they had succeeded in stopping the Confederates. He wanted nothing more than to assess his losses and was not in any mood to deal with traitors who had planned to sabotage the Union's efforts.

He was exhausted, and it showed around his eyes and the slump of his broad shoulders.

Lydia looked like a slip of a young woman to him, and she reminded him of his own daughter. "Sit down, young lady," he directed sternly. He didn't want to frighten her, but this was a serious charge. She obeyed and sat on the small stool in front of him.

"How did you get here?" he asked.

"I came on my own. I was staying with Carlos and his family at their ranch and discovered that he was sympathetic to the South. He had stockpiled guns and ammunition and supplies."

"Why did you come?"

"To warn the Union troops. I came to tell Eli, Lieutenant Colonel Stevens, what I had found out and try to warn him."

"Lieutenant Colonel Stevens never disclosed the information came from you."

"No, he wouldn't have. He was trying to protect me. He didn't tell anyone, except my brother, Eduardo, who was killed in battle today," she said as fresh tears ran down her face.

"Are you engaged to Carlos Aragon?" Chivington asked.

"Yes," she replied. "But I left the ranch because I do not want to marry him."

"Were you traveling with Mr. Aragon to deliver the supplies to the Confederates?"

"No," she cried. "I told you, I left before he did. My brother just died today, Major, all in the name of the United States. I came to warn everyone. I was not a part of any conspiracy."

There was still doubt in Chivington's mind from Carlos' testimony, and he was thankful the final decision would not be his. He gave the soldiers instructions to place her in a tent under guard until the next morning.

Lydia was shocked that the Major did not believe her. She moved as if in a dream as the soldier escorted her to a tent, securely closed the flap, and positioned himself in front. She needed to be free to be with Eli. *What is going to happen to me?* she wondered. All she could do was pray, exhaustion and grief overtaking her. She cried desperately into the pillow on the small cot, and eventually, tears gave way to a troubled sleep.

The next morning, the whole camp seemed calmer and more at ease. Word had come that the Confederates had suffered losses as well and were headed back to Santa Fe. They had scarce supplies since most of them had been destroyed by the Union troops.

Lydia woke to the many noises outside her tent. She was not sure where she was at first, only that the sleep had done her well. She stretched her arms and opened her eyes, almost expecting to see Eli there with her. The emptiness of the small tent greeted her, and then it all came back.

She sat up, thinking that someone would surely testify on her behalf. She had grown up here and knew many people. She would fight this battle. With a renewed sense of hope, she stood and opened the panel at the front of the tent. "Please tell Major Chivington that I would like to see him."

"I'm sorry ma'am," he replied. "He's headed back to Fort Craig. I was just about to bring this bread to you. You'd better eat before we leave."

"Where, exactly, are we going?" she asked with distress.

"To Las Vegas, ma'am. That's where your trial will be held."

*   *   *

Las Vegas, New Mexico was nearly seventy miles north of Santa Fe. It was a small community that grew from a land grant established in the early 1800s. Commerce was the mainstay, and the townspeople had easily welcomed the stagecoaches loaded with goods and supplies that could no longer get to Santa Fe. Governor Connelly had moved the Executive Offices of New Mexico to the plaza in Las Vegas just before the Battle of Glorieta Pass.

Judge Anthony Sims snapped his pocket watch shut. It was exactly noon and time for him to take his meal at the hotel. He gathered his black overcoat with a short outer cape hanging from the hook behind his door and pulled his stout arms through the sleeves, meticulously brushing lint from the front lapel. Reaching for his wool felt top hat, he took care to place it exactly on the top of his head. Pulling on his black silk gloves, he reached for his gold-topped cane before stepping out in the early afternoon sunshine.

He strolled along the same sidewalk he had walked on for the last thirty years. He was an institution in the small town, and he knew it. He had provided input in every major decision.

His family had been wealthy and affluent in the East. Sims had traveled to the territory as a young man for health reasons. He never married but rather studied law and read a great deal. Highly intellectual, he had helped shape Las Vegas over the years. In 1852, he was appointed one of five Chief Justices for the territory by the United States president and was confirmed by the Senate. It was a lofty appointment for a humble man, but he took his responsibility to heart. He also served as the judge for one of the three judicial districts that included Santa Fe.

The townspeople nodded to him as he walked by on this sunny afternoon. Word had come in that the Battle of Glorieta had been a victory for the Union army. Sims was pleased. He had always thought secession by the states was ignorant, and he believed in the United States and President Lincoln.

The judge walked through the doors of the boarding house and turned to the left to sit down at his regular table. He ordered his usual, beef with potatoes, sipped his coffee, and read the Las Vegas Journal while he waited for his meal to be served.

His clerk, a thin, nervous young man, came rushing through the doors and sat down across from him. "Judge, I am glad you're sitting down," he said excitedly. "We just received word that three adults are being brought here by soldiers. They have been accused of treason."

The waitress refilled the judge's coffee and set his lunch down.

"And they are going to try them here since we are considered the capital, at least for the moment?" Sims asked.

The clerk nodded his head yes.

"Let me eat my lunch in peace. I will be back to the office shortly," the judge said somberly.

*   *   *

Lydia slept much of the way between the camp near Glorieta and Las Vegas. It was a day's ride, and she was in the back of a covered wagon. The ride was bumpy, and she was extremely uncomfortable but did her best to rest.

The young soldier shook her awake. "We're here," he said.

She opened her eyes and let them adjust to the low light of dusk.

The jail was attached to the courthouse and the sheriff's office, which were in one building made of gray stone. He led her down from the wagon and directly into the jail. The sheriff, a stern and broadly built man, took custody of her and, wearing a look of disgust, let her know he didn't want any problems. He locked her inside one of the cells, which was damp and cold. "I'll try to see about something for you to eat," he said gruffly.

Lydia laid her head down on the hard mattress of the cot, and dark thoughts circled around her head. Eli wounded, Eduardo dead, her father's whereabouts unknown. How could she redeem herself from these charges?

The inside of the cell had no light of its own, except for a small window that was well above Lydia's reach. An eerie glow was cast by a lantern hung in the hallway. Lydia heard a slight motion in the next cell. She stayed quiet and still.

"Lydia," she heard her name called in a whisper and cringed when she recognized the voice. "I'm glad you're here now," Carlos said. "They will probably hang us together. You see, if I could not have you, no one else can." Carlos laughed softly.

She didn't respond and curled up into herself as great tears spilled out of her eyes.

*   *   *

Back at his office, Judge Sims realized he was under the gun to move quickly. Treason was to be tried and punished by order of the United States government. He decided to send a messenger to Canby, who'd been promoted to brigadier general after the Battle of Glorieta Pass, asking for a military commission to handle the case. The jury would be nine members of the Union forces, and he asked to be appointed Judge Advocate to oversee the prosecution and serve as advisor to the commission. Hanging a woman was going to be tricky, he knew. But, if the story were true, he'd make it work.

Word that Carlos had been captured traveled to the Aragon ranch. His father had selected a lawyer from Santa Fe to defend his son and hoped he could testify as a character witness on behalf of Carlos. He would not allow his son to die. He ordered his coach to be made ready.

In the meantime, word had also spread through Santa Fe that Lydia was being held prisoner in Las Vegas. Many of the Union soldiers were regrouping at Fort Craig. Cecil Murray was terrified for Lydia. He knew Eduardo had been killed, Manuel was missing, and Eli was recuperating from a severe chest wound. Cecil requested a meeting with Colonel Slough.

"This can't be true," he said as they sat in the Colonel's office.

"They have arrested her," the Colonel replied. "I don't know how much evidence they have against her," he said. "I will send a note to Governor Connelly to intervene on her behalf. We must also be prepared for the worst. She was privy to very damaging information. She could have chosen to share it. Maybe she loves this man, Carlos. I will let you know of any developments."

Cecil was overcome with worry as he stood to leave the Colonel's office. "There was a soldier I heard about, that Eli was looking for. A recruit who had come from the north. Let me see if I can find him."

Governor Connelly visited Judge Sims after he received the message from Colonel Slough the next day. They shook hands and sat down in the judge's well-furnished office.

"Judge, surely you see how preposterous this allegation is," the Governor began. "I've heard from many people in the last few hours," he said, "all telling me about the innocence of this young lady. Her father and brother fought for the Union. Her brother, Eduardo, was killed during the battle at Glorieta Pass. I have known Manuel for many years, and since we believe he is badly wounded or being held prisoner or dead, I must act in his stead. I have asked a lawyer, Mr. Dobbs, from Santa Fe to act in her defense. He is on his way and should arrive here this afternoon."

"I understand your concern, but I have interviewed Mr. Aragon myself and he assures me she was part of it. He claims she got frightened when they arrived at the pass and ran off to the Union camp." The Governor shook his head in disbelief. "I know this is frustrating, sir, but we have no choice and must let the judicial process take its course. The trial will begin tomorrow."

For the next few days, in a crowded courtroom filled with curious spectators, Judge Sims established that Carlos had indeed stolen cattle, purchased guns and ammunition, and hoarded food supplies that he intended to deliver to the Confederates. Mr. Sutton had come to the trial to testify about the death of his son, and Carlos eventually admitted to that crime.

Savina's testimony buried Lydia along with Carlos. "I met Miss Sena when she arrived at the Aragon ranch," she lied. "I have been a friend of the Aragon family for many years, and I have never seen a couple so in love and ready to enter the sanctity of marriage." Asked if she thought Lydia knew about Carlos' efforts, she replied, "I am certain of it. I overheard them discussing the plan to distribute the items Carlos had collected at the precise time to benefit the Confederates. Miss Sena was fully aware of his intentions."

Mr. Dobbs had spent hours with Lydia going over her testimony but knew there wasn't anyone available to verify her claims. He had sent a man to the Aragon ranch in search of Rosa, who had disappeared. Alita had offered to testify, but Dobbs thought it was conceivable that she could be seen to be lying on her mistress' behalf. Armstrong could not testify as he had also confessed, and Eli was still recovering from his chest wound and was battling an infection that left him in and out of consciousness. Dobbs knew it would be difficult to convince the jury of seasoned military men that Lydia was innocent.

The day finally arrived for her testimony. Dobbs made sure Lydia had a new dress and shoes and a shawl. She had been able to bathe with the help of the sheriff's wife, and her hair was pinned loosely at her neck—but her face was pale and worn. Well-rehearsed, Dobbs led her through questions about her treatment by Carlos at his home, how she learned of his plans, and how she decided to go directly to the Union troops. He spoke passionately about Eli and how he had chosen to protect her through the ordeal, how Eduardo had perished, and how she had found Eli after the battle. The prosecution and defense wrapped up with closing arguments and the jury was scheduled to begin deliberations the next day.

After the trial ended, the guards returned Lydia to her cell. Carlos was already locked inside his own cell. When the guard left, Carlos said in a harsh whisper, "It will all be over soon, Lydia. We will be found guilty. You will never see your home again or your family, or Eli."

Lydia had been clutching the steel bars of the cell that held her. Hearing someone else say his name out loud pulled at her insides. Tears poured down her face and she slid into a pile of misery.

Carlos' prediction was correct. After hearing the testimonies, the jury found Carlos, Armstrong, and Lydia guilty of treason and sentenced them to death by hanging. Lydia nearly fainted as Judge Sims read their decision.

Back in her cell that afternoon, she felt the weight of knowing she didn't have much time left on this earth. Even now, she could hear the hammers beating strong nails into the scaffold being built outside. She could not hold herself against it any longer. She had neither the will nor the energy to pretend this would not come to pass.

Small shafts of light from the tiny window seeped into the enormous darkness of her cell. It seemed out of place against the cold, lifeless gray walls. Lydia reached out and the light danced across her fingers like a delicate piece of lace. It transformed her skin, making it warm and glowing. She had stopped trying to warm herself days ago. She closed her hand and tried to capture the light in her palm.

The coldness once again assaulted her body and would not let go.

It blew right into her, twisting and turning, stopping just short of carrying her off with it. She wanted nothing more than to be a part of something else. Not this. She didn't know where the courage would come from to face the day that lay ahead.

She would never know Eli's touch again or feel the love in his embrace.

Each day that had passed had brought her closer to her fate. She had tried relentlessly to explain to anyone who would listen to her about why she had left the Aragon ranch. Only Eli could verify the facts of her story now, and she did not know whether he was alive or dead.

She would never know.

She shut out the sound of the constant water dripping and Carlos' breathing, to keep the maddening noises from bouncing within the walls of her brain. She closed herself off from this charade that had become her world. To still her racing mind, she searched for any thought that would bring her peace. Always, Eli's face loomed above hers with a soft tenderness that enveloped her. The darkness fell around her like a cloak that surrounded and embraced her small body.

She had faith in her soul, though, that he lived and would carry on for her in some way. Their love was strong, and their lives had been joined and intertwined, bound by passion and commitment.

That was enough for her. His love had touched her in a profound way, and it would linger in her soul forever. Her heart and mind were finally at peace.

≡ 19 ≡

The doctor bent over Eli and checked the bandages. His patient had been unconscious for several days. He had lost a great deal of blood and had been struggling with an infection in the wound. The doctor hadn't been sure about performing the surgery to remove the bullet when they'd brought him in; he could barely find the young man's pulse. Doctor Porter had been utterly exhausted from treating many men before him at the time. It had been a difficult choice, but the alternative to not performing the surgery would have surely meant death for this soldier.

Sister Cathleen walked in with a tray containing fresh bandages and morphine. Eli was still unconscious, but the doctor was not concerned. The wound had been deep and had gone all the way through his chest, just missing his heart and lungs, but the infection was clearing, and the wound showed adequate signs of healing.

Eli couldn't feel the doctor's hands on his body. His own mind was in a hazy place between consciousness and unconsciousness. The battle kept playing over and over, and then there were moments when all he could see was Lydia, her soft features and sparkling eyes. It was more though than just her physical beauty, it was her spirit, her strength calling to him. He wanted to be with her, to bask in the light that was only hers.

He tried to call out to her, but she was out of reach, not there, and he became confused and frustrated.

Doctor Porter finished cleaning and rebandaging the wound, and he looked to the nun in the dimly lit room. "Reduce the amount," he said, looking at the bottle of morphine. "We need him to start moving now."

As if on cue, Eli lifted his hand as though he was reaching for something or someone. The doctor was just about ready to administer the pain medicine when Eli's eyes fluttered open. Even the dim light was painful, but he kept them open, forcing them to adjust to the light.

"You're with us," the doctor said. "Welcome back. How do you feel?" he asked.

Eli moved his whole body slightly and felt the pain searing through his chest. His mouth was dry, and his face showed beads of sweat. He grunted and tried to sit up. "Lydia," he said roughly.

The doctor looked concerned and exchanged a glance with the nun. He continued to administer the pain killer. "Just relax, son, let me get this in you."

"No," Eli said as he pushed the doctor's hand away. "I need to find Lydia," he struggled with the words.

"Son," the doctor said firmly, "you need to lie down and let me give you this for the pain." Eli squeezed the doctor's hand with his own. Eli's strength surprised Doctor Porter, given the serious nature of his wounds.

"Her life may be in danger, send for one of my men. I must find her," Eli said through gritted teeth.

Doctor Porter could see the look of resolve in his face and motioned to the nun to come to his side. "Please check in with the officer overseeing the hospital. Tell him to try to find any man who was with Eli at Glorieta."

Captain Vigil was writing to his children from his hospital bed. He had fought alongside Eli during the battle and was recovering slowly from his own leg wound. He was in a makeshift ward placed in the hallway at the Loretto Chapel. He was surrounded by injured men, some wounded slightly and others critically. He tried to block out the noise of low moans and labored breathing around him and tried to re-call happier times with his wife and children. He rested his head back on the pillow and closed his eyes.

He felt a hand on his shoulder and opened them to see a young nun in her black and white habit, gently shaking him. "Sir," she called softly. "We need you; Lieutenant Colonel Stevens needs to speak to you."

Vigil did not hesitate to move towards the edge of the bed and, with her help, set himself into a pair of crude crutches. Eli had surely saved many lives in the battle, and he was honored to help. He fol-lowed the nun down the hallway, past the beds, to a separate room. He entered to see the doctor was there.

"Doctor Porter, this is Captain Vigil," said Sister Cathleen.

The captain greeted the doctor who said, "This young man is determined to get information from you, something about a woman whose life may be in danger."

Captain Vigil looked confused but moved his eyes over to Eli.

Eli motioned him to move closer. In a whisper he asked, "Do you know where the young woman who was with me is? She was dressed like a maid and was near my tent right before the battle."

Vigil, with his head bent to hear, said, "Yes sir, she was arrested and taken to Las Vegas for a trial. They suspected that she was with the man, Aragon, who brought guns and supplies to the Confederates the morning of the battle."

Eli asked, "Has the trial taken place?"

"Yes," Vigil answered. "They were both found guilty of treason and will be hanged along with Private Armstrong, who assisted them."

Eli thanked him and closed his eyes for a moment. He knew Lydia was not dead yet, for surely, he would have felt that in his heart. He knew, somehow, he had to get to Las Vegas. "Can you get word to Pri-vate Montoya. Tell him I need him with a wagon and guns first thing in the morning."

"I will find a way, sir," Captain Vigil said.

Eli tried to rest that night as he had decided he would travel to Lyd-ia himself. He forced himself to eat the broth Sister Cathleen brought to him, and he wrestled with the intense pain in his upper chest. He slept off and on through the night and woke early the next morning.

He asked Sister Cathleen to help him up and get dressed. She did so only after he ate the meager breakfast she had brought on a tray. He was filled with the promise of freeing Lydia, and he hoped in his own heart she was holding up. He heard footsteps coming down the hall as he pulled his shirt on over his head. He looked up and was never so happy to see Cecil Murray.

"Eli, you are up and around. Thank God. I found the soldier who knew about the supplies and Carlos' plan. He'd become very cozy with a woman there named Rosa, and she told him of Lydia's innocence and her attempt to warn the Union army. I have a sworn statement from him," he said as he pulled the document from a leather satchel at his side.

"Good," Eli said. "Help me finish dressing. I am going to Las Vegas and need your help."

The journey was hard for Eli. He often felt he would not make it, but Private Montoya, who had served with Eli at Valverde and Glorieta, was driving the wagon and he kept a good eye on the road, traveling at a slow, but steady, pace. Cecil rode his horse next to the wagon and made sure Eli was alert and comfortable. Doctor Porter had warned him the wound was not yet fully healed and any strenuous activity could open the stitches.

Cecil thought of his love for Claire and understood Eli's determination. He would have done anything to save his wife. He only hoped they would get there in time to save Lydia.

*   *   *

Lydia heard footsteps coming down the jail hallway. She knew the end would begin now. The guard's keys jingled against his side—the noise would have been cheerful anywhere else.

"Señorita," he called. They were not used to dealing with female prisoners, and he had been softened by Lydia's pleasant nature and natural beauty. "We have some food and water here." He stopped for a moment and drew a long breath. "We have been given instructions to get you ready, Señorita," he said as he let out a ragged breath, "for the hanging."

Lydia did not move. Hearing the words again from someone else paralyzed her. She heard the key move expertly into the lock that held her prisoner and the heavy metal bars were opened.

The hearty aroma of eggs, bacon, and tortillas drifted towards her. Memories of her home flooded her mind, like a wave that almost consumed her and shook her to the core. She had not been able to allow her mind to wander there, and she physically stiffened her body to steel herself against those memories. She had hoped she could return home someday.

The sheriff's wife, who had tended to her meals, moved the guard out of the way to personally deliver the hot steaming breakfast. "Señorita Lydia," she said calmly and kindly, "I have brought you some clean clothes and I will help you change when you are ready."

It was a mended skirt and a simple white blouse. Lydia's fingers toyed with the stitches as she sat on the wooden cot with the woman next to her. The woman put her arms around Lydia, and Lydia leaned her head on her shoulder. She stroked Lydia's hair with a hand that was rough from a life of hard work and drudgery.

Tears slipped down the sheriff's wife's cheeks as she hummed softly, and then words flowed out of her mouth in Spanish. She said a prayer asking God to spare Lydia's life. The guard, ashamed of what he knew would happen, sheepishly backed out of the cell.

Lydia had no more tears to cry so she got up and washed her face and combed her hair. She would leave this world with dignity and hoped Eli was alive to clear her name, for her family's sake, especially her father.

She heard Carlos stir. "It is the end now, Lydia, soon we will be together forever. I have even asked my father to bury us together at the ranch."

Lydia shivered and put her hands over her ears. "Please God," she begged, "let this madness end."

*   *   *

Just outside of Las Vegas, Eli's heart was beating furiously; he was almost there, and he knew in his heart she was still alive. They made their way to the plaza, where a large group of people had gathered. Cecil rode ahead of the wagon and cleared a path, moving people out of their way. The town was buzzing with activity; vendors on the street were selling baked goods and glasses of ale to celebrate the hanging.

Eli could finally breathe deeply, knowing he had made it on time. Private Montoya stopped the wagon in front of the courthouse. Cecil dismounted and helped Eli climb out the back. Cecil started to walk with him towards the entrance. Eli stopped and put his hand on Cecil's shoulder. "Stay here," he said. "You and Montoya guard this door until I come out with her."

He walked into the courthouse and removed his hat. He held his arm protectively over his injury. "I need to see Judge Sims immediately," he said to a young clerk behind a small desk.

The clerk asked suspiciously, "What do you need to see him for?"

Eli pulled out his pistol and pointed it at the man's head. "If you want to live, I suggest you find the judge. Otherwise, I will kill you and find him myself."

The clerk moved quickly, and within a short time, the doorway was filled with Judge Sims.

"I understand you need to see me?" he asked gruffly.

"Yes sir," Eli responded as he holstered his gun. "I have information that will free Lydia Sena."

The judge led Eli into his large office. The deputy stepped outside and made an announcement to the crowd that the hanging was briefly postponed, which was met with protests and shouting.

The two men sat across from one another, and Sims could see Eli was in immense pain. "Were you injured in battle, son?" he asked.

"Yes, I am Lieutenant Colonel Eli Stevens with the Colorado Regiment. I have been in New Mexico for the past several months helping coordinate the war effort for the Union troops."

"And what does Miss Sena have to do with you?"

"I know her father, and he asked me to escort her to the Aragon ranch after Christmas. I did and went on to meet the troops from Colorado in Taos to lead them back to Santa Fe. Just before the Battle of Glorieta, she arrived at our camp. She had escaped from the Aragon ranch and let me know Carlos Aragon was planning to help the enemy. I never disclosed her identity to anyone since we were not sure of Carlos' whereabouts, and I felt she was in danger." Eli pulled the document tucked into his belt. "This is a sworn statement from a man who knew of Aragon's plans and had contact with the Aragons' maid who took care of Lydia. See for yourself," he said as he unfurled the paper and set it on the judge's desk.

Sims pulled his glasses from his coat pocket and read through the page carefully. "Will you swear to this information, Lieutenant?"

"Yes sir, I will."

"Very well, I am going to call the jury back together. This may take a while, so make yourself comfortable."

A few hours later, Eli and the judge emerged from the courtroom with the members of the jury behind them. Eli was pale and visibly shaken from the exertion and the realization of how close Lydia had come to being hanged.

The judge asked the deputy to take Eli up to Lydia's cell while he moved to the entrance to address the crowd. Eli and the deputy walked up the narrow stairwell.

Lydia was straining to hear what was happening outside and what had made the crowd so excited. She was trying to pull herself up to the open window and hardly heard the footsteps behind her.

She looked up and saw the figure of the deputy in the dimly lit hallway. Then, her eyes rested on Eli. At first, she though he was just a figment of her imagination, then she knew it was really Eli, come to save her. Her heart fluttered.

A grateful smile filled her face, and she called out his name. "Eli, is that you? Could it possibly be true?"

He moved towards the bars and their hands touched. "Thank God you are safe, Lydia."

"I can't believe you are here," she said, and it seemed an eternity before the deputy unlocked the door and she was in his arms.

She looked up at him anxiously, afraid to ask.

"I have come to take you home, Lydia. You are free."

Tears spilled down her cheeks and onto Eli's uniform. They walked together toward the staircase.

She never looked back at Carlos. He was screaming her name, fear and anger alive in his voice. "You cannot take her; she belongs to me!"

Outside, some members of the crowd had become upset when they learned only Carlos and Armstrong would hang. Many had come to see a woman put to death, as it was exceptionally rare to see a woman killed in such a manner.

Cecil and Private Montoya flanked Eli and Lydia on either side. They pushed through the crowd to the wagon where they helped Lydia into the back. Eli heard the word "traitor" uttered loudly by someone in the crowd. He feared the crowd would attack them and ordered Private Montoya to fire a shot into the air. The gunshot settled the noise of the crowd.

In a strong voice Eli said, "This woman is innocent. The truth is, she risked her own life to save the lives of many men who just fought for you."

A guilty silence fell among the crowd, and Eli, taking advantage of the moment, joined Lydia in the back of the wagon. Cecil was quickly seated on his horse, and Private Montoya jumped to the front of the wagon and grabbed the reins, urging the horses to move.

As the wagon headed towards the main road leading back to Santa Fe, people moved to make a path to let them pass. Eli knelt next to Lydia, his hand on his holster.

It was only when they were a few miles out of the small town that Eli fell back on the bed of the wagon. This startled Lydia, and placing her hand on his chest, she realized he was in bad shape. She could feel the blood oozing out from his side.

"Stop, please stop," she yelled.

The wagon came to a halt and Cecil dismounted. "He was badly injured, Lydia. It's a miracle he was able to gather the strength to come for you."

"I need to get him home," she said, and Cecil nodded as he gave Montoya instructions.

She settled him on the bed of blankets as the wagon jolted forward and offered him a drink of water from his canteen. Lydia could see beads of sweat forming on his face and could feel the heat from a fever on his forehead. She knew she had to get him back to Santa Fe quickly.

Readjusting her position so his head would rest on her lap, she said, "You have done a wonderful thing for me today. Now I will get you home, and I will help you to heal."

They arrived at the Sena home a few hours later. After the grueling ride, Cecil and Montoya carefully removed Eli from the back of the wagon. Lydia called out to Alita for help. Alita's face was filled with joy when she saw her mistress and they clasped hands for just a moment before turning their attention to Eli. The men walked with Eli between them, his arms around their necks. He was not unconscious, but very weak.

Alita ran ahead and pulled the blankets down in Eduardo's room. All three worked to remove Eli's coat, pants, and shirt and get him into bed. Lydia was surprised at the thick bandages covering Eli's deep wound and the blood that was causing deep, red pools.

"Alita, please bring fresh bandages, brew some tea, and send for Doctor Porter," Lydia said as she began the slow, painful process of re-bandaging the wound.

"You will be well, my love," she said, and he weakly grabbed one of her hands and placed it on his lips.

Over the next few days, Lydia and Alita kept vigil over Eli, changing his bandages, feeding him broth, and caring for his every need. Doctor Porter came by each day to make sure Eli's stitches were healing well.

He examined the deep wound to make sure the infection was gone. "Lieutenant," he said as he snapped his medical bag closed, "I think you're going to be just fine. Several more days of rest and care from these two ladies, and you will be up before you know it."

"Thank you, Doctor," Eli said as he held Lydia's hand. "I am feeling stronger."

She and Eli slipped into a daily routine. Lydia would rise early and check on him. Each day his breathing was better, his color more robust, and his appetite increasing. He was a strong man, and Lydia knew they were past the initial scare of imminent death.

Lydia had much to contend with while Eli recovered. She and Alita would prepare breakfast together, and there were many times during their tasks they both broke down in tears for the loss of Eduardo and the uncertainty of Manuel. Cecil made it a point to stop by daily with news of Claire, movement of troops, and to visit with Eli. Lydia had not heard any new information about her father.

She had arranged for a small burial service for Eduardo shortly after she returned. His body had been returned to their home, and the women prepared him for his internment. With only a few family members present, Vicar Lamy had overseen Eduardo's simple coffin being placed in the family plot at the church. Lydia wore only black now in memory of her brother. Each evening, she would recite the rosary on her knees, praying for the safe return of her father and for the repose of Eduardo's soul.

She had also received confirmation from Cecil that Carlos and Armstrong had been hung the same day Eli rescued her. She had mixed feelings about their deaths but kept them in her prayers and hoped someday she could truly forgive Carlos.

Food supplies were scarce because the Confederate troops had passed through Santa Fe after Glorieta and had confiscated all supplies. Alita had been wise enough to bury some flour and dried pork and a few other staples a few weeks earlier. And they still had two chickens who continued to provide eggs each day.

The two women prepared small feasts with their meager rations as Eli's appetite gradually improved. He knew Lydia's heart was broken from the loss of Eduardo, and he tried his best to comfort her each day. Eventually, he was able to get up and sit in the parlor in the afternoons and evenings. They read together and played checkers or cards.

Many times, Eli would catch Lydia deep in thought. Her father had not returned, but Colonel Slough, after returning from Fort Craig, stopped by the house often to give them any updated information and to check on Eli's progress. He optimistically thought all would be well and Manuel was safe somewhere and would make his way home.

Lydia finally had time to check the inside of the mercantile store, which had been boarded up after being ransacked and vandalized by the retreating Confederates. She and Alita spent a day sweeping and throwing away the remnants. As Lydia cleaned a high shelf, a box fell off, and the yards of wedding dress material Carlos had sent spilled across the floor. Lydia exchanged a glance with Alita, who made the sign of the cross, and they quickly put the material back in the box and on the shelf. Lydia shuddered, thinking of how it might have been if the war had not come.

*   *   *

The fire roared as Lydia and Eli sat together, each reading their own books. They kept glancing up at one another, comfortable with their silence. Eli moved closer to her on the settee and put his hand over hers. "Lydia," he said, and she thought her name sounded like an early morning sunrise when it came from his lips. "I want to go back," he said.

Panic and fear ran through her mind. "Go back where?" she asked, not really wanting to hear the answer.

"To finish the fight," he said. "I'm well enough, and it is something I feel compelled to complete."

Her common sense left her, and she stood, trembling with anger and grief. "Eli, you go if you want to, I can't stop you, but I can't bear the thought of anything ever happening to you like it did to Eduardo. I couldn't go on if something happened to you," she said, beginning to weep.

He put his arms around her. "This war is not over. I've had word from Colonel Riley in Colorado. My regiment is preparing to leave for the Texas border. You fell in love with me when I was a soldier, and I am still a soldier. I love you, Lydia, and I want to spend the rest of my life with you, but I must see this through."

She buried her head in his chest and sobbed. He held her tightly until she pulled away. "I understand," she said between long gulps of air. "I know this is something you must do. I wouldn't want Eduardo's death to have no meaning. The Union must win."

Eli packed his things the next morning and donned his uniform. Private Montoya had been caring for Coal and brought the horse to Eli.

Eli hugged Lydia tightly and kissed her soundly on the lips. "I will let you know when I get back to Fort Craig. I love you, Lydia," he said, and she squeezed him with all her strength.

"I will be waiting here for you."

That evening, she and Alita were sipping the last bit of their tea together before the fire, each of them lost in their own thoughts, when there was a knock on the front door. The women exchanged worried glances, and Lydia quietly rose.

"Who is there?" she asked loudly through the door that was kept bolted from the inside.

"It's me, Lydia, it's your father."

She pulled hard on the bolt then pushed the door wide open. There he was in the flesh, looking small and old, with a worn blanket wrapped around his shoulders for warmth. They fell into a long, tight embrace. He kissed her cheek and couldn't seem to let go as she led him into the parlor.

"Papa, I am so relieved you are alive," she said with pure joy in her voice.

He held her tightly against him as they made their way to a chair, and she felt how thin and frail he had become.

"Alita, please bring Papa some tea and some bread," she said.

Lydia helped Manuel sit in his favorite chair and watched his shaking hands move to cover his eyes filled with tears. She removed the filthy blanket he wore and used one from the back of the sofa to wrap around him.

"I was captured at Valverde with ten other men. We were held in Socorro for many days and then transported to a small town in Texas. The conditions were deplorable. Others were brought there, and many died. I'm very lucky to be alive. They let us all go some time after Glorieta, and we found our way back home, step by step."

Lydia, kneeling at his feet, held his hands as he spoke, and tears streamed down her face.

"Papa," she said. "Eduardo was killed at Glorieta." She knew the news might be too much for her father, but she had to tell him, and she felt a release knowing he was the only other person on the earth who would know the same depth of loss.

Manuel looked at her, dumbfounded, and then his shoulders hunched over and shook with grief and loss as he broke down in tears.

"I was there, Papa," she said. "I saw him when they brought him back. He was at peace." She reached towards him to put her arms around her father, who felt so slight to her.

Alita poured tea for each of them, and father and daughter spoke through the night about what had happened over the last few months. As the sun rose the next morning, Lydia guided her father to his room for a hot bath, a warm meal, and a much-needed rest.

$\equiv 20 \equiv$

Lydia longed for Eli—she felt so anxious without him. A sullen sadness had spread over the Sena household like a thick fog. Her father moved in a slow manner, his body and mind wracked with lingering grief.

During the day, Lydia and Alita took care of the house and the few animals they had left, including chickens, a few sheep, a cow, and some goats. Sadie was the only horse left in the massive barn, and Lydia took time to tend to her each day. On most evenings, they prepared what they could for dinner and then called her father to the simple table in the kitchen.

Manuel spent much of his time going over and calculating the business losses he had incurred, including the cattle that had been taken to feed the soldiers.

After dinner one night, Lydia and her father moved to the parlor. Lydia worked on her mending, and her father tried to read from one of his favorite books. They sat next to one another in quiet comfort, yet there was a feeling of loss in the room, utterly silent and ever-present. They both sighed as they internally dealt with Eduardo's death.

"I am tired, Papa," Lydia said as she stood. "I think I will try to sleep."

"Yes, my dear," he said, but held on to her hand after she leaned over and kissed his cheek. "Lydia, I am so sorry for having sent you to Carlos. I don't think I have said that, how wrong I was to send you. Please forgive me."

Tears fell from her eyes and blended with his as they held each other's hand. "You don't have to talk about this, Papa," she said bowing her head. "I know you would never place me in harm's way. It was logical at the time. You could have never known the kind of man he had become. Perhaps it was my destiny." She raised her head. "Just as it was Eduardo's destiny, Papa, to die a hero's death. You must believe that. There was nothing we could have done."

Manuel's body shook with grief as he wept for his only son taken from him. Lydia's hands held his own, and she knelt to wrap her arms around him, rocking him like a small child.

In a whisper, she said, "Eduardo is with Mama."

Somehow, her words penetrated his mind, and they gave him great comfort.

Lydia helped her father upstairs and kissed him on the cheek. "Good night, Papa. Everything will be all right," she said as she closed the door to his room.

He nodded and forced a smile for her.

The next morning, Manuel's spirits seemed better and he felt more in control of his emotions. As he entered the kitchen, he did not see his young daughter before him, but a beautiful young woman who was already seasoned from life's experiences.

"Lydia," he asked as they were sharing a meager breakfast at the kitchen table, "how do you feel about Eli?"

Just the mention of his name sent her heart beating. "I love him, Papa, and I want to spend the rest of my life with him."

Manuel knew this was the case but needed to hear her say it out loud. The loss of his daughter to Eli would be painful. He hoped in his heart they would stay here in New Mexico, but he knew they could easily go back to Colorado when the war was over.

"You have been given the gift of love, Lydia. Hold on to it and make a beautiful life together."

Later that day, while Lydia and Alita were preparing supplies to take to the wounded in the local hospital, Lydia heard a horse come to the stable outside and went to the back door and opened it. The sun was shining, and the day's temperature was beginning to warm. Lydia held her hand up against the sun and made out Claire's smile from a distance. She ran to her, and the two women embraced with immense joy.

"Thank God you are safe, Lydia," Claire exclaimed. "My father told me of your ordeal last night when we returned."

The women walked together arm-in-arm towards the house. They leaned into one another as they made their way toward the house.

Claire stopped Lydia for a moment. "I am so sorry about Eduardo," she said. "I can't tell you how badly I feel." They hugged one another tightly.

Pulling apart, Lydia said, "I miss him every day. I saw him right before he died. I thank God I was able to tell him I loved him before the battle. We may still have a way to go with this war, but at least we are together now. I don't have much to offer you, but I'm sure Alita will come up with something."

As the war raged on, Lydia continued to receive letters from Eli describing his troop's activity at the border of the New Mexico Territory. There had been multiple skirmishes, but the Confederates never really made any real attempt to return. Most of their troops were fighting large scale battles in the southern part of the United States.

Eli wrote of his desire to return to her and start their lives together. She always read the letters many times over and prayed constantly for his safe return.

Lydia had also received a letter from Mrs. Aragon apologizing for her son's treatment of her and begging her forgiveness on his behalf. Mr. Aragon had returned to his ranch a broken man after Carlos' hanging. Mrs. Aragon did not think he would live much longer. On a happier note, she wrote that Rosa had returned to the ranch and was now her constant companion and caregiver. She assured Lydia that Rosa was well and happy and hoped they could visit her soon.

On a warm spring day in the middle of April, Lydia and her father walked together through the plaza. People were taking advantage of the warm weather and had congregated to enjoy the sunshine and catch up with one another. Lydia felt as though the town had returned to normal, even though many lives had been lost. She stood by as her father engaged in a discussion about the upcoming planting season.

Suddenly, a young man from the newspaper office ran out to the middle of the square with a sheet of paper in his hand. He yelled at the top of his voice, "The war is over! General Lee has surrendered. The Union has won the war!" Cheers rang out from the crowd and soon everyone was chattering with excitement and relief.

After word spread to the 2nd Colorado Calvary now stationed near Austin, Texas, defending against Confederate invasions, Eli could hardly get back to Lydia fast enough. He traveled night and day with a small group of men heading back to the Colorado Territory.

When he arrived in Santa Fe early one evening, he noticed how calm and peaceful the town was—settled now their encounter with the war was over. After the Battle of Glorieta and the retreat of the Confederate troops moving through their town, they had not seen any other Confederate soldiers.

Eli headed past the plaza and took the road to the Sena house. He could hardly wait to see Lydia, to breathe her in and hold her in his arms. He tied Coal to the post out front and knocked soundly on the door. Her father answered and they greeted each other warmly. Lydia, hearing the knock, ran down the stairs and now stood at the threshold with gratitude and excitement gushing from her face and eyes. Eli stepped inside and their eyes locked on one another. Manuel stood aside as the couple embraced.

"I am so happy you are back," Lydia said.

She pulled Eli out the front door to the arbor in the courtyard, now covered in tiny pink and yellow wild rose buds, so they could have some privacy. As they each took a seat, brimming with anticipation, they both began to speak at once.

Laughing, Eli said, "Let me go first, Lydia. I have only thought of returning to you over the last few years, and I want to be with you for the rest of my life." Before she could respond, he dropped to his knee and asked, "Will you be my wife, Lydia?"

Out of his pocket, he pulled a gold ring with a deep blue sapphire surrounded by rose petal diamonds. "This belonged to my grandmother, and my mother gave it to me when I left," he said. "In case I met the woman I wanted to marry, and that woman is you."

"Yes, yes with all my heart!" she exclaimed.

He rose to hold her and spin her around the arbor. He lovingly placed the ring on her left hand, and they returned to the house to tell Manuel of their plans. Her father kissed Lydia on the forehead.

"I have never known a more courageous and beautiful woman, besides your mother. If this is what will make you happy, I am in full agreement."

After Eli settled in, and over the next several months, he worked with Manuel to replace some of the cattle he'd lost, mend fences that had been torn down, plant a new garden, and fully restock the mercantile. Stagecoaches from the East had resumed delivering goods after the war ended. Manuel was impressed with Eli's general knowledge of livestock, and he realized Eli had a good sense for business. He knew Eli could never replace his precious Eduardo, but he had begun to forge a relationship with his future son-in-law as they worked to restore the family's livelihood. Manuel was certain he and Lydia would be happy in their new life together.

The young couple spent many an evening with Claire and Cecil, and the women planned and discussed all the aspects of the upcoming wedding. So much so, that Cecil and Eli often left them alone after dinner to make their plans.

≡ 21 ≡

The glorious morning sun announced the beginning of a new fall day. Drops of dew settled on the leaves and glistened in the early morning light. The trees stood tall and heavy with the weight of their colorful leaves. All the world was wrapped in the light of day.

Lydia looked radiant as she walked up the steps of the church with Manuel at her side. Alita, Claire, and Lydia had worked many hours restoring the cream-colored satin wedding gown that had belonged to Lydia's mother. The material had weathered well and still held its sheen. The neckline was rounded and trimmed in white Spanish lace, the sleeves were gathered, and the cuffs landed gracefully on her wrists; the lower portion of the wide skirt was encircled by the same lace. Lydia wore a long, flowing mantilla with a crown of roses on her head over her coiled hair held tightly at the back of her neck. Lydia's bouquet was a simple combination of late blooming red roses and snapdragons from her garden.

Claire, the matron of honor, wore a rose-colored gown and was smiling deeply as she walked up the main aisle of the church.

The church was full of townspeople and Sena relatives from afar who had traveled for this joyous occasion. Eli's mother, Anna, radiated with happiness when she saw Lydia at the entrance to the church.

She had traveled with his brother, Matthew, who now stood near him at the altar. Anna had met Lydia when they arrived and was astonished Eli had found such a lovely young woman while fighting in a war. Anna held a handkerchief to her eyes as Lydia and her father made their way into the church.

Vicar Lamy stood at the altar with Eli at his side dressed in his full uniform. With candles glowing from the altar, they both watched as the bride made her way up the aisle. Her father kissed Lydia's cheek and embraced her tightly before he gave her hand to Eli. Manuel brushed a tear from his eye as he took his seat.

When the time came during the mass, guitar music played softly as Eli lifted the veil from Lydia's face and they took their places, side-by-side. They exchanged their vows, and Eli placed a simple gold band next to her engagement ring. The group cheered when the couple kissed, and they followed the young couple to the Sena house to celebrate.

In the courtyard, long tables were covered in white linen and filled with the wedding feast. Alita had worked tirelessly on the food, and many of the other women had contributed.

Halfway through the meal, Manuel raised his glass to the happy couple. "We were so fortunate the day Eli Stevens stepped into our lives. I was proud to serve by his side in the war, but I am especially proud to call him son today. And to my beautiful daughter, may you both have endless happiness and love in your marriage."

Eli could not take his eyes away from his bride as the afternoon celebration continued with dancing and more toasts to the newlyweds.

Lydia stopped at each table to greet guests and thank them for attending. Mrs. Aragon and Rosa stood when she arrived at their table. "Lydia," Rosa exclaimed as she put her arms around her. "Thank God it all worked out, and I am so happy you and Eli found your way back to one another."

Lydia smiled broadly. "Thank you again, Rosa, for all your help, and I am so glad you and Señora Aragon are well."

"My dear Lydia," Mrs. Aragon said as she took her hand. "Your mother would be so proud today to see you so happy and the lovely young woman you have become. You are always welcome at my home."

Eli found Thomas Sutton at one of the food tables. He reached his hand out and was greeted warmly by the man who had been a beacon for Eli. "I want to thank you again for all your help," Eli said. "And for coming today. It means so much to both of us."

Sutton nodded. "Thank you for helping bring down Aragon," he said. "It helps to know my son's killers have been punished."

As the late afternoon sun glided towards the west, casting its final glow over the festivities, Eli decided it was time to take his bride home. He took hold of her hand and led her to the carriage as she waved goodbye to her friends and family. He stopped to embrace Cecil and in a low voice said, "Let's hope she loves it. Thank you for all your help."

"I have a surprise for you," Eli said as they sat close to one another in the carriage.

Manuel had purchased the property with the abandoned house as a wedding gift, and Eli had overseen the complete restoration over the past several months. Cecil had been instrumental in supervising the project.

In the glow of the evening light, they made their way up the narrow road leading to their new home. Lydia gasped with delight when they arrived.

"Eli," she exclaimed, "how can this be? It is beautiful." She looked up at the weathervane, now clean and restored, as it spun whimsically in the light breeze.

He carried her through the front door he had spent endless hours sanding and painting and into the large living room with white adobe walls and wood plank floors. A fire was burning in the central fireplace, and Lydia could smell a delicious dinner coming from the kitchen.

Eli placed her gently down on a cream-colored chair next to the fire. "Warm up my love, and I will take you on a tour of your new home."

She rose instantly and put her hand in his. He showed her the kitchen, pantry, and dining room, talking about how much work each project had taken. They made their way up the narrow staircase to two large bedrooms upstairs.

"Your father helped me these last few months. Many of the men from town worked on the weekends and their days off so it would all be finished before the wedding. Cecil spent every weekend here. There are still many things to complete, and Claire helped me pick out most of the furniture," Eli said.

Lydia was overwhelmed and reached out to him for a long, deep kiss. They walked into their bedroom, and both looked towards the beautiful brass bed longingly.

They stood facing one another, and Eli carefully lifted her crown of roses and her mantilla and then took the pins out of her hair. She unbuttoned his jacket and pulled his arms out of it. Piece by piece, they lovingly removed each other's clothing until Lydia was left in her chemise and he in his trousers.

"I think this is a good time to return something to you," she said as her hand reached into the small valise she had carried in with her and pulled out an item wrapped in a soft cloth. She handed it to him and explained as he started to pull the material away. "You gave this to me for safekeeping and the glass cover cracked when they tried to take it from me at Glorieta. I had the jeweler restore the glass and take out the nicks. It is your watch, Eli. The one thing from you that kept me from losing my mind when we were separated."

He held the pocket watch in his hand and reached for her. "This has even more significance for me now, Lydia," he said as he drew her into his arms. "I can't believe we are here and that it is all real." His lips trailed her neck.

"My Eli," she said, wrapping her arms around his neck and allowing her body to mold into his. "I always knew you would be mine." She took his hand and led him to the bed.

*   *   *

Eli woke from his deep sleep and reached for her. Even in her sleep she moved to him and nestled in his arm. He moved the curls from her face and thought to himself, *I have never been happier in my whole life.*

Lydia could hear his heart beating in her ear and, without opening her eyes, moved her hands lightly over his chest.

"You shouldn't start something you can't finish, my love," he said tenderly.

"I can see it through if it has to do with you," she replied.

≡Epilogue≡

Alita knocked softly on the door and opened it with care. The heavy curtains were drawn and let little light into the bedroom. A fire's warm glow radiated throughout the room.

Eli ran his hand through his hair. His eyes were misty as he looked up at Alita who placed a tray with steaming herbal tea next to the bed. Lydia rested her head against Eli's chest as he sat beside her in the bed. Her breathing had finally returned to normal, and the color was coming back to her face. Small beads of sweat still clung to her forehead, and with a sure and steady hand, Eli wiped them away.

He leaned down and kissed the top of her head as his eyes gazed into those of his newborn son.

"He is beautiful, Lydia," he said, his voice filled with emotion. "I have never seen anything so beautiful."

Lydia's own eyes filled with tears of joy; her arms full of the baby who was wrapped in a warm, soft blanket. His dark hair lightly covered the top of his head like a halo, and he could hardly keep his eyes open.

Eli tenderly reached down and stroked his son's pink cheek. His skin felt so fresh and vulnerable under his rough hand. He squeezed Lydia tightly.

I owe so much to her, he thought to himself. When he'd found her, he thought his life was complete and he never dreamed of asking for more. Now, he had a son, living proof of their love for one another.

There was a hard, anxious knock at the door, and without waiting for a response, Manuel rushed in, his face filled with worry and concern.

"Papa," Lydia said lovingly. "I am fine, the baby is fine. Come and see how lovely he is."

Manuel walked slowly toward the bed. Eli moved to pick up his son and easily placed him in his grandfather's arms after he was seated in a chair. Lydia watched as years melted away from her father's face. His features softened and relaxed as he cooed happily to his new grandson.

"I would have sent word earlier, but there was very little time, he came so quickly," Eli said as he and Lydia exchanged a glance.

They had not wanted to burden Manuel. Since they'd told him of the pregnancy, he had been so worried about Lydia, checking on her daily. They both knew why—he had never recovered from the loss of his wife during childbirth—and they were uncertain of the extent of Lydia's labor.

"Papa," Lydia said as she sat up against her pillows. "We would like to call him Eduardo."

Manuel looked at Lydia then at Eli, finally saying, "Yes, yes. I think that would suit him just fine. Eduardo," he said lovingly to the baby.

Lydia lay back against her pillow, physically exhausted but emotionally rejuvenated. She felt all was well.

She heard the unmistakable sound of petticoats rustling up the stairs and down the hallway. Claire burst into the room without warning.

"Why didn't anyone send for me? I had to hear the news from Mrs. Martinez' maid," she said, acting offended. "Uncle Manuel, let me see him," she said excitedly. "Oh Lydia, Eli, he is the most handsome baby I have ever seen," she said, looking over Manuel's shoulder.

"Eduardo, meet your Tía Claire," Manuel said. Claire leaned down and put her arm around Manuel and hugged him tightly.

Eli was standing over Lydia, and she took hold of his hand. "Thank you, mi amor," she said softly. "I can't think of anywhere else in the world I would rather be than here with you and our new son."

The love between them was shining in their eyes and in the tight grip of their hands.

Lydia sighed happily as she looked at her husband, father, Claire, and her son. *So much life ahead of me*, she thought to herself. Her glance moved to the photographs of her mother and brother. She knew in her heart they would always be with her—whatever came her way.

Author's Note

I based Lydia's home on La Casa Sena in Santa Fe, New Mexico. The enormous two-story structure is one of the oldest surviving homes in Santa Fe and is located on Palace Avenue right across from the St. Francis Cathedral.

The land was original-ly granted to Captain Arias de Quiros by General Di-ego de Vargas after the re-conquest of New Mexico in 1693. Over time, the land was divided among other families. In 1796, Don Juan Sena obtained all the land and it remained exclusively in the Sena family for some time. What is now La Casa Sena was acquired by Jose D. Sena, a major with the Unit-ed States Army during the Civil War. He built a home  and garden for his new bride, Doña Isabel Cabeza de Baca in 1864, and was one of the first two people admitted to the New Mexico Territory

241

Supreme Court Bar. The building was added to over the years to become a 33-room hacienda. It is now home to a prominent restaurant, La Casa Sena, offering dining, a piano bar, and seating on the patio. There are also several charming shops along the portal.

Every time I visit, I can the hear whispers of history speaking softly.

Acknowledgements

This novel took me many years to finish. It is based on a story my father shared with me when I was a child about his ancestor who arrived in Santa Fe as a Union soldier during the Civil War. The young man remained in Santa Fe, married a local woman, and they had several children, one of whom became my great-grandfather. My father was instrumental in shaping my appreciation of New Mexico.

Santa Fe has always represented home to me, and I have a profound respect and love for its history and its many stories. I know there are still many more to tell.

Writing is a lonely process and it comes down to the thoughts in my head and the words on the page, but I had many encouraging people along the way. I would like to thank my editor, Lisa McCoy, who brilliantly edited the novel and encouraged me, then expertly guided me through the publication process. Not only was she a guiding light but is also now a dear friend.

I would like to thank my beautiful immediate family who offered encouragement and support when needed and held a belief that I could finish. I would also like to acknowledge the support and excitement from my first readers who are sisters and friends. They read first, second, and third drafts and offered suggestions and positivity, helping me to tell this story well.

The historical academic books written before me were priceless in providing a baseline for the story. I would like to especially thank the Special Collections staff and section at the Albuquerque Public Library, home to many historical references.

Thank you to my readers for spending the time and energy. I hope you enjoyed *Touch of Glory!*

About the Author

Elizabeth Analise is a 12th generation New Mexican and was a fea-
ture writer for *New Mexico Magazine* and *La Herencia Magazine* for many
years. She is passionate about the history of our state and enjoys visiting all our most treasured areas. She lives with her husband and two
dogs in New Mexico.

Follow the author at **www.elizabethanalise.org**